The Ha-Ha

The Ha-Ha

TOM SHAKESPEARE

This edition published in 2024 by Farrago,
an imprint of Duckworth Books Ltd
1 Golden Court, Richmond TW9 1EU, United Kingdom

www.farragobooks.com

Print ISBN: 978-1-78842-477-6
eISBN: 978-1-78842-478-3

This book is dedicated to the memory of Dan Conway,
the original man in the van. I wish he'd been
at the party, and I hope that, wherever he is, he
forgives me for rewriting parts of his life

Chapter 1

A small but exquisitely stately home, set amidst an emerald pond of parkland, Threepwood Hall was the ideal marriage plot. Through that pillared portico, Emma Woodhouse could have orchestrated the local gentry. Behind those blue window shutters, Bertie Wooster could have resolved the most challenging affair of the heart. In that kitchen garden, Lord Emsworth could have pottered to his heart's content. An adornment to the county of Suffolk, Threepwood Hall exuded bonhomie, from cellars to chimneys.

This balmy day in May showed off the Hall at its very best. The raked gravel waited expectantly, as if for the carriage wheels of the propertied classes. Beams of sunlight swept languidly over the rose garden and dappled a pond on which ducks dallied. Somewhere nearby, a pig groaned appreciatively as an underling scratched his back. The Heritage Trust had restored this Regency jewel with loving care. No wonder that more than one production manager had their phone number on speed dial, it was the type of location that demanded an epic love story.

The village beyond the Hall featured an appropriate supporting cast. In the church belfry, a trio of teachers were persistently venting their classroom frustrations on their bell ropes. Opposite the pub, a fund manager in red trousers was rolling the cricket pitch in preparation for the coming match and his own coronary. A mother pondering alimony in a puce puffer jacket was walking her labradoodle through the park. Everything appeared to offer visitors a return to an idyllic England before agribusiness and house price inflation had made the countryside a monoculture. But by Monday morning, each extra would have returned to London.

In the back kitchen of the Hall, a man of nigh on forty summers sat with his laptop open, stressing about his spreadsheet when he would have preferred to have imagined the woman of his dreams. Unfolded, as it were, Fred would have been a tall man. He had once played wing on the school rugby field, such was the length of his limbs and his fleetness of foot. Now, he could lay claim to 'long' but sadly no longer to 'tall'. Worse, twenty years of paralysis had left his legs like anaemic twiglets, as he had confessed to a sympathetic friend. Despite this, he still had the grace of the great rugby player, that ability to weave through obstacles and avoid the bruising encounters and crunching tackles which sadden most lives. Excepting the undodged disaster of the car crash, the life he led had been charmed, for the most part. As a result, he retained a youthful grace which endeared him to staff, clients and above all friends.

Ordinarily Fred was as sunny as a globally-warmed summer afternoon, with the genial disposition of a small-town solicitor. Today, however, despite the wheelchair-accessible stately home of which he was proprietor for the weekend, he was as tremulous as a climate activist beset by melting icecaps and extreme weather events. He peered at his notes, while fiddling with his wheelchair push rims in a manner that his psychologist pal would surely have slapped a label on. Dressed for the part in a rugby shirt and green corduroys, he was temporarily lord of all he surveyed, and he wasn't sure he liked it.

It had been so difficult juggling everyone's needs. He had filled the Hall with people who had almost nothing in common, except him. Most had been to one of his previous birthday parties, except Alberto, Robin's partner, who was a completely unknown quantity. Fred just hoped that the Costa Rican would get on with everyone, and vice versa. Another potential problem was Hugh, his oldest school friend, who would rather be taken for a misanthrope than admit to being shy, and who resisted every effort to be included. And since shortly after graduation, Fred's glimpses of Heather had mainly come via television screens or computer monitors, though she had always loomed large in his imagination.

Then was the big problem of divorce clustering. In his parents' day, divorce had been something that happened like a V2 rocket, a single hit that devastated entire neighbourhoods. Now it seemed to be like a chicken pox epidemic for forty-year-olds. First one couple succumbed, and then before you knew it the whole peer group had come down with a nasty case of decree nisi, which made it extraordinarily difficult to plan a get-together. You couldn't invite Person A and Person B together, even though you liked them both, because now they wouldn't exchange a friendly vowel. And then if Person C was the cause of the split of A and B, you couldn't invite him or her either... Person D and Person E would have had children together, and whoever had the ferals that weekend couldn't come. It had been a minefield. Which reminded Fred why he steered clear of Family Law as far as possible. He did a disconsolate wheelie in front of his laptop.

Take Freya, for example, only daughter of Polly, who was another college friend. Polly was bisexual and her ex, Fred's other friend, Georgina, was off with her new beau, or rather belle, that weekend so there was no alternative but to bring Freya along. Polly was one of his oldest friends and he loved her to bits. She was always going to attend; she had to, despite the seven-year-old in tow. It wasn't as if it was a problem for Freya to be hanging out with a bunch of adults. She'd seen everything and could swear in several languages. Thankfully there were enough twin rooms for her to share with Polly.

Thinking of Freya reminded Fred of catering, and he switched to another page of his spreadsheet. Freya must not have animal products of any kind, he'd noted. Not because of an allergy, more because Georgina would see red if her daughter were ever to sample cadavers (her words). In his experience, Freya seemed to follow her own unique dietary code, largely based around mashed potato, sweetcorn and vegan ice cream, a nutritional wasteland in which she apparently thrived. Fred glanced around the kitchen. He'd already allocated the left-hand fridge as vegan, and stocked the freezer compartment with Kinderglace, a wincingly expensive soya-based ice cream. If a birthday party was now impossible without a spreadsheet, did that say more about him, or about the modern age?

Chapter 2

The Skype chat with Heather had happened a month or so ago. Fred had been in his flat on King Street, in Norwich. She'd been overseas somewhere exotic and dangerous to broadcast news from, as always.

'It would be so great if you could come,' Fred repeated, hopefully. 'It's been ages.'

'Wouldn't miss it,' replied Heather, vaguely. 'Always depending on the geo-political situation of course. I'm just sorry to be such an appallingly useless friend.'

'I can imagine you've been busy…' said Fred, not daring to hope she'd actually make it. 'One global crisis after another!'

His heart still beat faster when he was talking with her. Either that or it was the new brand of coffee beans he'd used at lunch. If only he could come up with something less banal, *wittier*. When he rehearsed this in advance, he had some great lines.

'That's exactly how it feels! Coup – Putin – Pandemic! No rest!' said Heather, who seemed to be inspecting her appearance on the screen. 'The years have flown by.'

'Forty!' groaned Fred. 'Forty! What have I got to show for it?'

'But I feel terrible that I haven't been there for you,' Heather said, now buffing her nails with an emery board. 'You've had some crises…'

'Don't even think about it. Plenty of people rallied round,' said Fred, who could have done with a little less rallying at times.

'And here we all are, on the verge of middle age!' said Heather, reaching for the nail varnish. Centaur Blood, that would suit.

'But it's all gone very well for you,' said Fred. 'You're certainly in the public eye…'

'I am rather, aren't I?' agreed Heather. 'But there are things I've missed out on.'

'Most of us have,' replied Fred. 'Although I do have two nephews, of course.'

'I didn't necessarily mean that,' said Heather, who thought of little else. 'But sometimes I think it would be nice to settle down. Find the right guy…'

'Ah… so… no one on the scene at the moment?' said Fred, cautiously pleased.

'Nobody serious,' replied Heather airily, discounting the video editor in Kabul and the diplomat in Paris. 'Guys come and go. But it's difficult to make anything *work*, when you're on the road the whole time.' She didn't think it was the right moment to mention Clancy.

'Mostly off-road, as far as I can see,' said Fred.

'You should see my schedule, darling! Sometimes, I think one might do better being a solicitor in a quiet country town.'

'Oh,' said Fred, with a laugh as light as his mother's pastry, 'you could always try marrying one!' He blushed, but she did not seem to have heard his heavy-handed quip. 'Anyway, it's more colourful than you'd think. In fact,' he now felt embarrassed, as if admitting to a penchant for light S&M, 'I'm writing a book...'

'A book?' said Heather in surprise. 'About rural farm sales? Conveyancing delays?'

'Well, partly. Trying to weave in the humour. Like James Herriot or something.'

'Oh god, don't mention Herriot. I'm from Yorkshire, remember. Terrible stereotypes.'

'And there's a lot about... becoming paralysed.'

'Oh, yes...' She paused meaningfully, muting the sound so she could blow on her nails. 'That must have been a hard time,' she continued. She could do sincerity, she thought: it was all in the eyes. George Burns had it right, if you could fake sincerity, you had got it made. She checked out her face on screen. *She* believed in her.

'I'm going to call it *Wheels of Misfortune.*' said Fred. 'I thought it might help people to hear that life goes on, even if... you know... you can't walk?'

'Sounds a marvellous idea, darling,' said Heather, distractedly. Maybe she should get tints in her hair again? 'I think Frank Gardner did something similar.'

'And there's a lot about our student days, of course. I've been working on it for ages. All about Roderick and Charlotte... You.'

'Me?' said Heather in alarm. 'What would there be to say about me? I was a dull little mouse at College. A nobody!'

'Exactly! And here you are, saving the world... or fiddling while Rome burns... or something.' He felt it was just the narrative arc that the book needed. Some soared, others

7

stumbled, but only one crashed. He could imagine the back cover copy. Now he just needed a happy ending.

'Not sure I like the sound of that,' said Heather, frowning. 'I'd rather you didn't mention me at all.'

'Oh, there's not much about you,' said Fred, trying to be reassuring. 'There's more on the others... parties and student politics, you know. Of course, I've mentioned that time when you came into the bar at the end of first year and asked everyone what heavy metal records were made of...'

'Jeez, I was such a dork! I can't believe I said that.'

'You were naive,' said Fred, wistfully. 'Endearingly so.'

'Naive?'

'Sweet,' confirmed Fred. It was a quality in her which had once been compellingly attractive, and which he feared had now evaporated. 'Like when we had to explain that a blow job was nothing to do with hairdressing. Or when you sat in that tent at Glastonbury in a sea of mud, putting on your blusher.'

'I'm not sure that either naive or sweet would do much for my viewing figures,' said Heather, choosing not to dwell on that image of her first festival. Tents were an unknown quantity back then. In the last decade or so, she'd worked hard on her rugged, battle-hardened look, all flak jackets and urgent concern.

'Oh, I don't know,' said Fred. 'You can't do wars forever, and I imagine someone has to present *Countryfile.*'

'I do wish you'd leave me out of it,' said Heather, earnestly. 'My editors are pretty nervous about our public profile.'

'I wouldn't worry, Heather,' said Fred, wishing he hadn't mentioned it all. 'I'm not daft. I didn't mention that nasty scandal on the student newspaper.'

There was a pause. One silently digested that memory, and the other suffered acid reflux.

'All the same, could I just have a look?' pleaded Heather. 'The manuscript I mean? I'd love to see it.'

'I just gave it to my friend Sonia to read. I'm hoping she might do something with it. But you could read it on the laptop...'

Fred felt as tall as he'd ever felt in his wheelchair. At last, Heather seemed to be showing an interest in his life. Because that book was his whole life, right now, however casually he talked about it.

'Oh god!' she said, thinking about internet privacy. She'd done a piece on it only the previous week, got right up close to Russian cyberwarfare. Would there be recrimination? 'Please don't tell me that it's just sitting on a computer which anyone could hack into. Some people would like nothing better than to discredit me.'

'You don't have anything to worry about,' said Fred, firmly. 'I've read all about fishing and dogging and so forth.'

'Not so fast, Mr Naive. Dogging is something else entirely,' said Heather. 'Or so I'm told...' she added quickly.

'The point is, I'm terrified of people seeing it. I've kept it all on a single memory stick, which is password protected. It's not even on the laptop hard drive, let alone the Cloud. I don't want anyone in the office to read it, until it's finished. I have just the one print out. It's all quite safe. I can bring it with me, if you're interested.'

'Remind me, who's Sonia?'

'I met her on a bus. She went to Cambridge and married my school friend Anil who she actually met at my last birthday party,' said Fred, proudly. 'Anyway, she's an agent...'

'MI5?' Now Heather was completely at sea.

'No! Literary! She thinks publishers are ripe for disability memoirs. They've had Chick Lit, Lad Lit, Grunge Lit, now it's time for Crip Lit.'

'Grunge Lit? Is that even a thing?'

'Apparently. I'd value your opinion as well. Being a journalist and all…'

'Don't worry,' said Heather. 'I'll tell you straight.' She doubted whether Fred would welcome her opinion.

'So, I'll definitely see you at Threepwood?' he beamed. 'Can I put you down to help with a meal?'

'Not sure I am quite cut out for the little woman role, to be honest. Been eating out for years. I'll tell you what: why don't I organise for a crate of fizz to be delivered?'

'That would be extraordinarily generous!' This was the sort of rapport he longed for.

'Consider it done. And don't forget to bring that manuscript.'

'Right. Sonia will be there, you know. In case you need any help with your own ideas. I'd think that your memoir would be worth reading too.'

'Hold that thought!' said Heather, and gratefully hit the red button.

As the Skype call ended with its usual dying fall, like the sigh of misguided optimism escaping from the Whoopee cushion of aspiration, Fred felt that, yet again, the conversation hadn't quite attained the fluency for which he had hoped. However much he planned his answers in advance, his actual dialogue with Heather remained wooden. It was like trying to speak in a different language with her sometimes. Still, they had the whole weekend ahead of them. He was not one to give up. If he'd had a middle name, it would have been Persistence. Although he supposed that would have made him a girl. Either way, he had a scheme.

As he wheeled into the kitchen to make coffee, he realised how anxious he was about Sonia's feedback on the book. She was the most literary person he knew, having studied at Cambridge and everything. Showing Sonia his manuscript was a bit like showing her his penis. Not that he'd ever actually done that, contrary to the jealous fears of her partner Anil. He knew it wasn't the most impressive book in the world. Nowhere near! But he was proud of it. And more importantly, if this wasn't good enough, he didn't have anything better. He hoped she'd bite.

Fred and Sonia went back a long way, since they'd met in that coach station, in their student days. Cambridge was far away from St Warburg's, but they had written long letters and been to the Edinburgh Festival, and even holidayed in a rented cottage in the rainy Lakes. But now Fred had begun to worry that Sonia and Anil's relationship, which had blossomed since they'd met at his thirtieth birthday, had come at the cost of his own friendship with each of them. He realised that he had never known Sonia closely when she was going out with anyone. He was used to her being his special friend. Trusting her had become a habit. But now she was with someone else, who in turn was no longer only his own close friend from school. Sometimes, it felt as if they had closed ranks against him, as past witness to their privy thoughts and therefore someone who could not be permitted to know their present ones.

Fred realised that perhaps it was he who was feeling jealous. Anil and Sonia had something with each other that he didn't have with them – or anyone else for that matter. Although, if the book worked out, he hoped it might bring him and Sonia together, and begin a new stage of their friendship. He'd drink to that, he thought, wheeling uncertainly back to his desk one-handedly, while holding his freshly brewed coffee in the other.

Three thousand miles away, Heather sat biting her vermillion nails, Lady Macbeth in an executive suite. A memoir of the past? Her past? Who even wrote their own essays, anyway? The naivete was bad, but the perjury of her college days was more than shaming. It could be career-destroying. Those anecdotes were dynamite, and not in a good way. Fred obviously had no respect for privacy whatsoever. Her best hope would be that, despite featuring the student antics of the subsequently famous, the memoirs of a small-town solicitor were unlikely to appeal to a publisher. But there was always a risk that a publisher took a punt. Scandal and embarrassment, not just for her, but for Clancy too. That would be an utter disaster right now. A plan was required.

Cold in, or as, her overly-air-conditioned suite, Heather wondered what Sonia would think of it all. Fred's early life at any rate was highly original. But the last twenty years had been rather derivative, with little interest to the casual reader. He'd ended up working as a solicitor, and Heather couldn't remember any bestsellers featuring rural litigation. His parents, Mr and Mrs Twistelton, had spent their retirement exploring England's borders by local bus. It all added up to a distinct lack of plot development.

While Heather was aware that Fred harboured hopes that were, well, unrealistic, that certainly wasn't her fault. She had hardly encouraged him. In the fantastic future that she had mapped out for herself, he didn't feature at all. It was all a matter of lifestyle. In the words of the immortal Paul McCartney, Fred would soon be experiencing a 'You say goodbye, and I say hello' moment.

Chapter 3

'Hello, hello… Not a bad neck of the woods, this…' Roddy craned his head to look back at the village street as they passed. 'Pretty quick out of London too. All Tory voters of course. Such a shame that so many of the nicest areas seem to have the wrong electorate…'

Roderick Twistleton, politics lecturer at a North London FE College, road safety activist and would-be Labour party election candidate, with his wife Charlotte, columnist, were driving their Toyota Corolla along unfamiliar East Anglian roads towards the birthday weekend at Threepwood Hall. Roddy was no less tall than his younger brother Fred, clean-cut and extremely handsome, but nature appeared to have endowed him with more elbow than was strictly necessary. To call him a bull in a china shop would have been to libel any passing livestock. When he gave a lecture, let alone a political speech, his contortions were more fascinating than his rhetoric, and far more dangerous to public safety.

'Local colour,' replied his wife, her eyes on the road, her hands firmly yet gently adopting the recommended 'ten to two' position on the wheel. 'As in, I need some. If you spot anything, be a dear and jot it down, would you?'

'Planning another novel?' said her husband in the passenger seat, as he pulled another batch of papers out of his briefcase. 'Let me guess... this time it's the vicar who's having crisis of conscience and the lady of the manor is shagging the farmer? Or the other way round? Careful! This is a twenty zone.'

'Certainly not,' said Charlotte, with all the froideur of an impatient vivisector. 'The bonkbusters are all behind me. I said local colour, not off-colour. Oh, that's good, "local versus off". Make a note, please. I was thinking I could do one of my columns based on our weekend away. You know, "Guardian-reader types in rustic idyll, twenty years on, what have they made of themselves, true meaning of life to be found not in worldly goods but in spiritual growth, Colossians 3, verse 5."' She paused to break sharply so as to avoid the peloton of lycra. 'Sodding bikes. It's nearly as bad as Hackney.'

'Now, now,' said Roddy. 'The Gospel according to Saint Karl Friedrich... Benz, I mean,' he added. 'All road users are fuelled by the Holy Spirit. We must live and let live. Except SUV drivers, of course. We should tax the hell out of them.'

The Toyota had been a good compromise between petrol and electric. Excellent safety record. Roddy was good with compromise, which is why he felt he had a bright future in the modern Labour Party. He managed to be both young and middle-aged simultaneously, like one of the Miliband brothers. And he was extremely telegenic, even when eating a bacon sandwich.

'I hope the boys will be OK with my parents,' fretted his wife. She loved her sons, particularly from a distance.

'Oh, stop worrying!' said Roddy. 'The boys will be fine. Less sure about your mum and dad though...'

'Adolescence is just around the corner,' considered Charlotte. 'Which will be good for their vocabulary, I suppose.'

'They'll not be using any of those words at dinner parties,' said Roddy. He wished that he had the sort of offspring who enjoyed canvassing with him. Or enjoyed anything at all with him, for that matter. His men's group had suggested he get on their level, so he'd had a go at Fortnite. It felt like vertigo with a pickaxe. With two boys, he'd had enough of zombies to last him a decade.

'Well, I think their swearing's vastly improved recently,' replied his wife.

'The boys, or your parents'?' asked Roddy, and guffawed.

Charlotte made a face. Not the least among her husband's annoying tendencies was his habit of laughing at all his own jokes, even the weakest ones. She decided to let it go.

'Do you have the directions there, carissimo?' she said, silkily. 'Only I thought we had to take a turn off somewhere near Haverhill?'

'Why the hell Fred couldn't have given a postcode that the Sat Nav would recognise, I can't imagine,' grumbled her husband, as he fumbled with his notes. 'Surely no one has bothered with written directions for at least the last decade?'

'You're certainly out of practice, Roddy. Pay attention and stick to what you're doing. And no deviations. We'll get there in the end. Even if it takes a bit longer.'

'Much like sex then', muttered her husband, darkly.

'What, dear?'

'Nothing, darling…' said Roddy. For him, sex had been postponed more times than the British road to socialism, and both prospects depressed him greatly. He had abandoned youthful zeal, but felt too young for gravitas. 'Anyway, if that was Much Flittering, I think we're fine on this road for another five miles… Can I leave you to it while I read these Party text messages?'

'About the weekend? Are there even more instructions?' wailed Charlotte. 'The dress code was complicated enough! I defy anyone over thirty to look her best in an Empire line dress. I'm so relieved Fred is only going to be forty once.' She glanced over at her husband. 'When we hit forty, please let's do something simple. Are we going to have a joint thing?'

Roddy shot her an incredulous glance. Luckily her eyes were back on the road. He resumed his reading with a snort.

'No, not *that* party. *The* Party.'

Roddy was not entirely sure about how to play his hand within the Labour Party. He was confused about his image and messaging. For a start, he liked to be known, in Labour Movement circles, as Rod. He felt that sounded, well, more blue-collar. Rod wanted to suggest that he was aware of allotments, he might even have visited an allotment, but also that he could identify a fish knife in a line-up, and had had at least one meeting in Brussels. He just hadn't yet decided how he was going to play it. He also had a certain nervousness about affiliating with his leader. In a maelstrom of indecision, Rod had run aground on the shoals of ideological branding.

'Bugger the Party,' said Charlotte with feeling, as she allocated another pound coin to her virtual swearbox. Forty-seven was it? Forty-eight? Mothers of the World would be able to afford a new bouncy castle in no time.

Charlotte was worrying about clothes again. So was her husband. Middle-age was a sartorial maze. For example, Roddy was in a perpetual crisis as to whether to wear a Lands End brushed cotton checked shirt or a Hugo Boss suit with a Paul Smith shirt. And should he carry a handkerchief? If so, what type? Red could be a radical option, but might risk him looking strangely Tory when in his top pocket. He wanted to be seen as a safe pair of hands, but also a dynamic innovator, at the same time. Mature, but forever young. A feminist, but not wet. Sexy but not sexist. He had been trying to cultivate a wildflower meadow of different messages but had unwittingly created a monoculture of stinging nettles.

Not far away, on a winding by-road, a battered Luton van was spluttering along like a Geordie with emphysema. On the dashboard was a selection of plant pots – basil, thyme, oregano and mint. At least one police officer had sternly expressed scepticism as to whether Hugh had a clear view of the road, given the window box, but so far Hugh's sullenness had won out. He had always been resolutely defiant of other people's opinions. He wore his perennial fatigues of worn corduroy trousers, plaid viyella shirt and frayed tweed jacket. His look was only enlivened by the odd, sometimes very odd, jumpers knitted for him by his sister, which he never threw away. This one was in lilac and orange stripes, and it already had holes in. Hugh would have been fascinated by the medieval proverb 'For clothyng oft maketh man', but in his case, clothyng oft maketh scarecrow. He had not the slightest interest in his appearance, and dressed only to keep comfortable, as the weather demanded. More than once, a stranger had requested of him the latest copy of *The Big Issue*.

The back of the van was all panelling and shelves and fold-out bed. In the corner, a wood-burning stove sat on the reinforced floor, its chimney neatly poking out of the roof.

On the bookshelves opposite sat some very battered copies of the Moomin books and a complete set of Pevsner, as well as a much-thumbed edition of *The Wind in the Willows* dating from his childhood. Hugh considered the loyal Luton his nest, his home from home. In earlier years, he had actually lived in it, going from one cabinet-making job to another, making shelves and pulpits and doors and wardrobes as his clients demanded. Now, he squatted in his brother's garden studio in Richmond, though the battered van parked outside was always enticing him with the prospect of a cosy escape from the confusing demands of modern life, such as tax credits and the opposite sex.

The coming weekend definitely came into the category of confusing demands. Why did he feel obliged to attend? Probably because Fred was his oldest friend, indeed the only school friend he was in touch with. Hugh shuddered at the thought of boarding school. They'd met properly in Mr K's sculpture studio. Fred had been bashing out the same Easter Island head from a block of soapstone for most of his sixth form career, while Hugh was carving a series of wooden blocks into versions of the woman of his dreams. No eligible women in sight, of course. Intimate knowledge of the sculpted feminine form was of zero benefit when he finally got up close and personal with a woman on his degree course. Should have talked less about Rodin and more about sex, back when he was hanging out with Mr K – who must surely have had some relationship wisdom to impart, given that he himself was married to a shy odalisque of monumental beauty.

In their gap year, Fred had been Hugh's companion on a grand tour of Europe, courtesy of the Interrail pass, enduring the youth hostels of the Continent while investigating Fra

Angelico and Gian Lorenzo Bernini, and the cheapest ways in which two impecunious teenagers could get drunk in any given European city. Then, Fred had gone to St Warburg's, and Hugh had gone to study philosophy at Balliol, partly for want of anything better to do, and partly to fulfil what his parents expected. After all, they were looking for a return on ten years of private schooling.

Oxford behind him, he'd been able to reject the stuffiness of his upbringing. There'd been the stone quarry in Swanage, the Luton van and now Existential Woodwork (trademark not applied for), so he'd not really seen Fred much, after years on the road. But Hugh did show up once to lay a patio for him. After all the poor guy could hardly manage that sort of thing himself, and solicitors obviously could pay for that sort of thing. Shame he'd scraped the bloody Luton in the driveway. And of course, Hugh had built some bookshelves for Fred's front room. But this weekend with Fred and his college and work pals sounded far too much like one of the old school reunions. Hugh could doubtless expect lots of dismissive reactions from city types.

'You'll like them,' Fred had promised. 'Well, some of them. My brother Roderick will be there, you know him.'

'That's not persuasive…'

'And Polly, my college friend. You met her at my thirtieth. She liked you. She's a bit, you know, unconventional herself. And of course, then there's Heather, remember her? I had a serious crush on her all through third year.'

'Was Heather the one who dated pop stars? The only person I've ever met who was impervious to Glastonbury mud?'

'Yes, that's her,' said Fred, wistfully. 'You must have seen her on telly, reporting from some global hotspot. Very… charismatic, Heather.'

'Not without having a television.'

'Ah. Well, I've not actually seen her in the flesh myself since finals. We Skype from time to time.'

'You have mentioned her once or twice. Bit of a soft spot?'

'Well,' started Fred, and stopped in embarrassment.

'She's OK with the whole wheelchair thing?'

'Broadly. Although she rather sweetly sent me a box of fruit when I was in rehabilitation hospital.'

'I look forward to meeting her,' said Hugh.

'As do I,' said Fred. 'As do I...'

Polly Nobbs and her daughter Freya, seven going on seventeen, had chosen to hitchhike. This decision was mostly involuntary, given that they had managed to get as far as Sudbury by train, and then missed the bus. Freya was wearing dungarees and a T-shirt, and her mother was equally androgenous in black jeans, Doc Marten boots and a checked flannel work shirt. She felt she was rocking the feminist social worker look.

'It's not far,' said Polly, hopefully.

'Can I sit on your shoulders?' said her daughter, who Polly felt was getting too big for that.

'Only if you stick out your thumb like you really mean it,' said Polly, hoping that the presence of a child and a large rucksack would cause a kind motorist to pull over, and scare off the creeps. It might compensate for her crewcut, which she'd concealed under a bandana.

'Am I going to have to wear fancy dress?' said Freya, after a few minutes of laborious progress down the A131.

'Well, you are going to have to wear *a* dress,' said her mother. 'It's all I've brought.'

'I don't like dresses, I like jeans! You know that.'

'I know darling, so do I,' said Polly, patiently. 'But tomorrow night's a special party for our friend Fred.'

'Is he going to wear a dress?'

'I very much doubt it, Freya. For one thing, I think he'd probably get a dress tangled up in his wheels.'

'Well, I don't want to wear a dress either then…'

'The dressing up is all because the house we are going to stay at is special,' said Polly. 'It's very, very old… like in a Jane Austen film.'

'Jane Austen? Will there be zombies?!'

'I think you've got that wrong, sweetheart. And I don't think you should be watching films with zombies in.'

'Mummy let me!'

'Well, Mummy Georgina shouldn't,' said Polly, making a mental note to have stern words with her ex-partner when they next met up for fennel tea and vegan fruitcake. It was hard enough single-parenting, without the tensions of shared-parenting added.

'I like horror films!' pouted Freya. 'Anyway, I bet there weren't any children in Jane Austen.'

'Well, she certainly didn't have any…'

'See!'

At that moment, Freya's literary education gave way to frantic thumb waving. The Mini Cooper that had just passed them at high speed carried on, with an apologetic arm flapped out of the window.

'Damn!' said Polly. 'I wish I'd brought the bike. This is going to take all afternoon.' She let her daughter down off her shoulders and rubbed her neck. 'Keep hold of my hand.'

'I'm not a baby, Polly,' said her nearest and dearest.

Just then they heard another car approaching. Polly took off her bandana and waved it hopefully. Freya shrieked. The vehicle slowed down. It was a battered Luton van, with a chimney pointing out of the roof and fiddle music on the tape deck.

Ten minutes later, Freya was slumbering gently in the back, and Hugh was trying to think of things to say to her mother.

'Remind me how you know Fred?' he asked, finally, as the Luton struggled up a hill. East Anglia was far bumpier than its reputation suggested. 'It was college, wasn't it?'

'I knew him in college. We were both studying law,' said Polly. 'We went out briefly. I think Fred was smitten with me for about a month, although he wasn't what I was looking for back then. But after that we ended up as great friends. Soul mates, in a way.'

'Sounds good to me,' said Hugh, feeling a bit envious of Fred's skills at soul-matery.

'We cried on each other's shoulders a fair bit. And then we lost touch. We've only reconnected over the last couple of years. And here I am. A single parent, or at least a part-time single parent, Betty Bothways if you like, but thankfully still friends with Fred. He's as close as Freya gets to having a godfather... a sort of constant in our lives.'

'Constant is about right,' agreed Hugh. He didn't think he'd met Betty Bothways. 'Sometimes I think Fred's super-power is friendship.'

Chapter 4

None of the party guests having arrived yet, Fred was taking Humphrey for what passed for a walk back at the Hall. He was impatient for action, as was his owner. Fred shared the pug with his next-door neighbour in King Street, and it was his weekend for custody. Although officially Humphrey wasn't here at all. The Trust were quite clear that no dogs were allowed, because of the livestock in the local fields, but then they'd never met Humphrey, who rarely chased anything more lifelike than an inflatable rubber pig. Humphrey was less of a dog, more of a pop-eyed hot water bottle. Being legally trained and anxious about rules, Fred had had qualms of conscience, but then he'd decided that if the Trust staff turned up unannounced, they could probably just hide Humphrey under a duvet or in a closet. Thankfully, pugs were as placid as they were stubborn. Offered a comfortable cupboard, Humphrey would likely just go to sleep.

Lorna, his King Street neighbour, was insistent that their pet shouldn't eat proprietary dog food. Humphrey had an enviable diet of organic free-range chicken breast. Fred regretted he had no time to make the sort of exotic meat loaf which Lorna lovingly prepared for the dog. Not for the first time, he wished he had chosen to celebrate his fortieth birthday with a simple drink down the local pub. But that way, he couldn't have inveigled the globe-trotting Heather into the party. It was just a shame that Lorna herself was away on a week-long meditation retreat.

Humphrey, who on a good day was very popular with the ladies, sniffed the flowers appreciatively, before selecting the best of them to cock his leg on. He'd also left a deposit on the croquet lawn, which his owner had carefully scooped up. Now Fred patiently followed after the pug, pondering his random assortment of friends. Did forty mark the beginning of the end or the end of the beginning? He hoped the latter. His life was frustratingly incomplete. Sometimes it was more like a half-life. The problem came down to women. Although women weren't the problem.

The challenge of how to appear manly to the opposite sex had often perturbed Fred during the eighteen years that followed the onset of his paraplegia. His arms and shoulders and chest were certainly as muscular as anyone could possibly wish for, now that he wheeled everywhere, as he had thought in the shower that morning. He could crack nuts with his fingers. Given some chemical assistance and an hour's advance notice, he could muster a rather impressive erection. He knew other paraplegic men who were almost hyper-masculine – going sit-skiing, which verged on suicidal, or playing wheelchair rugby, which appeared far more homicidal than the standing kind. He had even taken part in a few marathons himself, but he didn't really have a very sporty nature. Sweat and blisters weren't appealing.

He was less of a jock and more of a listener, which meant that women liked talking to him, and as a result he had some very close friends. But all too often, he found that women tended to see him as a sympathetic companion, rather than an object of desire. He'd listened to a lot of relationship problems, he'd even helped draft a few lonely-hearts ads, but he himself remained slim, successful, but frustratingly single. So much so, that he'd had no need to worry about how he might overcome his slight phobia of naked femininity. That was still a brassiere too far. First, he needed to break out of the friend zone and he'd come up with exactly the plan for that.

Fred's life had been marked by the tragedy that had befallen him and his family during the summer of his Finals, nearly twenty years ago. Fred's father David had been driving through the winding roads of Tenerife with the two brothers and their mother Effy. David Twistleton was a GP, a Methodist lay minister, and somewhat straight-laced. Unfortunately, on leaving the café where they had lunched, and being an absent-minded driver at the best of times, he had made a turn onto the wrong side of the road. As they passed the neighbourhood nudist beach, he had prudishly averted his eyes from the naked flesh adorning the foreshore, ignoring the tourists who were urgently flagging them down. Coming around a bend at a moderate speed, they had smashed head-on into a jeep driven, as if on the Nürburgring, by two German tourists.

The hire car was a complete write-off. Dr and Mrs Twistelton miraculously avoided the worst, walking away with cuts and bruises, a nasty case of whiplash, and everlasting guilt. Roderick was saved from serious injury because he was wearing a seatbelt. Fred, however, who was not, was flung out of the vehicle and landed in the nudist colony. His spine was fractured at the lowest thoracic vertebrae, and he was med-evacuated back to a Spinal Injury Unit in Middlesborough, thanks to the travel insurance in which Dr Twistelton had prudently invested. Life with paraplegia awaited him, and a shiny new lightweight wheelchair was his prize.

Ever since, the unfortunate Fred had associated nudity with tragedy. On top of being unable to walk, he found romance all but impossible. The problem was not physical, but psychological. He had indeed tried everything, even weekly sessions of post-trauma counselling in Swiss Cottage. The therapist had been a Canadian lady, who would very slowly undress while making reassuring noises. Fred passed out every time. Unfortunately, his 'little difficulty' was with intimacy, not insomnia. Plus, he had a marked antipathy towards Middlesborough, where he had spent the worst three months of his life: the nurses were lovely, but Teeside was ever after destined to be a closed book to him.

The Germans who had been driving the jeep were miraculously unharmed, although very put out by the incident. To them, it was entirely the fault of the ignorant British driving on the left, violating the European rules of the road. It was a most inconvenient mistake which had all but ruined their vacation. In 2016, they celebrated Brexit with gleeful schadenfreude.

Now, twenty years on from The Accident, Fred saw, as he and Humphrey rounded the corner, that his older brother Roderick had just parked the Toyota Hybrid, with characteristic care, outside Threepwood Hall. Flinging open the passenger door, Charlotte rushed out to greet her brother-in-law. He was much less tiresome than her husband, and so much easier to escape from. She pecked Fred on the cheek. Then, most obligingly, she was swept off her feet – not by Fred, but at the sight of the Hall.

'Oh. My. God! This is place is amazing!' Charlotte looked around her in disbelief. '*Country Life* will love this! I wasn't even sure that we'd come to the right address. That long drive through the parkland!'

Fred chuckled. This was exactly the reaction he was hoping for.

'Isn't it great?' he beamed. 'Straight out of *Pride and Prejudice?*' He didn't mind spending money on his family and friends, but he particularly loved it when they appreciated it. All that was missing was the discreet butler with the tray of chilled drinks.

Charlotte flung her arms around Fred and gaily kissed him again on each cheek, which was rather more forward than he was used to. No doubt due to relief at being out of a car with his brother.

'Here! We brought you a present!' she said, handing over an expensively wrapped cube. Fred made appropriate noises as he unwrapped it. And then looked blank.

'It's a scented candle,' said his sister-in-law. 'And don't call me twee. My life has been changed by scented candles.'

Fred was taken aback. This was an unexpected revelation.

'I have two pre-pubescent sons who fart more times in a day than they shower in a month,' she spelled out. 'And while you may not suffer those precise indignities, I seem to remember you do have a dog... Oh, there he is,' she said, backing away from Humphrey.

'This is certainly quite the gaff!' said Roddy, bringing up the bags. 'Hello, bro. Happy birthday!'

'Thanks, Roderick!' said Fred. They didn't kiss. 'Great to see you too. How are the boys?'

'Obnoxious,' replied his brother, stroking the dog. 'They're with Lottie's parents this weekend. A respite from their perennial sulking.'

Charlotte had flung open the main door and was looking around the entrance hall, and the beautifully restored rooms off it.

'No wonder you wanted us to dress up!' she said.

'Look at that dining room,' said Fred, proudly. 'The table alone is spectacular!'

'Can we go and explore?' asked Charlotte. 'Or do you need help? I've brought some nibbles, I'll get them from the car in a minute.'

'Make yourselves at home,' said the temporary Lord of the Manor. 'Your room is on the first floor. It's the one with the view.'

'Oooo, I want to check it out!' she squealed in excitement. 'Roddy, bring the bags!'

Without stopping for a reply, Charlotte was away up the staircase.

Roddy glanced at his brother and rolled his eyes.

'Glad the comrades can't see this, to be honest. But Lottie's right, this is very special. Shame about the Wi-Fi and phone reception... You'd have thought they could have invested in a router, in this day and age. Also, they need speed bumps on that drive.'

'According to the visitors' book, you can get a mobile signal if you stand next to the Smithson statue on the ha-ha,' said Fred.

Roddy brightened up. He hated being out of touch with Party Head Office.

'Excellent! That will make all the difference, going forward!'

'A relief for us all,' replied Fred. 'Careful with that bag!' he said, lurching forward to save the pricey-looking Art Deco standard lamp which Roddy had knocked off the hall table as he hefted the second grip onto his shoulder. Roddy was a living exponent of the proverb: 'If it ain't broke, it soon will be'.

Her room inspected, face refreshed and *Daily Treasures* installed on the bedside, Charlotte was soon back downstairs, bringing in things from the car with her husband.

'I'm on a mission from Marks!' she said, entering through the back door into the kitchen. Fred was hovering to greet other guests. Being the host seemed to be a tiring business. Charlotte went out for another couple of carrier bags. She came back smiling warmly: 'I brought some hummus!'

Coming up behind her with the cool box, Roddy winced. His wife used the word for leaf mould whenever she referred to the Mediterranean chickpea dip. He'd given up trying to correct her.

'I do love hummus myself...' continued Charlotte. 'Classic hummus, not the onion sort, it's got kilos of sugar in it... although of course the crisps are sooo bad for you too... and I can't have my hummus without my crisps'.

She looked around for her cool box and bags.

'Where are the crisps, people? What have I done with the crisps? And I got olives, you can never have too many olives... It's a bit like a messy, really...'

'MEZZE!' hissed Roddy at her in irritation.

Charlotte continued, as oblivious to the parlous state of her marriage as she was to pronunciation rules: 'I'm sorry, I'm sure it's all disgusting, but if we get some drinks down us, nobody will know...'

Charlotte continued unpacking Marks and Spencer's picnic food from her cool box. Fred had cheerfully suggested a

Geordie buffet for the first day's lunch: home-made pork pies and black pudding and pickled onions, ham and pease pudding sandwiches and bits of pizza. He had assured Roderick and Charlotte that it would be ironic, and that his metropolitan friends would love it, especially if it was sourced from Borough Market. Except the vegans, though it was impossible to make them truly happy. But now, true to form, Charlotte was piling the table with plastic containers from a supermarket. Nothing home-made, not even the soup. Poor Robin would be horrified. Polly would be scornful that it was M&S not Lidl.

Fred went outside to have a sly fag. The weekend was feeling more and more stressful.

Chapter 5

The battered Luton chugged up the drive, spluttering dyspeptically. It finally made it to the gravel sweep in front of the portico and unloaded Polly and Freya, who flung her arms wide and dashed all around the park that surrounded the great house. Fred quickly stubbed out his cigarette and concealed the stub about his person.

'It's amaaaazing!' shouted Freya, as she scampered. Hugh stood in awe, of child and view.

'Rather better than our ex-council flat in Hackney,' agreed Polly. 'Room to run around, for a start. And no danger of needles in the long grass.'

'Only pine needles,' said Fred, who was waiting for them under the portico. 'Although I hate gravel! And mind the ha-ha!' he added. 'There's a fall of several metres.'

'What's an aha?' asked Freya, puzzled, pulling up short.

'Ha-ha,' corrected her mother. 'It's a sort of wall in the ground. It looks as if it isn't there. You think you are on solid ground, and then everything gives way, which is presumably why it's called a ha-ha. But be careful, because it's quite a drop.' said Polly.

Hugh nodded.

'I had no idea what one was,' said Polly, 'but the Trust website mentioned it. I thought at first it might be a bouncy castle.'

'Bouncy castle?!' repeated Freya, still panting from her circumnavigation of the building. 'Where?'

'Sorry, darling. No soft play. And please mind the edge. But there is a dog…'

Freya looked excitedly around her.

'Humphrey's certainly soft,' agreed Fred.

The dog looked about him in some disgust, and then returned inside. His sole ambition in life was to sleep next to an Aga, within sniffing distance of his dinner bowl.

'Really, it's all about eighteenth-century property values,' said Hugh. 'If you have a ha-ha, that means that you don't need a wall or a fence to keep out nature. The view is intact – in fact, it looks as if you own the whole landscape. It's like an infinity pool, only in grass.'

'Are you going to lecture us for the whole weekend?' asked Fred. 'Only, if you are, I'd better go get my notebook.'

'I was interested, actually.' said Polly.

'But seriously, the Trust is fantastic,' said Hugh. Cynicism was fighting a losing battle with wonder. 'Just look at that guttering!'

'They reclaim all these old houses and put them to use,' said Fred, who just hoped the plumbing was as good as the guttering.

'I'm surprised they've never brought Hugh in to help with restoration,' said Polly, who had warmed to him on the drive. 'Aren't you a cabinet maker? Couldn't you do the shelves and so forth?'

'There's still time,' said Hugh. 'I'll leave my business card in the visitors' book. Should I park around the back so as not to disturb the Regency effect?'

'Oh, yes please,' said Fred. 'There's parking next to the kitchen door.' Hugh drove around in the van, as Polly and Freya talked to Fred.

A few moments later, a black cab puttered up the drive and disgorged Sonia at the front door. Her outfit signalled that she was a 'motherly-support-to-troubled-artist' kind of an agent, rather than a ball-breaking deal hound. In the office, she had taken to wearing reading glasses on a cord around her neck, even though she was a year short of forty. There were few Sinhala women in publishing, which made her distinctive, and she was as beautiful as ever. Her long cardigan reached her mid-thigh, over dove grey leggings and a batik tunic dress. Her clothes, like her, were vaguely ethnic but acceptable anywhere.

'Reunion time!' called Sonia, beaming at her old friend with unfeigned affection. She held out her arms to Fred, leant down and squeezed him awkwardly.

'Welcome to Threepwood!' said Fred, with equal feeling, as he untangled himself from her beads. 'Thanks for coming.'

'Anil sends his love,' said Sonia, 'from his business trip to Denver.'

'Your tenth anniversary must be around now, given that you met at my thirtieth?' asked Fred.

'How could I forget that awful field in Northumberland?' said Sonia. 'Freezing cold, and I've not used a composting toilet since.' Hugh, back from parking, nodded approvingly. He knew far more about wild camping than was good for anyone.

'Maybe it's your turn?' Fred said to Polly.

'For what?' she said, blankly. She had one eye on her daughter, who was cartwheeling across the lawn.

'To meet the... person. Of your dreams,' he said. 'At my party.'

'Oh, I never remember my dreams,' Polly said blithely. 'All men are bastards, remember? And women are complicated. It would be better to make peace with being a single parent. Freya's a full-time job.'

'She'll be well looked after this weekend,' said Fred, looking round to see where the child had got to. 'Heather has no children, we're still waiting for Sonia to produce, and Charlotte's got girl-envy. Freya will have as many aunties as she wants.'

Sonia studied her feet rather than catch anyone's eye. That familiar failure feeling crept up again.

'And uncles?' said Polly, frowning.

'Of course,' said Fred and Hugh, in gallant unison. Freya was an enchanting child, thought Hugh, surprising himself. And you could always give her back to Polly when it got too much, felt Fred, who'd had more experience of feral nephews. Perfect.

At that moment, a VW Polo drove up to the small group who were standing in the sun, surrounded by daffodils. Fred's former housemate Robin bounced out of the hire car, smiling earnestly, while his new boyfriend Alberto stepped out more formally, looking around first to check his surroundings. Alberto was dressed, styled, accessorised and finished as if he had walked straight out of the pages of GQ. He draped an expensive-looking leather jacket over his striped T-shirt. He had the tan and build of a professional tennis player, although he was rather better in conversation, and he walked in the skinniest pair of jeans with the unconscious elegance of a dancer. Robin wore an ill-advised tight salmon pink T-shirt under a suit jacket.

Alberto glanced around, and nodded approvingly at what he saw. This was more like it. He carefully arranged his most becoming smile and stepped forward to shake Fred's hand.

'I am Alberto Rivas,' he announced with a flourish, enunciating his words precisely. He gave a small bow from the waist. 'Thank you for... accommodating me, Frederick. Robin has told me everything about you.'

'Really?' said Fred in surprise at the formality. 'Well, you are very welcome. It's a great pleasure to meet you. Robin is one of my dearest friends.'

'Does the house have a good oven?' asked Alberto.

'An oven?' said Fred in surprise. 'I suppose it must have, but I confess I haven't checked.'

'No matter,' said the Costa Rican. 'Just leave it to me.'

Mystified, Fred turned and smiled warmly at his old housemate. Robin ignored the hand, put an arm around Fred's neck and kissed him on both cheeks.

'Good to see you looking so well, Freddy darling. Happy birthday!'

'Your room is on the top floor, guys,' said Fred. 'Apparently, you have a fantastic bathroom. Make sure you take a photo for me.' He ushered them into the house. Alberto went on an inspection of the kitchen appliances. Sonia, Hugh, Polly and Freya were left on the drive outside Threepwood Hall.

'Freya,' pondered Sonia. 'That's an unusual name, isn't it?'

Freya glowed.

'You'd have thought so,' said Polly. 'We certainly did when we came up with it. But it turns out that there are three of them in Freya's class.'

'Freyr was the goddess of rain and sunshine,' offered Hugh. 'You're obviously an outdoors person then?'

'I guess,' replied Freya, doubtfully. 'Although I prefer my Nintendo.'

'There's rather a lot of pollution in Islington,' explained Polly.

'But not here!' said Hugh, wondering if the little girl would turn out to be more sunshine or showers.

'Is anyone this weekend going to be married with 2.4 children?' enquired Polly, with interest. 'Because so far, it's evident that Fred is failing at heteronormativity.'

'I'm doing my best,' thought Sonia, who was hopeful.

'What's heteronormativity?' wondered Hugh.

'Can I play my recorder now?' asked Freya.

Chapter 6

As they deposited their bags in their room, admired their view over the gardens from the window and freshened up, Robin explained to Alberto the parameters of their future life together. They'd had versions of this conversation before. Alberto reluctantly put aside his iPhone to listen to his boyfriend's briefing.

'I might take you to a dinner party with the Vice-Chancellor. And it's not impossible that I get invited to be the keynote at the British Psychological Society annual conference, and they'd definitely wine me and dine me.'

Alberto looked at him witheringly.

'Will there be paparazzi outside? Will the chef have at least one Michelin star? Will I even have to wear a tuxedo?'

Robin shook his head in embarrassment.

'No, no, of course I know it doesn't compare to what you're used to…'

'Querido, I may be in a different world now,' Alberto sighed (a little too theatrically Robin thought). 'But driving here in a hired VW… Polo,' – he spat out the last word in disdain – 'is a bit of a… how you say, go down?'

'Come down,'' interjected Robin. 'In English, you must say "come down".'

'Exactly,' said Alberto, not entirely certain where the difference lay. 'In the old days, someone would have sent me a limo. Or possibly even a jet.' He smiled wistfully. Jean-Francois had been fond of the grand gesture. 'And everything so spectacular! The cameras! The cocaine!' He sighed.

'Well, I don't think you can expect Class A drugs at Fred's fortieth, Alberto. But I think I've got a bottle of poppers somewhere,' Robin said defensively, as he brushed his teeth.

Alberto rolled his eyes.

'These days I am beyond that. I eat nothing but organic. I drink only mineral water. I've had...' he did a rough calculation and halved it, 'ten years of excess... Nearly. It's time to be kind to my body.'

'Let me be kind to your body!' said Robin, eagerly. Too eagerly? He was incredulous that he was now permitted to lie in bed alongside someone so... lithe and taut and... and... He gulped and looked away. Life's poker dealer had finally passed him a good card, and he wasn't up to bluffing.

Alberto mournfully considered the many puddings he had been eating. His sweet tooth was his downfall. He turned his chiselled features from one side to the other, while inspecting himself in the mirror. He sucked in his stomach experimentally.

'Should I have some work done, Robin?' He corrected himself. 'More work?'

'Certainly not,' said his partner. 'You look like a... spring chicken!' That analogy was all wrong. 'You have lovely eyes! And dimples...'

Alberto tried fluttering his eye lids at himself. Was it possible to flirt with yourself? He flashed a grin at the mirror and scowled.

'Botox would solve the crow claws…'

'But for god's sake!' protested Robin. 'That would mean you couldn't even smile properly! Expressions are feelings!'

Alberto remembered one friend from his escort days, who had had so much work done that he was left with the emotional range of a greyhound. He turned to Robin, with the sincerity of a Club Class flight attendant: 'Daaarliing… being with you is enough to make me feel beautiful'.

Considering himself to have regained Perfect Boyfriend status, Alberto fired off another message from his iPhone.

Robin sighed. He wasn't sure whether he should worry about whether he was competing with another man – or men – or whether his partner was merely suffering from advanced social media addiction. It might be better not to know. Robin felt now his only job was to make Alberto happy. It was unfortunate that he'd never had even basic training for this tricky role. Being a consultant clinical psychologist was clearly not enough. His companion was well out of his metrosexual comfort zone. He wondered what he'd think of his fellow guests this weekend.

'So you never actually slept with him?' came the voice in Sonia de Saram's ear. She was having a lie-down in her room, and Anil had phoned from America before he started his working day.

'No, Anil, I said to you before, we were only ever pals,' said Sonia, patiently. She pulled her Missoni cardigan over her, wishing that the Hall had better central heating. British summer was as chilly as an evening in hill country.

'Because it sounds very romantic… like some Bollywood movie,' said her husband down the line.

'It wasn't a song and dance number. It may have been hot and dusty that summer, but Cambridge bus station is not exactly the sub-continent. I was sorting out accommodation for my final year at uni. He'd been visiting Robin I think, he wasn't in a wheelchair back then. We got talking in the queue for the London coach. Then there was one space left and the bus driver asks "Are you two together?" and although we'd been getting on like a house on fire in the queue, both of us were too shy to say yes.'

'And then you met again at an SWP meeting? That dates you rather!'

'Everyone interesting was briefly a Trot,' said Sonia. She had only lasted one summer with the comrades, who took an objectional line on the Sri Lankan conflict, among other problems. Plus, they were sleazy as hell.

'He was a wheelie by then, of course. Anyway, we became firm friends, wrote loads of letters, went to the Edinburgh Festival together, that sort of thing... We might have gone further, but there was this weird thing where he found it challenging when I took my top off.'

'I find it challenging when you don't take your top off.'

'Yeah, yeah,' said Sonia, who could find her husband trying sometimes, 'I have no sympathy for you.'

'Don't deny it! You long for the tickle of my moustache on your inner thighs...' She could imagine Anil smirking. 'How could he resist you topless? At school he was always absolutely desperate for a girlfriend.'

'We were going to go swimming, somewhere very ill-advised, I think it must have been the North Sea. It was our first trip up to the festival and we were taking a break from driving. I didn't have a costume, so I said I'd just skinny dip in my knickers, there was no one around. But when I pulled off my T-shirt, he practically vomited.'

'Charming!'

'Well, it certainly didn't do much for my ego. I mean, I know my boobs are probably smaller than yours are…'

'Thanks, darling. Blame it all on the dahl makhani.'

'Well, we didn't proceed any further towards intimacy, let's put it that way. At the time, I wondered whether it was because of him being paralysed.'

Anil murmured sympathetically. 'I think I can guess the problem… You do know about The Accident?'

'You mean the crash? Vaguely. What's this got to do with me being topless?' asked Sonia.

'That's what I am explaining, no? According to Roderick, ever since The Accident, poor Fred has connected nudity with disaster. You remember, the crash was right outside a Nudist Colony? Fred now finds nudity very traumatic. On top of being unable to walk, relationships are no end of trouble.'

'That's wonderful!' Sonia exclaimed, before quickly correcting herself. 'I mean, what an awful story!'

'Would have made you a lot less paranoid, eh?' said Anil.

'Yes, but the main thing is that it sounds like the poor guy needs support… psychological help.' And a publisher, she thought to herself.

'Oh, I think he's tried,' said Anil. 'Psychotherapy. Hypno-therapy. Aversion therapy. Everything. I suggested yoga, myself,' he added.

'Poor Fred,' sighed Sonia. 'So sad. But at the same time, this sounds like powerful stuff!'

'What do you mean?'

'Well, Fred's written this all up… he wants me to look at his manuscript this weekend. See if I can place it. I didn't realise the material was so strong… Well worth reading. There's lots about you in it, apparently!'

'Me?'

'Your friendship, his visit to your family in Mumbai… that's what he said anyway…'

'Oh no,' said Anil, in alarm. 'You wouldn't want to read that at all. I don't think anyone needs to read all that.'

'I'll be the judge of that, darling. Although, it's not a great time for me to go partying…'

'How are you feeling?' The voice in her ear seemed anxious.

'A bit tired after my week,' she replied, guardedly. 'Endless holding of anxious authors' hands… Metaphorically, you understand,' she added quickly. Anil did have a tiresome tendency towards jealousy.

'Not feeling sick?' he asked, solicitously.

'Not at all,' said Sonia.

'Oh.' He seemed disappointed.

'Well, maybe a little bit,' she admitted.

'Excellent. That's the spirit.'

Chapter 7

As the clock in the hall chimed twelve thirty, and his guests gathered in the hall, Fred Twistleton was playing the role of country squire. Almost everyone had arrived and now he could relax and enjoy himself. His voice rang out across the ground floor.

'Welcome, everyone! Thank you all coming so far. Most of you have met before… at my thirtieth and thirty-fifth and so on. Now it's time for a lunchtime tipple. Charlotte has made her special fruit punch…'

'Punch was more of a Victorian thing, wasn't it?' called out Hugh. When he hammered home a point, it stayed hammered, thought Fred – as one might expect of a carpenter.

'We may have just the odd anachronism this weekend,' responded Polly. 'Like phones and laptops. I think I can cope with a glass of Charlotte's punch. If that's OK with our local historian?'

'And a buffet lunch, thanks to Lottie and Roderick,' Fred ignored the interruption, smiling weakly at his sister-in-law, 'is all laid out in the dining room. It's a Geordie buffet, to honour my Northern roots. With some Crouch End additions. So, come and go as you please. But please be careful not to spill anything. We're responsible for leaving everything just as we found it.'

He thought to himself that everything had begun reasonably well. It was a bit like being a rural auctioneer, but without the gavel. And entirely metaphorical sheep. Loudly debating the latest actions of the American president, the parlous state of the BBC, the contribution of climate change to the recent balmy weather and the plague of electric scooters in London, his guests moved into the panelled dining room. The spread was laid out on the unfeasibly long walnut dining table. Fred sighed. At least Charlotte had decanted the dips into bowls from the kitchen. He just hoped his friends would all get on, for his sake, and not try and score points off each other. He put most of the awkwardness down to nerves. But he felt there would be rather too much label-checking this weekend. At least with a few drinks inside them, people would surely start to relax.

Charlotte circled attentively with trays of the punch, in proper glass punch cups, with accompanying cheese straws. She'd had to quickly whistle up a non-alcoholic version for Freya. Though the drinks hadn't been the only problem. Sonia had wandered into the kitchen to enquire about the menu.

'Only, I am a bit anxious about taramasalata…'

'Anxious? Meaning you don't like it?' said Charlotte, impatiently. 'Or you're concerned about codfish stocks?'

'Oh, I love it, I'm just not sure I can *eat* it,' said Sonia, significantly.

'Are you vegetarian?'

'Well, Sinhalese are mostly Buddhist, you know, so yes, I was brought up vegetarian, though I started eating meat some years ago now. I'm not sure if I'm allowed fish *at the moment* though… I know I can't have sushi.'

'But we don't have sushi,' said Charlotte, in indignation.

'I *can* eat pigeon.'

'We don't have pigeon either! Who has pigeon? M&S don't even stock pigeon!'

'It's not that I *need* to eat pigeon. Just when I Googled, it said I could.'

'You can get reception?'

'No, but I checked on the way down. You can't be too careful.'

'Oh, I see,' said Charlotte, who found allergies a bit tiresome. She'd written a column about them, which made her practically an expert. Taking a platter out to the dining room, she called back: 'Do you have a list of what you can't eat?'

'Yes, listeria is a bit of a worry,' said Sonia, gazing out of the kitchen window absently.

'No, a *list*!' said Charlotte, coming back for another tray.

'Oh, I just keep it in my head. But it's constantly changing. They will keep on revising the rules.'

'Well, just keep us posted,' Charlotte said, 'day by day…'

'I'll be sure to update you,' said Sonia. 'When I can get reception.'

A few moments later, fortified with their drinks, Robin and Roddy were discussing their outfits for the birthday dinner. Robin was enthusiastic about his efforts:

'I tried very hard to get a totally authentic Regency look. Brocade waistcoat, I even have a stock tie… it's made of yards of silk. Beau Brummel eat your heart out!'

Robin worried maybe he'd overdone it. Alberto was standing beside him, poised like an attentive impala, displaying his best profile and ignoring the conversation around him much as an antelope ignores lions.

'Ah, I think Lottie and I may have got our historical enactment thing a few decades out,' admitted Roddy, sipping his punch. 'I mean, it's obvious we've made an effort, but they were all out of Georgian at the fancy dress place. So we're more like Louis Quatorze, I think. Or do I mean Quinze? Eighteenth century, anyway. The boys thought we looked bad. Not bad as in good, they kindly clarified. Bad as in shit. But I think it's mostly about making the effort.'

'Louis Quinze? I am trying not to picture you as a pair of dining chairs!' said Sonia, in surprise. 'No wonder your boys laughed.'

'Alberto knows actual fashion designers,' said Robin airily, as he reached out for another of the cheese straws which were so moreish. 'He went for a modern take on the Regency style.'

'Ooo, aren't you swish Alberto?!' said Polly.

'You have Beau Brummel to thank for men wearing trousers,' said Alberto, in an offhand way. 'He hated frills on men.'

Fred thought that Robin's new guy seemed to be fitting in fine. He'd obviously done his research. He smiled at Alberto as he passed.

'We do have an actual prize, you know! For the best period costume!'

The Costa Rican shrugged his shoulders, nonchalantly.

'It was nothing. I always try to fit in.'

Robin smirked at him, although his expression was lost on Alberto. Robin felt it was a shame that Alberto seemed so... cool. He had always thought Latinos were meant to be passionate, but Alberto took off-hand to a different level. What was a different level of off-hand? Off-elbow?

Polly walked over to look out at the park through the bay windows. There were trees swaying in the breeze, clusters of cows ruminating. It was all most satisfactorily the countryside. She was relaxing, now that there were a dozen people to look out for Freya, instead of just one stressed social worker. They were definitely going to have to do a group photo later, she thought, glad she had brought her camera.

'Who are you coming as?' asked Hugh, who was taking refuge from the more boisterous members of the party in the window bay.

'Well, I have a headdress. And a rather shapeless shift,' said Polly. 'I look quite like Jane Austen, I'd like to think. Quiet spinster sort of thing. Sexuality ambiguous. What about you?'

'I'm just wearing a velvet smoking jacket I picked up in Oxfam,' said Hugh. He tried to keep his wardrobe to a minimum, so he didn't have many options. And he didn't have a mirror in the van. 'I think it's maybe more Victorian than Regency. No idea whether it's the right thing.'

'And how about you, Freya?' asked Charlotte, who was sitting on the sofa next to them. She hadn't had much in common with Polly at college. Polly was always on Iraq war demos, and she was, well, busy with parties and essays and things. The one thing they had shared was their mutual friendship with Fred. But it was impossible not to adore Freya. Charlotte wished, not for the first time, that she'd had a girl.

'I'm going to be Grace Holloway…' said Freya.

Everyone looked blank.

'Doctor Who's assistant!' said Freya, proudly. There was a glimmer of recognition from Roddy and Charlotte. They'd seen the show, back in the days when the boys had conde-scended to watch TV with them.

'Apologies, everyone,' said Polly, wearily, 'I seem to have raised a nerd.'

'I'm not a nerd!' pouted Freya. 'You listened to the story with me! The Doctor goes back in time to meet Mary... Mary... Mum, what was her name again?'

'Shelley?' said Polly.

'Yes, he met her by a lake... She was the lady who wrote *Frankenstein*,' added Freya proudly. 'I was going to come as the Monster, but Mum said not to.'

'Quite understandable,' said Fred, wheeling over to their corner. 'No monsters this weekend, please.'

'Except for that vile statue in the garden!' exclaimed Hugh, his passion rising to a surprising level. 'I'm glad you didn't tell me about it, Fred. I definitely wouldn't have come if I had known one of Smithson's solipsistic monstrosities was anywhere near the premises.'

'Ah yes,' said Fred, making a face. 'It is a bit awful isn't it? Wasn't here last time I visited. It was installed by the Trust to celebrate an anniversary or something.'

'We called him Wally Smithson when I was at Art School,' said Hugh. 'I have no idea how he came to be regarded as the best British sculptor. All his work is so utterly trite! And it ruins the view over the park!'

Fred turned to Polly and Charlotte.

'You just have to remember, Hugh is completely house-trained, except when it comes to contemporary art. Be careful about parroting received opinions. He'll lose all respect for you.'

'I won't!' protested Hugh. 'I'll just show why you're wrong.'

Polly smiled. She hummed 'That's the Way (I Like It)' by KC and the Sunshine Band. Where had that come from? She shifted from side to side and bobbed her head. Passion! That's what the world needed.

'Would you like to listen to me play recorder, Aunty Charlotte?' asked Freya, with a calculated sweetness that was hard to refuse.

'Well…' began Charlotte.

'Oh thanks!' said the seven year old, and whipped out her plastic descant recorder. A moment later, the wobbling notes of 'Frère Jacques' filled the air. Glances were exchanged as Polly tried to indicate by her body language that the recorder was not her first choice, and that though she was proud of her daughter, she couldn't be held responsible for the noise she produced.

Wheeling away, Fred looked around the room to check that everyone else seemed happy and that his older brother was kept well away from the more delicate fixtures and fittings. He flinched and called over: 'Roderick, please do be careful of the fireguard. Those porcelain dogs look rather precious.'

His brother was slouching by the fireplace, millimeters from the Trust's best period detail. He leapt forward in alarm. There was a small crash and a yell.

'Quick, can we have a cloth, please?' called Charlotte. 'Roddy's knocked over my punch.'

There was an awkward silence as spillage and breakage were cleared up.

'We tend to only drink wine from workers' cooperatives,' Roddy announced to no one in particular, as he mopped up his drink, trying to look nonchalantly committed as he did so. Was that a thing? he wondered.

Meanwhile, as she listened to the third consecutive rendering of the French folk song, Charlotte was worrying again about her clothes. She had ordered virtually a new Boden wardrobe for this weekend. Her outfits had arrived wrapped in spotty tissue paper a couple of days before, but now she was at Threepwood Hall, they felt charmless and ill-fitting. She wished she'd not bought the sleeveless dress. Her upper arms, not being used to carrying anything heavier than a cottage pie for four, were not as toned as she might have liked. Generally, she favoured pink and red floral prints. She fancied that they were warm and inviting, although at a subliminal level, the colour combination was alarmingly like a cry for help.

As always when a group of people are thrown together, the chat was slightly louder than necessary. Several of the smiles concealed incipient panic, and the conversational forays were closer to chess gambits than the meeting of minds.

Having exhausted her repertoire, and now exploring the dining room, Freya edged closer to the pork pies, with all the boldness of a seven-year-old in training to be a secret service agent. She felt this was a more promising career option than 'minstrel'. She had already fashioned a gun from a handy tree root she had found in the garden. Later, she thought she would probably have to assassinate the little black piggy who she'd seen in the sty behind the great house. Now, while no one was watching, she thought she'd fill her face with meaty snacks. She felt that they would go well with the ice cream she had been promised later on, and Mummy Georgina would never know. Her Mum was off talking about constellations with the speccy guy from the van, so she figured the coast was clear. M15 could wait. Or was she with the FSB? She wasn't sure where her allegiance lay. Maybe it was more fun to be a double agent.

Fortified by alcohol, noise levels were rising back in the draw-ing room. Conversations were becoming more confessional.

'I have to say, I think having children is overrated,' said Charlotte, who made it a rule to ignore her husband wherever possible. Sonia listened politely. With Charlotte, you did get the feeling sometimes that she was trying out a new column on you. Getting a word in edgeways could be difficult.

'I felt that Freya's recorder could prove a bit trying,' admitted Sonia. 'She only seems to know one tune.'

'If you could call it a tune,' interjected Roddy, passing by on his way to the drinks.

'But it's better than what comes after,' Charlotte continued, ignoring her husband. 'Herod missed a trick, he should have focused on the adolescents. The myth about childbirth is that all the screaming stops at labour. Children are almost bearable until they hit puberty. Then the shit hits the fan.'

Sonia looked alarmed. She hadn't thought that babies grow eventually into bolshy teens, any more than besotted puppy owners anticipate the farting, snoring hound their darling little dog will become.

'Or the shit hits Granddad, as the case may be, if they get talking about the European Union,' Charlotte explained. 'Apparently, it's happened a lot more since Brexit.'

Robin was dining out on his new partner's contact book, although he wished he'd chosen someone other than Polly as his audience. Roddy or Sonia's partner Anil might have been properly impressed. He ploughed on regardless. Polly could only admire his enthusiasm, which made a change from his glumness at Fred's previous gatherings:

'He even says he might be able to get us ticket to Cannes – I am sure someone like you has been, of course. But it's new to me,' Robin issued a little squeak of pleasure. 'Imagine me, being on the Croisette! Following in the footsteps of, oh, I don't know, Jude Law or Antonio Banderas or some heart-throb…'

'Sounds like… heaven, I suppose,' said Polly, cautiously. 'If you like that sort of thing.'

She didn't think she would at all. Lesbian home life was so… well, homely, compared to what some of these gay guys aspired to.

Robin beamed at her. He had proudly watched his boyfriend sashaying into the dining room a few minutes earlier. To him, that was brilliant. All his life, he had appeared rather straight-acting, and now he could learn from a master and live a little. He felt he was finally himself. Robin swelled with pride. He felt like a lucky man.

As conversation flagged, Roddy spotted Charlotte talking to Sonia at the other side of the room. Emboldened by drink, he turned to Alberto.

'Look over there. My wife. The one with the plastic necklace…'

'Yes?'

'Well, put it this way, if I were choosing again I wouldn't go for blonde. £100 a month in Headmasters.'

'She looks charming,' said Alberto, who didn't understand the reference to the hairdressing chain. 'The belle of the ball, so to say.'

He didn't mention that Charlotte's hair was so dry it looked flammable, like a tiny haystack atop her head. She also seemed to be wearing a charmless necklace of hunks of misshapen coloured Perspex. Everything bad about man-made materials on a rope, he thought. He mentally rolled his eyes, as he searched for the *mot juste*.

'You would call her glamorous!' Alberto concluded.

'Oh, I suppose she's not so bad, really,' agreed Roddy, feeling a twinge of guilt. 'With her hair down, on a good day she looks like a ladies' golf captain. Attractive-ish.'

At that moment, a clatter began to impinge on the conversation. All eyes turned back to the french windows of the drawing room. Then there were lights, and a deafening racket, as if a very large washing machine had begun its final cycle.

'Wow!' gasped Freya, running over to the windows in excitement. 'It's a chopper!'

Sure enough, a small helicopter was descending onto the croquet lawn in front of the drawing room. Half a metre from the ground, a door slid open and a familiar figure leapt out, landing crouched and turning to give a thumbs up signal to the pilot, who shot up skywards, before banking to the west. As the vibrations abated, the figure straightened up, pulled off a baseball cap which sported the logo of a major media chain and shook out a mane of auburn hair, a tip she'd internalised from a youth watching *Challenge Anneka*.

Clustered around the french windows, more than one male gulped nervously as Heather Crisp, special correspondent, veteran of a series of wars and natural disasters, strode across the lawn, her famous carpet bag tossed casually over her shoulder. At the terrace doorway, she paused for effect, waiting until all eyes were on her. She tossed her hair again.

An epidemic of gallantry broke out. Roddy leapt forward first.

'Welcome! I'm Fred's older brother, the name's Rod, can I get you a drink? We have beer, wine, there may sherry somewhere...' He didn't pause for breath.

'Sherry?' Heather responded in disgust. 'Who still drinks that muck? Bring me a gin!'

'Don't think we have that,' called out Robin, standing by the drinks table. 'How about a whisky and ginger ale?'

'Easy on the ginger,' said Heather. 'I've been dry for two weeks in the bloody Hadhramaut. Never again. The insurgency didn't even get going properly, damned waste of time. Should have stayed in Aden, only it was getting a bit hot.'

Freya gazed at her spellbound. Heather was definitely the sort of person who she thought would have a gun.

'Are you from the CIA?' she said. Heather looked down at the child and flashed an expensive set of teeth.

'No, sweetheart. GTN. Global Television News. I'm a war correspondent.'

'She doesn't start wars,' said Roddy helpfully. 'She just tells people about them.'

'Well, to be honest, I have precipitated the odd minor conflict,' said Heather, gratefully taking a deep gulp of her drink. 'There was one interview I did in... when was it? 2008 in Eastern Europe... some shit hole in South Ossetia. They had plans to secede from the Russians, it's tricky in the Caucasus, always has been. The boss of the South Ossetian Oblast or whatever it was, Sergei, he was trying to impress me, he had a huge crush or something, called up a whole military parade with MiGs and stuff, and it freaked out the neighbouring enclave, and the whole thing escalated from there... The second President, the one from Georgia, he was so disgusted that he shelled a Russian troop carrier on the border, just to show he could, and then all hell broke loose. I mean they're always fighting in that corner of Europe of course... but it was quite a car crash.'

'Cool!' said Freya, who didn't understand international relations but knew a military engagement when she heard of one. 'I'd love to do what you do,'

At that point, having placated Charlotte, who was holding a warm basket of part-baked bread rolls as if they were primed hand grenades, Fred rolled over to say hello. It was the moment he had been anticipating ever since Heather had accepted his invitation. She beamed at him.

'I always forget your wheels,' she said. 'When we Skype, I can never see them.'

'Part of me now,' said Fred, in embarrassment. Heather was as intimidating as ever. But the auburn hair still did it for him, and he felt the familiar foolishness in her company. 'Wouldn't be without them. Not much good in a war zone of course. But ideal in a flat place like Norfolk.'

What banal nonsense, he thought. Twenty years hadn't changed a thing. Well, this was the time to speak up or shut up. He just had to choose his moment.

Chapter 8

Following the buffet lunch, by tacit agreement most of the party dispersed. Having tidied up, hindered as much as helped by Roddy, Charlotte went upstairs to lie down in a darkened room. Sonia, Robin and Alberto did likewise. Polly loitered politely, although what she really wanted to do was to march out of the house and put as many miles as possible between her and her temporary housemates. She never thought she'd miss social care law or Deprivation of Liberty Safeguards, but she almost did.

Once he'd made his domestic contribution via washing up – he operated a strict dishwasher boycott – Hugh went out to his van to play his fiddle. He needed space. When he arrived at a big group like this, he started off feeling like the Unabomber. He knew it was really him being terrified of others. People were chatting away happily to each other, talking superficial nonsense, and he despised small talk. So, he took himself out. He went for walks, sat in the kitchen, or occupied himself with a task, like chopping wood or laying a fire. He disliked himself for being unable to join in, but at the same time he loathed everybody else for their banality.

But as he tuned up, the thought struck him that perhaps this weekend might turn out to be bearable after all. These people were mostly more congenial than he remembered. Roddy was as tedious as ever, but Heather was quite something. Although a celebrity like her would definitely have a boyfriend. He put her freckles out of his mind and concentrated on mastering a particularly tricky Irish jig.

Impervious to exhaustion, Freya dragged Polly out to play hide-and-seek in the gardens. She was determined that they would both improve their jungle skills, although Polly drew the line at climbing the ha-ha, which Freya insisted on calling the ah-ha. Endearing one moment, enduring the next, that summed up parenthood, as far as Polly was concerned. She had already had to hide the recorder.

After a rest, Charlotte decided to walk down to the village and inspect what looked very much like a Saxon church. As she had explained to Sonia over lunch, she had taken up walking to get fit. Now she looked ruefully down at her curvaceous legs. It was the only part of her that truly undulated and not in a good way. Really, she wished she could be stretched by about a third.

As usual, Roddy had begged off, saying that he had to read the motions for his spring conference and do some composit-ing, whatever that was. All his talk about movements and motions sounded more lavatorial than political, Charlotte giggled to herself, as she wandered down the endless drive. Better laughter than misery about her marriage or anxiety about her outfits. Time to sit quietly in a church, she thought, and do penance for her superficiality.

Fred and Heather sat on the terrace in the sun. Humphrey was catching some rays. Fred felt as content as he ever did. His anxieties about the weekend had dissipated. All would be well, and if you kept out of the breeze, it was really quite nice outside.

The house was in a slightly raised position, offering a view over rural Suffolk that would gladden an estate agent's heart.

'Thanks for ordering the fizz,' said Fred. 'I'm sure it will make our Saturday evening go with a bang.'

'It's the sort of bang I prefer,' agreed Heather, stretching out in her chair. 'Although Lottie's lunchtime punch was fairly heavy-duty too. Now everyone will have to doze away the afternoon.'

'No bad thing,' said Fred. 'Takes the pressure off somehow.'

'It's a great place for you, this,' said Heather, looking around. 'Access-wise, I mean.'

'Yup. Unless I want to head off across the fields on a hike.'

'I suppose you could manage a quad bike? Most of these farmers seem to have one, these days… You even get them in Mongolia.'

'No doubt an improvement on a yak? Maybe that's something I should do before I'm fifty. I do think of getting a second home sometimes.'

'Where? South of France?'

'No, that's just a middle-class cliché,' said Fred. 'I meant somewhere like this. Somewhere in the real countryside.'

'I think of moving to LA. Or even DC.'

'Well, that's an ambition,' said Fred, feeling a twinge of concern. He'd never aspired to live in America. 'I suppose you would have friends there?'

'One or two,' said Heather, thinking of Clancy. He was mainly on the West Coast at the moment. Of course, after the election, he would be in Washington.

'I've thought a lot about you over the years,' said Fred, choosing his words carefully.

59

'That's nice,' said Heather, vaguely. 'Of course, I have wondered about you... occasionally,' she added, for the sake of accuracy.

'I've missed having that Special Person by my side,' said Fred. Special Person? What a cliché, he thought to himself.

'Ah yes,' said Heather. 'Neither of us has proved adept at snaring that Special Person.'

Fred nodded. For different reasons, he thought. He loved looking at her profile. Her green eyes were so distinctive. And those famous freckles. He was trying to look without staring, which gave him a bit of a squint. At that moment, she heaved a sigh, and tossed her auburn hair again.

'Maybe things will change in the next couple of years,' said Heather. She felt things were certainly about to change for her. She couldn't talk about Clancy until his ex-wife had signed the non-disclosure agreement, but a *Hello* feature would no doubt soon follow. It would all be great optics for his senatorial bid. Fred would no doubt stay marooned in East Anglia. But each to their own.

Fred thought that the idea of change sounded promising.

'Well, it's about time,' he agreed. 'It would be great to see more of you—'

'More?' said Heather, surprised. That wasn't part of her plans. Not that she made plans as such. More... calculations. Wasn't that what they meant by mental arithmetic?

'—in Norfolk,' continued Fred.

'Well, I'll certainly try and drop in,' said Heather, carefully non-committal. 'When I can.'

'That would be terrific,' said Fred bravely, although her lack of enthusiasm was obvious. 'You're always welcome. And Stansted's just down the road.'

There was a pregnant pause as Heather contemplated Stansted. A shopping mall with a runway. To call it a London airport was to stretch language beyond its elastic limits.

'How about your literary efforts?' asked Heather, changing the subject as nonchalantly as she could. 'Did you get tired of all that?'

'The writing?' enquired Fred, brightly. 'Not at all. I get up at 6 a.m. I do at least an hour before going to work. Like Trollope.' The more he wrote, the more he felt that this was where his real future lay.

'Joanna?' asked Heather, confused. She thought Aga sagas were more Charlotte's cup of tea.

'No, Anthony!' said Fred. 'He had a job in the Victorian Post Office, but still churned out several thousand words every morning.'

There was a pause.

'I thought it might be a flash in the pan,' said Heather, wistfully.

'Oh no,' said Fred. 'I'm quite serious about it.'

'I see,' said Heather. They fell back into a silence which felt more ominous than companiable.

Chapter 9

When they gathered later for afternoon tea and cake – a Nadiya Hussain recipe, baked by Sonia as her contribution to the party – Heather managed to attract the attention of Roddy, and then Charlotte. It wasn't very hard to attract Roddy's attention, given that he spent most of his time gazing at her chest as if he was trying to work out her bra size.

The three of them took their tea and found the smaller sitting room empty. Having first ensured that Fred was committed to a game of Beggar My Neighbour with Freya, Heather carefully shut the door behind them.

'Children have their uses,' said Charlotte, sitting at the furthest end of the sofa from her husband. 'Oh, and word to the wise, Heather? Don't pat Fred on the head. He doesn't like that sort of thing.'

Heather looked at her blankly, recalled and winced.

'What's this about, Heather?' asked Roddy.

'Look guys, we all enjoyed our youth, didn't we?' Heather was standing with her back to the door, arms folded, every inch the authoritative foreign correspondent.

'I think you've forgotten I wasn't at St Warburgs,' said Roddy, who'd never got over going to Exeter, and then having to watch his younger brother flourish at St Warburgs, founded back in 1321, even before most of the Oxbridge colleges.

'OK, school then. With Fred,' said Heather.

'Well, mostly,' said Charlotte, thinking of her college days. 'But I'm a different person now... Thank the Lord.'

Roddy rolled his eyes. 'You never get in the same river twice, yadda yadda. What's the point of these heart-warming reminiscences? We're all gathered here like conspirators? It's beginning to feel like party conference...'

'Fred says he's written a memoir...' said Heather, glaring at him.

'A memoir? Of what?' asked Roddy, in confusion. Only ex-Cabinet Ministers wrote memoirs, wasn't that the rule? Very useful for propping up bookshelves, or making a backdrop for Zoom meetings.

'...full of stories about us,' continued Heather.

'Us?' asked Charlotte, confused.

'Yes. His colourful friends. And, in my case at least, his memories of student days aren't going to help my reputation.'

'Oh god,' said Roddy, suddenly leaping to his feet in alarm and knocking over a small table lamp. 'I bet he's going to mention the EUCC story. That would completely torpedo my chances of being selected for Stoke Central next month.'

'Yuck?' queried Heather, confused by Roddy's acronym.

'Stoke?' wailed Charlotte. 'You never said Stoke. I'm not moving to bloody Stoke!'

'Exeter University Conservative Club,' explained Roddy. 'In a moment of drunken idiocy, I signed up in the first week of my first term.' He paced the room nervously.

'Ha ha ha!' laughed his wife. 'Tory Boy!'

'And, I seem to remember you were quite the floozy at St Warburg's, Lottie,' said Heather, suddenly grinning at Charlotte, quite unnecessarily she felt.

'Oh no!' Charlotte blanched, as memories flooded back. 'He wouldn't! That would be nasty. After all, I've put all of that behind me.'

'Wasn't there a nickname?' said Roddy, turning to his wife. 'You've always been a bit reticent regarding the details…'

'I've forgotten,' said Charlotte, who hadn't.

'OK, enough backstory,' said Heather. 'I'm going to look like a loser. Roddy's going to come across as a toff. And Charlotte's going to sound like a slut.'

'Heather! It wasn't anything like that!' protested her old friend.

'I'm just going to say two words to you, Charlotte: Boat Club.'

'Boat Club?' said Roddy, with interest. 'You never mentioned you were a rower. Or were you a cox?'

'Cox is about right,' said Heather, grimly. 'Anyway, the point is, we have to nobble this book. Fred even mentioned that Sonia, who went to Cambridge and is an actual damn literary agent, was interested in getting him a publishing deal. So, it's not just a pipe dream.'

'Oh crapola,' gasped Roddy, knocking a porcelain statue of the infant Samuel off the mantlepiece. 'He never told me!'

'He thinks it's his chance to get out of conveyancing and set himself up as a writer.'

'Not if I've got anything to do with it,' said Charlotte. She had definitely rediscovered her inner ruthlessness. 'I'll kill the bastard.'

'Wow!' said her husband. He was impressed despite himself. He looked at her admiringly. Ruthless Lottie was rather hot.

'Guys, this is serious,' said Heather. 'Very bad.'

There was a pause as they each pondered the consequences of publication.

'Can we get hold of the manuscript?' asked Roddy. 'Destroy it?'

'You could be the Cain to his Abel' said his wife. Her husband looked blank. 'Was that the mess of pottage?' asked Roddy.

'Whatever!' said Heather. 'We have to burn it or something. Fred told me there's only one hard copy.'

'We could make like his laptop was stolen. It's probably insured…' replied Roddy, feeling disloyal to his younger brother. But needs must.

'It'll all be on a Cloud somewhere,' said Charlotte, gloomily.

'No, it's all on a password-protected memory stick. We talked about it. For some complicated reason to do with intellectual property, he's very anti-Cloud.'

'Right, that's the answer,' said Charlotte. 'We trash the manuscript, smash the memory stick and that's probably the end of it. Takes blooming ages to write a book, as I know to my cost. I can't see him having the energy to start over again.'

'He'd have to write fiction instead,' said Roddy. 'Which would probably sell much better anyway,' he said brightly. 'Nobody wants to know about how a bunch of middle-aged nobodies started out…'

Heather and Charlotte glared at him.

'Speak for yourself,' muttered Heather. There was a moment of silence. They looked at each other.

'Well then, we're agreed. Now, who is going to do the deed?' asked Charlotte, looking at the others.

'I was thinking Rod could,' said Heather, giving him her most winning smile. For a millisecond, he looked dopey enough to be compliant, but then he shook his head.

'He's my own brother. If he found out, the repercussions would be awful. I'd really much prefer if I could honestly say I was completely innocent. I want no Suffolk-gate in my past!'

'Well, I hope you don't think I'm going to do it?!' said Charlotte indignantly. 'I'm a columnist, remember? We just don't steal each other's manuscripts, I have some journalistic integrity, plus it looks awful if anyone finds out. Besides which I'm a Christian, which means "Thou Shalt not Steal" is a total deal-breaker!'

They stared at each other, a three-way face off. Who would be first off their high horse?

'Hugh…' said Heather, thoughtfully. The sum immediately looked more positive.

'Hugh?' asked Roddy in surprise.

'I think he's got a soft spot for me,' said Heather.

'Seeing as you've been encouraging him,' said Charlotte.

'I certainly have not!' retorted Heather.

'Lottie, don't you think you're being a bit unfair?' said Roddy. 'It's not Heather's fault if Hugh gets the wrong end of the stick.'

Charlotte wasn't sure that Roddy should be taking Heather's side, and glared at her husband.

'He is a bit of a lost soul on life's highway,' she said.

'But at the same time, he's very practical,' said Roddy. 'In a nerdy kind of way. Although I'd call him more of a flake than a nerd,' he added. 'His heart's in the right place, but his head is on another planet. We used to call him "Who" at school.'

'Vacant but somehow practical,' said Heather. 'Exactly what we need.'

'So you're going to bat your eyelids at him some more,' said Charlotte. 'And you think he'll just go and burglarise one of his oldest friends? How exploitative!'

'I may do rather more than bat my eyelids,' said Heather. 'I'll do whatever it takes. This is my career we're talking about.' Not to mention her chances of a prestigious marriage, she thought to herself.

'Respect!' said Roddy, in admiration. 'You should really have gone into politics. We need mean bastards like you.'

Heather gave him her iciest stare.

'What makes you think I'd be on your side?'

Roddy felt it was probably time he shut up. He hadn't felt so small since the time a stranger had opened his toilet door on the early train to London.

'Look, I can keep Fred distracted over dinner tomorrow,' said Heather. 'Get him talking about school or something. It's been ages since we really had a proper chat.'

On the path outside, a certain Costa Rican former model, ex-high-end-escort and aspiring international businessman, was sauntering past, illicit cigarette in hand. Thanks to the warm of that spring afternoon, the windows of the sitting room were open, or he would have missed the sound of voices. As it was, he stopped in his tracks, and listened in shameless fascination.

'But we'll still have to get rid of it!' said Charlotte.

'Cut it up so it's easier to dispose of?' suggested Roddy.

'Takes too long...' said Heather.

'What about just burying it?' asked Charlotte. 'You know, somewhere in a flower bed?'

'Digging holes is a bit conspicuous. And Humphrey might just dig it up again,' said Roddy.

'I really can't see Humphrey being bothered,' said Charlotte.

'Fire might be good?' said Roddy.

'We'd just draw attention to ourselves,' said Heather. 'Unless we went down the barbecue route?'

'I wish it wasn't Fred. It makes me feel awful. After he's been so kind to us,' said Charlotte.

'It's his fault,' said Heather. 'If he'd just left us out of it, we wouldn't have to do this.'

'If only it wasn't real life, if only it were a corny novel...'

'Please don't try to make me feel guilty' replied Roddy. 'Us politicians don't do "guilty". This way will be better for everyone in the long run.'

'Not for Fred,' wailed Charlotte.

Having heard more than enough, Alberto quietly walked away, hardly glancing at the rose garden. His heart was beating fast. People thought that Latin America was full of violence and political assassinations! But behind the polite English exterior, Threepwood Hall was obviously a seething cauldron of badly dressed revenge and betrayal!

'Hey, I've had a thought,' said Roddy, for whom this was not an everyday occurence. 'I was having a walk around the grounds earlier. There's a pigsty behind the garages. Near the kitchen garden. Hugh could toss the manuscript to the pig. Don't pigs eat anything?'

'Good idea,' said Heather. 'I'll give him clear instructions. Steal the book, feed the pig. Job done. It would probably take too long to burn it, and also way too obvious if there were some unburned pages left in the fireplace.'

'I still don't like it,' said Charlotte. 'But I am not sure we've got much choice.'

Macbeth moment done with, the three conspirators got up to rejoin the others.

'Were you really a rower, Lottie?' asked Roddy, as they filed out. 'Only, you don't seem to have the height for it.'

Heather turned round and grinned at them both. 'I think you'll find it's mostly about rhythm…'

Charlotte glared daggers at her. She could see exactly how homicide had become habit forming for Lady M.

Chapter 10

'This garden is perfect,' said Polly, stretching out on the bench next to Hugh. 'Facing south makes it a total sun trap.' She undid two buttons on the Fred Perry shirt which made her look like the keyboard player of a post-punk band. Freya was in the kitchen, learning how to make custard with Alberto, and her mother was relishing her freedom. She'd taken a book off the Library shelves about John Constable, who'd apparently painted in the vicinity, but she suspected she wouldn't be reading much of it. Not like poor Sonia, holed up in her bedroom, reading manuscripts.

Polly and Hugh were sitting in the late afternoon sun at the far end of the garden, next to the ha-ha. They could look back at the house, or they could look over the farmland beyond. The place and the moment were deeply National Trust, except devoid of crowds. Hugh stood up and flapped his arms like an animated scarecrow, inhaling deeply. He was pointedly ignoring the corten steel statue which dominated the ha-ha.

'Ozone,' said Hugh. 'That's what you want. Not pollution.'

'I guess that's the advantage of living in a van,' said Polly, sleepily. 'You can take up off somewhere unspoiled.'

'Somewhere less spoiled,' Hugh corrected her. 'To get unspoiled you need… well, the wilds of Scotland or Wales, or across to Ireland. Too many people in the south of England.'

'My professional life is spent worrying about some of them.'

'I rather agree with Sartre. "Hell is other people",' said Hugh.

'You're a bit of a loner, really, aren't you?' said Polly. 'Not that that's a bad thing,' she added quickly. 'But most people are dependent on someone else.'

'I don't generally find people easy, no,' confessed Hugh. 'Not my family, nor the folk I was at school with, at any rate.'

'Or at this party with?'

'Probably not,' said Hugh. 'Present company excepted,' he added, blushing.

'I love the idea of just setting off on a walk from here… to the coast,' said Polly, twirling around the points of the compass with her arms outstretched. 'A backpack with a bivouac tent.'

'Well, you could do it,' said Hugh, suddenly enthusiastic. 'There's probably a footpath. You could just sleep under the stars. Escape this bunch!'

'Not this weekend. And not with Freya.' Polly felt like such an adult. She found it so tedious always having to be the grown-up in the room.

'Ah, yes. I forgot that. I've always imagined it might be better to bring up a child in the country,' replied Hugh. 'Freedom. Imagination. Fresh air.'

'Yeah, well. Tell that to Georgie.'

'Georgie?'

'Freya's mother,' said Polly, shortly. Hugh was not sure what to say about that. What did that make Polly? He said nothing.

'Plenty of social work need in the country, of course. There must be rural poor folk hidden around here somewhere,' added Polly. 'And probably loads of drug addicts and disabled people too.'

'Isn't this weather fabulous?' Fred was wheeling out to join them, with Roddy at his side.

'Global warming!' warned Hugh, for whom no silver lining was without its darker cloud.

'Are you sure I can't give you a push, bro?' asked Roddy. 'It's a rather hard going on grass, isn't it?'

'Not the easiest,' admitted Fred. 'But you know, I prefer to do it myself, thanks.'

'Independent as ever,' smiled Polly.

Hugh just looked over at his old friend and nodded in welcome. It was one of the things Fred liked about Hugh. He didn't make a fuss.

'How did you find this place?' said Polly, eager to change the subject from something that sounded suspiciously like social work. 'It's just perfect for a party.'

'Friends of mine rented it for their wedding anniversary a few years back. A holiday let that has enough rooms, plus access, and a downstairs bedroom and bathroom… well, let's say it's pretty hard to find.'

'Shame about the phone reception,' muttered Roddy.

'Three days should be just right,' said Hugh, who had been thinking he might leave after two.

'Must have cost you a fortune,' said Polly. 'Thanks for treating us all.'.

Hugh grunted in appreciation.

'Don't mention it,' said Fred, glowing. Even naturally generous people get more satisfaction if somebody notices.

'You've certainly picked the best spot!' They turned to see Heather had joined the party. She sat down at the edge of the ha-ha, with her feet dangling over the drop.

'Where were you?' asked Fred. 'Having a nap?'

'No, I was trying to find reception. Suffolk has worse mobile coverage than Somalia.'

'You are now in exactly the right place,' said Fred. 'Right next to the statue.'

'Oh, thanks, darling,' said Heather, glancing briefly at the statue before burying her head in her iPhone. Fred quietly glowed. Silence reigned for a few minutes until she thrust her phone into a pocket.

'I just had to check in with the office,' Heather said airily. 'See where I'm off to on Monday, you know.'

'I think people would be better off staying in one spot,' said Hugh. 'Too much flying about these days…. Carbon footprints, and all that.'

'Could you tell my editor that?' said Heather. 'He seems to have a different opinion.'

Hugh blushed and played with a twig. Fred raised his eyebrows. Roddy gazed admiringly. Heather thought suddenly that it wouldn't do to alienate Hugh, given that he was the only burglar they could lay their hands on at short notice. Luckily he seemed extremely susceptible.

'The climate emergency is, of course, completely dreadful, but isn't this marvellous sunshine?!' said Heather, and in a smooth movement pulled her top off to expose an expensively lacy bra. She hung her shirt off the statue and then, with a sigh of pleasure, she lay back down on the grass, eyes closed, and stretched out her arms.

There was a moment's silence. Fred was breathing noisily, and looking anywhere but at his old friend. Roddy was gazing at Heather's scantily clad form with undisguised interest, like a farmer appraising a heifer he might bid on at auction. Hugh was staring intently into the middle distance, but shot the occasional glance back at Heather. She appeared oblivious to all of them.

Polly thought to herself that Heather knew exactly what effect she was having. On everyone. She wasn't sure whether she was disgusted with middle-aged men having the hots just because a pretty woman showed some flesh, or whether she was irritated at Heather deliberately going for attention, or whether she was annoyed with herself, feeling aroused every time someone showed her a glimpse of lingerie. That was the problem with libido. It was like an eager puppy, widdling where it liked.

Fred turned and wheeled away. A few moments later, Heather opened her eyes and gazed in his direction.

'Where's he off to in such a hurry?' she asked, idly.

'Probably to walk the dog,' said Polly.

'I've never heard it called that before,' said Roddy, with a leer. His smut landed awkwardly. Everyone felt he was best ignored.

'I think it's, erm… because you took your top off,' said Hugh.

'What?' said Heather, sitting up and draping her shirt over herself. 'Aren't we all grown-ups? He must have seen a woman in her bra before.'

'He still finds nudity a bit tricky. Probably worried that you were going to reveal all,' replied Hugh.

'Remember the accident,' said Polly. 'It's left him rather traumatised about… about naked female flesh.'

'Oh, of course!' said Heather, who rarely spent much time worrying about Fred's sexuality.

'It's... unusual' replied Polly, cautiously. 'He's liable to... vomit.'

'What?' said Heather. 'You're saying my boobs would make him throw up?'

'It's not a family trait,' smirked Roddy.

Heather looked at Roddy and raised her eyebrows. He looked innocently back at her. Polly scowled in disgust. An attractive woman seemed to bring out Roddy's inner lothario, which was not a pretty sight.

Hugh was still looking intently at the landscape.

'See there!' he said, sotte voce, and pointed.

'What?' said Heather and Roddy, in unison and looking wildly around. Polly's gaze followed where Hugh's finger was indicating.

'Oh... yeah...' she slowly replied, staring with interest.

'What are we looking at?' asked Roddy. Nature was rather less appealing to him than naturism.

'Kestrel,' said Hugh, shortly. 'Hovering over the edge of that field.'

As they watched, the bird plunged to seize its prey. Heather shivered. Polly looked again at Hugh.

'You know the names of all these birds?'

Hugh nodded.

'And the trees?' She waved her hand around the amply forested landscape. Hugh nodded again.

'Wildflowers too,' he said. 'Hours in a van with a lantern and the Observer book of this and that. Nothing else to do with my time.'

'I think that's admirable,' said Heather. 'Wish I knew stuff like that. My mother would do for sure. Lots of walking in the Dales does that for you, I suppose.'

'I'm sure there are things you know about,' said Roddy. 'Politics and so on. I find all that much more interesting myself,' he said with an ingratiatingly boyish grin.

'Oh, I can usually tell whether a particular explosion is an IED or a landmine or a mortar,' replied Heather. 'But that's not a talent that gets you very far in Suffolk.'

'I think you'll find that taking your top off will get you anywhere you want to go, even in Suffolk,' thought Polly to herself. She rose, and wandered off in the direction that Fred had disappeared in.

Heather was left sitting between Hugh and Roddy. Hugh was still surveying the landscape, looking for birds. Roddy was smiling suggestively. Smirking had never done it for Heather. She indicated with a flick of her head that he should buzz off. He looked momentarily hurt, like a small boy being denied his iPad. She looked meaningfully over at Hugh and raised her eyebrows. Comprehension dawned, and Roddy got to his feet.

'Well, I'll see you later then,' he said, and nodded at Heather. She gave the smallest of nods in return. Hugh ignored him, and Roddy sauntered off towards the house.

There was a few minutes of silence. After a moment's thought, Heather quietly put her top back on, while Hugh gazed determinedly at the trees. The silence continued. She sat there expectantly. It took another five minutes, but finally Hugh turned around and looked at her. There was a pause. She cleared her throat.

'Hughie, sweetie, there was a little something I wanted to talk to you about...'

Chapter 11

One of the chief advantages of Threepwood Hall, Fred had discovered on his first visit, was that the gardens were well-appointed with paths. Lots of paths. The firm, smooth, stoned kind, and with barely any camber. He hated camber. Here he could wheel easily around the roses, and onwards to the kitchen garden. When you were in a wheelchair, things like that made a difference. Which was why he had chosen to work in East Anglia instead of, say, the Peak District.

Brought up in the North East of England – another hilly region – he had happy memories of visiting National Trust gardens with his parents. Back in the days when he could walk, of course. They'd visited Belsay, and Wallington, and Cragside, with all the rhododendrons. His poor father had been particularly keen on rhodies, as he called them. No rhodies here, but an impressive array of tulips, and in a month or two, those roses would look fantastic, he thought. He should send his mother some roses. She would like that, she hadn't forgotten her gardening and nor had he.

It was quite a strain being the host, even with everyone taking their share of catering. He felt entitled to half an hour on his own. He was also keen to inspect this famous pig.

Sure enough, beyond the broad beans and behind the potting shed was a sty, and although the shelter at the back of the sty was in darkness, and the open area was pig-less, the sound effects suggested a small-to-medium size animal was catching forty winks. The snoring sent a low rumble through the surrounding area, such that the bars which Fred gripped to pull himself up and look into the shelter were vibrating. He wished he brought... What would work, a carrot? Presumably not leftovers from lunch – he'd read somewhere that you couldn't do that anymore.

'Hello!'

Fred pushed back from the gate and wheeled around. Standing in front of him was a woman wearing what appeared to be a tie-dye boiler suit, and a Barbour jerkin that had seen better days. She was laden down with two zinc buckets, one full of feeding pellets, the other of water.

'I'm Nel. Sorry, can't shake hands. Just come to feed Vin Pong,'

She had a strong Birmingham accent, as if she'd walked straight out of The Archers' recording studio. He looked more closely at her. She had a nice face, he thought. Although more muddy than tended to be fashionable these days. He looked back through the bars.

'Vin Pong? You mean the pig? I thought they were normally called things like Empress or Babe.'

'Well, it's a boy not a girl. And this is a Vietnamese pig, and Vin Pong basically means His Lordship in Vietnamese, apparently. It wasn't my idea. They're very clean animals, not pongy in the slightest. I call him Vinny.'

'Is Vin Pong your pig?'

'Not my pig. His Nibs.'

'His nibs? Your husband?'

'Nooo! I'm not married. I mean Mr Cheeswell, the guy who owns this place. The farm, the house, the land... the big house near the Church. The moat. All that.'

'I though the house belonged to Heritage Trust? That's who I rented it from.'

'Oh, you're the party at Threepwood Hall? No, the Trust just have a long-term lease from Mr Cheeswell. He's a city man. A billionaire with half a dozen houses dotted around the world, apparently... Seems to collect them. And lots of other things.'

She strode past him and put down her buckets to open the gate.

'Sorry,' said Fred, wheeling out of the way. 'I'm Fred. A bit of a foreigner here. From Norfolk.'

Nel smiled, and tipped the pellets into the trough. The snoring stopped abruptly, and seconds later, a small and very hairy boar looked out into his al fresco dining area, showing more interest in his supper than his visitors. Humphrey watched through the bars feeling sorry for himself. Breakfast seemed such a long time ago.

'You feed pigs for Mr Cheeswell?' said Fred, with interest. 'And your day job is presenting children's TV?' He indicated the tie-dye boiler suit.

She giggled.

'I forgot I must look pretty damn odd.'

'Just... unusual.' Vin Pong was now getting stuck into his dinner, chuntering happily as if to approve the evening selection. Tentatively, Fred reached a hand through the bars and scratched the pig's black and bristly back. Vin Pong wriggled appreciatively.

'Reminds me of my dog!' said Fred. 'Humphrey here is also rather well-padded. And keen on his dinner.'

'Only Vinny is rather cleverer,' answered Nel. 'Don't suppose you'd eat slices of dog in a bun with brown sauce, would you?'

Fred looked with interest at the pig. Now you thought about it, eating these creatures was rather barbaric.

'I saw one doing a jigsaw puzzle the other week. On YouTube.'

'What?' said Nell, in surprise.

'A pig. Not sure what breed. But it was rather pleased with itself when it got all the pieces in the right slots. If that's what squeaking furiously means. Nearly put me off bacon and sausages for life.'

She looked at him again. Her daily life was not well-endowed with people you could have conversations with. And Fred seemed sound on pigs.

'Would you like a cuppa?' Fred looked around. There was no café in sight.

'I'll make you one,' said Nel. 'Give me a second.'

After she had supplied Vin Pong with his own beverage of choice, she carefully shut and bolted the gate to the sty and beckoned Fred to follow her.

Beside the kitchen garden was a rusting red freight container. Once Nel had swung back the heavy door and turned on a light, Fred could see that it had been fitted it out as a living unit. Bed... shelves... books... A table with kitchen supplies.

'Cosy,' he said, in some admiration. 'My mate Hugh would probably like this.'

She glanced around it.

'It's a bit dark. And gets damn cold in winter. Though I'm only really in here in the summer months. And then when it gets to August, it's way too hot, so last year I pitched a tent right outside here. It's nice to be out in the park rather than stuck on a housing estate in West Bromwich.'

She turned on a small gas stove and filled up her kettle.

'Anyway. I have to explain the outfit, or you'll think I'm a total berk.'

He hadn't thought she was a berk at all and was about to say so, but she raised a hand to stop him.

'Mr Cheeswell, between ourselves, is a bit of a creep. Wandering hands. Worse if he gets half a chance. Has lots of money and thinks he can buy anyone. The tie-dye boiler suit is mainly to put him off. If I look very ghastly or childish or whatever, he's less likely to be interested.

'That's awful! Sexual harassment is a crime!'

'My word against his,' she replied. 'Not worth pursuing.'

'The Suffolk version of "Me Too" – I'm very sorry to hear that. But it's a relief that it's not your idea of rural dress.'

'Right, said Fred...' she replied, 'what did you say your surname was?'

'Twistleton.'

'Unusual name...' She pondered for a moment. I think there was a guy called that at the first uni I went to...'

'Where was that?'

'St Warburg's. Near Hexham. Went up in 1998. Just after Blair was elected. Not that the College had noticed.'

Fred beamed at her delightedly. They were birds of a feather.

'That must have been me then! I was at St Warburg's.'

'Were you? But that guy wasn't in a chair.'

'No, I wasn't, then. Got my wheels after Finals.'

'Ah. That explains it. I'd left by then.'

'Left?' Fred was mystified. 'I thought you were younger than me?'

'All of thirty-eight. I only did the first year. In fact, only two terms of the first year. We parted company because of my rabbit.'

'Your rabb…?' For a second, he thought that he must have misheard. 'You left because of your Rabbi?'

'Not Rabbi. Rabbit! Flemish Giant.'

He paused for a moment, trying to compute.

'Sorry Nel, I've only just turned forty and I am clearly losing it already. What was a Flemish Giant doing with your rabbi?'

'OK. Stop! I was – am, really – a bit crazy about animals. I came to college with Bugs, my Flemish Giant rabbit.'

'Giant?'

'It's a breed. Big. They can weigh up to about six kilos. The College hated it. The Bursar kept on showing me rules and regulations. In the end, I left the university. Well, sent down actually. Stupid really. Not sure I'd do it now.'

'You took a bullet for Bugs?'

'Yup.'

'Are you insane?' He shook his head. Disbelief was tinged with admiration. She giggled. He liked a woman who laughed a lot.

'But I did get to be the poster girl in the PETA magazine.'

'PETA?'

'People for the Ethical Treatment of Animals. They're the campaigners who do adverts with semi-naked celebrities in them.'

'You were semi-naked?' He felt a frisson.

'Noo!'

'Well, I still think that's kind of admirable,' he said. 'Bonkers. But admirable.'

She chortled again as she passed him a cup of tea.

'What did you do next?'

'The following autumn I went to Aston to study ecology. They didn't mind you having a pet. Basically, I traded my St Warburgs education for five years in a bedsit with a massive lagomorph…'

'A what?'

'People think rabbits are rodents. But they aren't.'

'Good to know.'

'Plus, to be honest, I hated that place. Too many nobs.'

He cleared his throat in embarrassment.

'Folk like me?'

'Well, I am sure you're not actually a nob. You sound a little Northern, actually.'

'Novocastrian rather than Geordie, I am afraid. Dad was a doctor.'

'People made fun of my accent. Being from the Black Country and all that. The kind of people who hung pheasants out of their bedroom windows. That sort of thing. My dad was a shop steward at Longbridge. I spent most of my time at St Warburgs being a Hunt Sab across the North of England.'

'Sounds like you made a stir. Though I'm not sure I actually remember you…'

'I was the one with a rainbow mohican and big doc martens?'

'Oh yes!' He had a dim memory of a debate about animal rights in the Junior Parlour. 'Didn't you wage a campaign to get proper veggie food in the dining hall?'

'Yup. That was me.'

He thought back twenty years. It was coming back to him.

'And wasn't it you who stamped the letters "Down With Brown" in the snow on the bowling green one morning?'

'Right again! Mr Brown was my nemesis.'

He looked blank, so she helped him out: 'The catering manager, remember?'

'Oh yes…'

'And then, there was a girl who was into taxidermy… her parents used to visit her with roadkill, and she would sit in her bedroom stuffing them. Total goth of course…'

'And?'

'I threw paint over her leather jacket. That got me into a bit of trouble, actually. Her family were going to press charges, but the Pro Vice-Chancellor talked them down. Although I didn't like him either… he was a vivisector – worked in the Physiology labs. I tipped off my mates, and they left a sheep carcass on his front doorstep.'

'Charming!'

'I wouldn't have done that myself. You have to draw the line somewhere… And of course, I'm not like that now,' she said hastily. 'I'm not even a vegan anymore. Woke up one day in my mid-twenties and "woke" was over for me, basically. Took out all my piercings. I'm pretty bland these days. Boring haircut. Still love our furry friends of course. For a while back there, I was just very… angry.'

'Yeah. Well, maybe I should have been more angry myself. Maybe I wouldn't have ended up as a rural solicitor. Dull or what?'

'At least you avoided being a nob. And anyway, look at me! Almost middle-aged, looking after a rare breed boar with a bad case of spoiled pig syndrome, on a toy farm for a rich business type who does his best to sexually harass me, and for whom I ghostwrite ecology papers… You think I can talk?'

'You do what?' Fred had not been playing close attention but thought he had heard something about the paranormal.

'Ghostwrite. Mr Cheeswell has lots of money, you'd think that would be enough, but what he really wants is respect. His daddy was probably nasty to him when he was a little boy or something. So now he employs little oddball me to do surveys of his land and the river, find out how many dragon flies there are, or toads or whatever, and I write them up as academic papers along the lines of "*natrix natrix* population in the Yare Valley" and then they get published in ecology journals with his name on.'

'That's terrible!' said Fred in outrage. 'There's pretty sound legislation about intellectual property these days.'

'Well, he pays me. I live here on his land. And it's perfectly good science, which is the main thing I care about. I don't want a proper academic career anymore. Don't like working alongside animal researchers. It's a bit frustrating in some ways, but this arrangement suits me fairly well. So long as he keeps his hands off me.'

They sat in silence for a few minutes and drank their tea. Fred wondered what to say next. She glanced over at him, her head tilted on one side in what he thought was rather a sweet way.

'And you? What would you really like to be doing? If you weren't a solicitor?'

'Well…' He felt a bit silly admitting it. 'My first love is writing. I dream of getting published one day. Being an author, you know… Short stories. Perhaps even a novel. I realise it's your standard bourgeois dream. Probably don't have the talent.

But it's about my only genuine ambition in life... Now that I'm unlikely to represent England at rugby.'

Nel looked at him in surprise.

'Joking!' he said. Though Robin would probably say that what someone cared about most, they joked about most. Underneath the self-deprecation, it mattered to Fred very much indeed. Mattered more even than Heather. He wasn't sure why he was now sharing his deepest dreams with a pig-herder. But it was very easy to talk to her.

Nel smiled, and said slowly, 'Well, I don't see why you couldn't be a writer. Someone's got to write all those airport novels. And if Alan Titchmarsh can do it...'

'Exactly!' he said enthusiastically. 'Thank you for taking me seriously! I've already made quite a start...'

'Great! What have you written?'

'It's a memoir, actually. What you would call "literary non-fiction", I think. About my life. Becoming disabled. All that. My thinking was that it was a way into being... a proper writer.'

'I'd like to read it,' she said.

He looked at her intently.

'No, really, I would,' she replied. 'I'm not just being polite.'

His face relaxed and he smiled.

'OK. You can be my first "member of the public" reader. I've got the manuscript up at the Hall. My friend Sonia's giving it a professional once-over.'

'Good. It would be an honour.'

'But it's such a coincidence, you being here!' said Fred again, shaking his head in disbelief. 'I can't get over it. Wait till I tell the others! They'll be amazed. Charlotte Howells? Heather Crisp? They went to St Warburgs too.'

'No, sorry, names mean nothing. Maybe I'd recognise the faces.'

'You must come and have a drink with us... Better still, come to the big dinner, tomorrow night?' He looked her over. 'I'm afraid you'll have to dress up a bit.'

'Dress up? I haven't agreed to come yet. Not at all sure it's my scene. I bet the rest of them are nobs, even if you're not.'

'You'll definitely like Polly. She's an actual Nobb. I mean, that's her name, Polly Nobbs. But she's dead down to earth, really... Lottie's sweet as anything, but much less hip than you... And Heather's just amazing, she does a lot of telly. You know, the foreign correspondent at GTS. My big brother Roderick will be there, he's married to Lottie, met her through me.'

Nel shook her head doubtfully. He went on regardless.

'So anyway, Saturday, tomorrow night, I've told everyone else, it's the Jane Austen character lookalike fancy dress competition.'

She raised her eyebrows:

'Definitely not my thing!'

He continued talking. 'Just a bit of fun. I got the idea because the Hall is like something out of *Pride and Prejudice*. You don't need to bother with a costume. Just come regardless. As you are.' He looked at her muddy attire. 'Well, maybe not quite as you are... But I really would love it if you came!'

He reddened. He'd only just met her after all.

'I'll check my social calendar and see how I'm placed. It's hectic out here in rural Suffolk.' She smiled at him. 'I do have proper clothes, you know. But I'm not sure there were any Brummie peasants in Austen.'

'Maybe you could come as a zombie.'

'Thanks for that!' she laughed.

'We have a kid with us, Freya, she's Polly's daughter, she'd be thrilled if you turned up looking like one of the undead.'

'It's a deal. It's hardly a stretch to manage that.'

'Do come. In return, I'll really try to give up eating pork.'

'Promises, promises...'

Chapter 12

Having failed to find Fred, Polly was talking to Freya in their bedroom. Her daughter had consented to washing her hands and generally tidying her appearance, removing sticks, leaves, dust and other garden waste from about her person. Satisfied she had not raised a Neanderthal by mistake, Polly smiled at her daughter.

'Are you enjoying yourself then?'

'Oh yes, Mum. I've had loads of adventures!'

'That's good, darling.'

'Hugh is making me a bow and arrow!' Polly made a face. In her day job, this was the kind of thing which demanded at least a risk assessment, possibly a Community Protection Notice. Well, it was her weekend off.

'Just so long as you are careful.'

'And I found my recorder under the bed. I have been practising my tune!'

'Oh, good. I have been meaning to talk to you about that…'

'Yes?' said her daughter. There was a momentary pause, as a brilliant idea came to Polly, an idea of which Screwtape would have been proud, and which would not have been out of place in a CIA manual. The scheme was certainly unworthy of her, but then again, in the words of Aphra Behn, 'Advantages are lawful in love and war.' Polly felt that combat had been entered upon, once a certain person had removed her shirt. But she had the secret weapon.

'Freya, darling – you remember Aunty Heather?'

'Yes! She was the one with the helicopter!'

'Exactly! Well, Aunty Heather happened to mention to me earlier today that she just loved hearing little girls play the recorder...'

'Really?' Now Freya was practically jumping up and down with excitement.

'Yes!' said Polly, who could be as devious as anyone, when she felt so inclined. 'And by an amazing coincidence, you'll never guess what her very favourite tune is...'

'Tell me!'

'Well, darling, her very favourite tune happens to be...'

'Frère Jacques?'

'Yes!'

'Oh yay! That's great!' said Freya. 'I should play it for her *all the time*.'

'The more the merrier!' said Polly, now feeling a tiniest soupçon of sympathy.

'I'm going IMMEDIATELY!'

And with that, Freya grabbed her recorder and rushed out of their bedroom. Lying back down on her bed, Polly smiled.

Heather and Robin were taking the air, strolling around the lawn peppered with daisies. Heather was unaware that the descant recorder of fate was at that very moment rushing towards her. Sonia was on the garden seat outside the dining room, still reading the coveted manuscript. Every time she laughed, Heather glanced over anxiously. Robin seemed oblivious, presumably pondering some mystery of Child and Adolescent Mental Health. In the distance, Alberto was standing on the edge of the ha-ha, phone gripped to his ear, next to the Wally Smithson statue, a contorted twist of wood and steel which apparently signified the existential predicament of the Millennial man. Heather didn't think much of it. It was crying out for a traffic cone on the head, in her opinion.

'What's your fella doing?' asked Heather, aimlessly.

'Oh, he's always on the phone' said Robin, his forehead creased in anxiety. 'Business, you know...' He hoped she did, because he certainly didn't.

'What's his line of work?' asked Heather, doing her best to appear polite.

'Uh...' Robin didn't think he should disclose Alberto's past life. 'He started out in International Relations,' he said, which was broadly accurate.

'Oh, really?' said Heather now more interested. 'I'd like to talk to him. That's my sort of thing, of course. He's from Costa Rica, isn't he?'

'He doesn't do that anymore' said Robin, hurriedly. 'Now that he's got me. He's more... business oriented.' Robin just hoped it was a legal trade. He'd heard his partner talking on WhatsApp about Latin American import/export operations. But Alberto was rather evasive when pressed. Maybe there really was another man...

'Anyway, what do you think of him?' asked Robin, eagerly. 'Quite a looker, isn't he?'

'He's certainly a catch,' admitted Heather. 'Must have great genetics... I wonder whether he's got a high sperm count.'

'I'm sorry?' said Robin, thinking he'd misheard.

'Oh, did I say that last bit out loud?' said Heather, absent-mindedly. 'I really must stop doing that.'

Robin stared at her with concern.

'We're talking about my boyfriend here. Who is entirely gay,' he said sniffily. '100 per cent,' he added, in case there was doubt.

'Oh, don't mind me, Robin,' said Heather, airily. 'It must be my time of life. I can't help sizing up all men as potential fathers, or rather sperm donors.'

'Very flattering, I'm sure. But generally, there's some rather complex discussions involved in sperm donations,' Robin said. 'Things can go badly wrong. I've seen it often, in the LGBT world.'

'Those lesbians make it all seem simple,' said Heather, enviously. 'People like Polly and her ilk. Can't be good for the sprogs.'

'Actually, the evidence is very positive, speaking as a psychologist.'

'What do you mean?'

'Children reared by lesbians do just as well, or better, than more conventional nuclear families.'

'Well, it doesn't seem to have done Freya any harm,' admitted Heather. 'She's a very mature and sweet young lady.' She hadn't yet had the chance to appreciate Freya's limited but distinctive musical talents.

'As long as you have two loving parents – of either gender – then there's no reason why things can't go very well.'

'What if there's one?' said Heather, who was aware of her clock. She might not want to put all her remaining eggs in the Clancy basket, as it were.

'One what?'

'Only one parent?'

'Well, could be a bit more difficult. You know, financially, in most cases. Which causes stress, of course. And if Mum has a new relationship, step-parenting can be fraught. Most importantly, children usually want a relationship with their father, however limited.'

'And what if they don't know who the father is?'

'Well, evidence on anonymous sperm donation is rather mixed.'

'Mixed?'

He spelled it out: 'Some children born of these arrangements get very distressed in later life about not being able to locate a biological father.'

'Oh, I see.' She pondered. 'I can understand that. Personal identity etcetera. But fine if they know who the squirter was?'

'Yes, if you have to put it like that,' replied Robin. His professional opinion of Heather's maternal potential would not have been high, had anyone asked him for a reference. She seemed a trifle narcissistic, to him. Although he'd want to run some personality tests before coming to a firm conclusion.

At this point, Alberto returned, beaming.

'Everything OK?' asked his partner.

'Gufeao!' said Alberto. 'Nitido!'

Judging by his boyfriend's facial expression, Robin thought that this sounded positive, although his Latino slang wasn't up to a translation. Nor did he want to probe. He'd tried asking questions about Alberto's activities before, and it hadn't gone well. He put out his hand and squeezed his boyfriend's outstretched fingers. The connection held. He sighed happily.

Heather was still thinking about sperm. She appraised Alberto. Were those cheekbones original? With a wave, she left them, and wandered off into the garden.

The problem was, she was so rarely in the right place. And it would need calibration with her menstrual cycle. Could be tricky, without a captive donor. Husbands did come in useful sometimes. But they didn't have to be your own, she thought, and giggled. Although if things went well with Clancy, and soon, then...

The two men watched her go.

'Not sure I like her attitude,' said Robin.

'Great outfits though,' said Alberto, appreciatively. He knew how much effort it took to look so glamorously windswept.

They watched as Freya skipped up to Heather, brandishing her recorder. They smiled approvingly and wandered hand in hand off into the distance, a trill of strangely familiar notes following on the afternoon breeze.

Then Alberto suddenly remembered what he'd heard earlier.

'Ah, cariño, there was something I wanted to ask you about... I was having a stroll and overheard a conversation. Of course, it's very naughty to drop eaves... but it worried me, you know.' He gazed, his face sincere, his head rather sweetly on one side, at Robin.

'Why?' said Robin, too captivated to correct him. 'What did you hear?'

'People plotting...'

'What?'

'Mi rey, it sounded like a murder!'

'You're joking, darling. You must have misheard!'

Alberto realised that it sounded ridiculous. He was addicted to *Inspector Morse* and *Midsomer Murders*, but even he thought that this conspiracy sounded too far-fetched for the English, more like the telenovelas that his mother liked. He persisted nevertheless in sharing what he'd overheard.

'They were going to kill Fred! They were talking about how to dispose of the body… they spoke about cutting it up… burning it… burying it!'

'Killing Fred?' Robin was aghast. 'Cutting up a body? That's fantastical, Alberto. Have you been smoking weed again? Or taking that Kambo powder of yours?'

'Certainly not!' said Alberto, defensively. 'Well, not Kambo. I save that for very special moments. I may have had a teeny weeny joint. Although I really did hear them up to something!' he added, plaintively. If only he had recorded them on his phone, he thought.

'And who were they?'

'That one. The smart reporter.'

'Heather?'

'Yes. And the badly dressed couple.'

'Roddy and Charlotte. And they were really plotting to dispose of a body?'

'That's what they were saying!' Alberto insisted, plaintively.

'You must have got your wires crossed, darling. I don't know them all very well, but I can't believe they'd do anything violent,' said Robin. 'Stupid, possibly. But not violent.'

'I'm going to watch them closely,' said Alberto, determinedly. 'I've seen violence. It bubbles up from nowhere. We must guard Fred at all times! I am going to stick to him like a barnacle!'

'He might not be very keen on that,' said Robin, who knew how his old friend hated overprotectiveness. 'But I'll certainly keep my eyes open.'

Walking along the path which ringed the house and went through the woods beyond, Polly was catching up with her old friend Fred. Humphrey strolled along, leaving his mark on every tree, and generally ignoring his lord and master. Having lost Heather, Freya chased after him, and tried to interest him in fetching sticks. He wasn't having any of it.

'Is Humphrey your assistance dog?' asked Freya.

'More of persistence…'

'Could you train him?'

'I doubt it,' replied Fred. 'If he was a bit bigger, he might pull my chair. If he was more obliging, he might do something useful. He could pick bits of paper up off the floor. If I had epilepsy or diabetes, he could alert me before I got ill.'

'So clever!' said Freya admiringly. She was a big fan of dogs, so long as they weren't called Malice or Fang.

'Not this dog! Pugs are lazy, obstreperous and obstinate. Sorry, Freya. And any dog is only as clever as the human that trains him, frankly,' said Fred. 'It's a tedious process of breaking the task down into steps, and then rewarding the pooch for getting it right, repeatedly.'

'A labour of love?' said Polly.

'Well, put it this way, it would take more shredded chicken than I have time to prepare to teach Humphrey to do anything useful… I suppose I could call him a comfort dog.'

'And then he'd get to wear one of those purple bibs and you could take him anywhere! Like that woman who tried to get on Delta Airlines with an emotional support peacock!'

'I'm not sure you can get a pug-size assistance bib,' said Fred. 'Although they probably come in different sizes. Some people have small ponies instead of dogs as their service animals…'

'They do not!' said Polly in disbelief.

'They do. I think it's for people who are allergic to dog hair.'

'A small pony? Really? Like a Thelwell Shetland pony?' Polly shook her head in amazement.

'Yup,' said Fred. 'Imagine the poo from that. Better off with a pug.'

There was a pause while Freya had a pee behind a tree. Fred turned tactfully aside, while Humphrey sniffed the leaves interestedly. A herd of black and white bullocks were chasing each other in the field beyond the ha-ha. One of them saw the people in the Park grounds and stopped. Then the bullocks all started edging their way towards the ha-ha. It was slightly uncanny, the interest that these cattle were taking in the humans, like some sort of bovine Hitchcock film. Fred felt glad of the six-foot height that separated them. Humphrey gazed, pop-eyed, over the countryside. Freya was now dancing about around them, trying to entice the lazy dog, while Polly came back to where her friend was waiting, gazing out over the open landscape.

'Any normal dog would be barking by now,' said Fred, in affectionate disgust. 'He looks more like a loaf of bread than a hound. Look at those snuffling nostrils. The wind blows, and his brain gets cold. Not that you could call what he has a brain.'

Freya squatted on her heels and gave Humphrey an indignant cuddle.

'He's a lovely pug!'

'Well, he's a bit rubbish at being a dog,' said his owner. 'And let's face it, that's not a hard job.'

'Strange to think all dogs, even Humphrey, are descended from wolves,' ruminated Polly.

'Really?' said her daughter, eyes as big as saucers.

'I think so,' said Polly. 'I read that they were domesticated in Siberia about 3,000 years ago.'

'You'd have thought he'd have got the hang of it by now!' grumbled Fred, who nevertheless loved Humphrey for his foolishness.

They walked on, Fred wheeling, Freya collecting things to throw, Humphrey puffing along in pursuit.

'He's not really accustomed to strenuous exercise,' Fred said to Freya, after Humphrey had disdained her latest stick. 'He's probably just looking for a lap to sink into.'

Once Freya had rushed ahead once more, Polly turned to her friend, evidently still thinking about their earlier conversation.

'You know the assistance dog training thing... Do you think you could use the same Pavlovian approach to get you over your little nudity problem?'

She was the only person in the world who would home in on this most sensitive of topics. He was about to glare at her, but resorted to the classic scarcasm defence:

'What, give me a bit of cheese to reward me for not passing out at the sight of female flesh?'

'Well, it's worth a try. Couldn't you reward yourself with malt whisky or After Eights or something?'

'Believe me, I've tried,' said Fred, sadly, giving up the pretence that he didn't care. 'We're talking about the bane of my adult life.'

Polly looked about until she saw Freya, out of earshot, trying to climb a tree.

'And really, for twenty years you've not had a sexual relationship?' asked Polly.

'Not with a third party,' said Fred. Polly was someone he could be frank with. But it took a big effort to admit his weakness.

Polly made a face.

'Well, at least the mechanics work, I suppose.'

'The mind is weak, but the flesh is willing to give it a go,' said Fred. 'There's no physiological problem at all, the neurologist assures me. Which almost makes it worse.'

They wandered along side by side in silence. He was glad he didn't have to say anything, because he was already on the verge of tears. Polly reached out and put her hand around the back of his neck, a gesture of gentle and genuine friendship. Fred hated people who patted his head, but liking this moment of sudden warmth, he didn't try to shake her off. But if she was any nicer to him now, he would definitely weep.

'One more thing,' said Polly, 'am I mistaken, or are you a bit keen on Heather?' As always, she spoke with the directness for which she was famed throughout the E8 postal district. She seemed blithely unconcerned about Freya falling out of the tree. Fred went redder than an organic beetroot in a weekly veg box.

'Is it that obvious?'

'Pretty much. At least to me. She's a bit... callous, don't you think?'

'I must have a thing for dominant women, I suppose.... She does stride around as if the landscape owes her a favour.'

Polly rolled her eyes. Fred was looking dangerously gooey-eyed to her.

'I love that thing she does on the telly... the gesture with four fingers in the air.'

'Well, when Heather does scare quotes, the quotes certainly stay scared,' said Polly. 'I think you could do better, to be honest. In the unlikely event that she did fall for your charms, wouldn't it just be the vomiting story all over again?'

'I did worry about that,' conceded Fred. 'But I've decided not to think about it.'

'I think she might be broody…' warned Polly. 'She has that glazed look in her eye whenever she sees Freya.' She turned around to check her daughter.

'Really?' said Fred in surprise. 'I wouldn't have thought that dependents were her thing.'

'True, she's more of a prima donna than a mother,' said his friend, brutally. 'But would it be a problem to be a dad?'

'Noooo…' said Fred. 'I do very much like kids, as you know.'

He looked over at Freya, who was now playing happily with Humphrey, and smiled.

'Although forty is a bit late in the day to be having them. I suppose I'd thought… that particular boat had sailed.'

'It can be rough, but the voyage is worth it,' said Polly, firmly. 'But first things first, eh?'

'Yes,' said Fred. 'I don't want to count all my chickens before they're in the same basket.'

'First catch your hen,' said Polly. 'Or rural wisdom to that effect…'

'Exactly,' said Fred. There was a pause before he went on. 'And when it comes to relationships, the words "pot", "kettle" and "black" come to mind, dear Polly…'

'Touché,' said Polly, glumly.

Fred smiled sympathetically. Polly was just about his greatest friend and he loved her dearly. He knew she hated being single, and thought she was probably in the search for a suitable woman. Shame she was unlikely to find one this weekend.

'Now, we'd better be getting back. It's nearly supper time. Come on Humphrey! Stop dawdling! Race you home, Freya!'

Chapter 13

It was 7.30 p.m., and Robin and Alberto were squabbling in the kitchen. Alberto had wanted to go into the nearest town and get bugging devices. Robin had pointed out rural Suffolk's limitations when it came to surveillance technology. But that wasn't what they were arguing about now.

'I want to do it!' said Alberto.

'Well, I was looking forward to it myself actually!' replied his boyfriend.

'You could do it tomorrow! We're here for two nights,' said Alberto in indignation.

'I can't believe two grown men are squabbling over this,' said Robin, resignedly.

A few moments later, the rippling tintabulation of the dinner gong was heard through the house. It began tentatively, but then as Alberto got into a familiar rhythm with his wrist, it rose in a crescendo, faster and faster. Fred came out of his room and waited in the entrance hall, slightly anxious that Alberto might be overdoing it. Could you break a gong? Humphrey, who had been wandering around the kitchen carefully hoovering up anything that had fallen on the floor, came out in a run, screeched to a halt in the hall and started barking in panic.

Nobody had checked with him that it was OK to make such a racket.

Upstairs, doors opened.

'I think it's a sign,' said Charlotte. 'Come on, Roddy.' There was a crunch behind her. 'Oh, for goodness sake, that was one of the house water glasses…'

Heather joined them on the landing. The three co-conspirators exchanged significant looks.

Behind them, Sonia stood waiting for Freya to come down, watching anxiously in case the little girl slipped on the stair carpet.

'We're coming!' shouted Freya, skipping down the first staircase from the top floor landing. Polly followed after her, holding a Tupperware of vegan snacks, thinking that for a child who allegedly never had sugar, her daughter's energy levels were prodigious.

Heather flinched as the seven-year-old passed her. She couldn't possibly have that recorder on her, could she?

Polly gestured for Freya to lead them down the main stairs. The others followed, as they processed down the wide staircase, and into to the sitting room.

The front door opened, and Hugh stood in the doorway, wearing a frayed sports jacket over a shirt that was clearly a stranger to the iron. The evening rushed in after him on the slight breeze, bringing assorted rural noises, and some flies. Outside, a blackbird was tunefully asserting his property rights. In the twilight, they could see rabbits were idly grazing the lawn that ran down to the ha-ha. Humphrey, still on high alert following the shock of the gong, stiffened, and then made a dash for freedom. Hugh reacted fast enough to grab his collar as he went past.

'Thanks, pal,' said Fred, picking up the lead from the hall table and wheeling forward. He bent down and tethered his dog. 'Come on, Humphrey. You're staying with us. I know you want to play. But those rabbits don't realise you're a wuss, and we're keeping it that way.'

Moments later, everyone was gathered in the drawing room. Robin was announcing cocktails to the crowd. Beside him, Alberto shook the cocktail shaker with his customary style, while indicating with his eyebrows that all this was rather beneath him. He found his boyfriend's enthusiasm a bit... gauche. It was only a house party. None of these people would count as a real celebrity, not even Heather.

'We have martinis in the shaker, very dry,' said Robin. 'We also have a big jug of rum punch, if you want a long drink... gin and tonics of course, they're easy... and some chilled and salted glasses for the margaritas.'

Freya gazed at Alberto in admiration, and pointed to a ginger ale, although she felt secret service agents should stick to martinis. Flashing her a glance of complicity, he poured it out in a cocktail glass, which went some way to assuaging her. Polly took a glass of the punch from Robin. The others shuffled after her in line. After taking their drinks, the guests swirled around the room, looking out of the window, inspecting the house, and generally failing to socialise. Robin and Alberto were left wondering if there was anyone to come. They looked around the room and tried to count heads.

'Sonia is not drinking alcohol,' whispered Robin to Alberto.

'Of course not!' said his boyfriend, who was not looking up because he was trying to get a signal on his phone. 'La niña!' he tutted. 'Children never should be drinking!'

'No, not Freya! Sonia... The woman over there.'

'Oh,' said Alberto, looking over. 'The one with the Missoni cardigan?'

'Yes,' said Robin. 'She is married to Fred's old friend Anil.'

'Married?' said Alberto in surprise. He whistled between his teeth.

'But still,' said Robin, 'not having a drink. Everyone in the literary world drinks.'

'She might have dark secrets in her past,' ventured Alberto, hopefully. 'Closeted skeletons! I watch Fred closely.'

'I very much doubt there are skeletons, or closets,' said Robin. 'And please *mio carissimo*, don't tell anyone your fantasies about them.'

'But you like my fantasies!' pouted Alberto.

'Different kind of fantasies,' said Robin. 'Those kinds are just fine.'

With that, they left their drinks station and joined the party, ready for the toast. As people gathered with their glasses, there was some jockeying for position amongst the guests. Fred wanted to be near Heather. Alberto wanted to be near Fred. Freya had decided Sonia was lovely and wondered if she too was partial to 'Frère Jacques'. Nobody wanted to be run over by the chair.

'To Fred!' said Polly, seeing that everyone had a drink. Everyone chimed glasses with their host, and mumbled in unison. Determined to follow suit, Freya thrust her ginger ale into the air, and shrieked as it splashed onto her wrist. Polly shushed her and dabbed at her with a napkin.

Fred felt he should say a few words. He gestured with his glass of punch.

'Thanks to Robin and Alberto, for the, uh, "mixology", as I think you call it these days. And to everyone else for pitching in with the food. It's wonderful that you could join me here for my birthday. So nice to see Heather again in the flesh.'

There was a titter from someone, which Fred ignored.

'You know I've had my ups and downs over the last twenty years.'

There was another giggle from someone unsure as to whether Fred was trying to joke.

'Anyway, the point is, I am so grateful to you, my dear friends, for sticking with me, and you're the best people in the whole world to help me celebrate my fortieth.'

'Life begins!' called out someone.

'Three cheers for Fred!' exclaimed Roddy, and they cheered Fred to the rafters, before sinking into the soft furnishings. Fred wheeled after them.

'So, what did you all do this afternoon?' he asked his friends. 'Polly and Freya and I took Humphrey for a walk around the grounds.'

'I read a book,' said Sonia. 'I thought it was rather good'. She smiled at Fred. That sounded promising, he thought.

Others in the crowd thought her response ominous. Heather looked anywhere but at her co-conspirators. It was mortifying to Heather that Sonia could be laughing at her past mistakes. Charlotte pretended she hadn't heard, but her smile became fixed.

'We played a hand of Scrabble,' said Robin. 'We like our games'.

Someone giggled. His boyfriend gazed around the room defiantly. Alberto knew some very on-trend people who simply adored Scrabble, but this crowd couldn't be expected to understand that. It had seemed cool in Biarritz, but here it was probably childish. Which was just so frustrating.

'I watched the rooks roosting in that copse of trees beyond the Park,' said Hugh. 'There are at least a thousand of them. I always find corvids amazing. They roost in such massive numbers. The largest roost ever recorded was something like a million. Not in one tree, of course,' he added.

Everyone was silent for a minute. No one actually knew what a corvid was. 'It's a sort of bird!' whispered Polly to Sonia. 'Wasn't there one in Jurassic Park?' Roddy asked his wife, puzzled.

'Corvids are extremely intelligent, you know,' Hugh continued, not known for his audience sensitivity. 'You can train starlings for example. I think they're the third cleverest non-primate, or something. And crows use tools, you know.'

'Tools? Like screwdrivers?' asked Roddy, with interest.

'Well, no, not *those* tools. Sticks and things. Poking ants' nests,' said Hugh. Really, some people were so dim. No wonder the political class were useless.

'Speaking of bright animals, I met the pig today.' said Fred. 'And his handler too. Nel. You might even remember her? She was in the first year at St Warburgs when we were in third year. Not that she stayed – apparently she was sent down!'

Fred looked at Charlotte, Heather, and Polly. Heads were shaking and shoulders were shrugging.

'Well, you must admit, it's an odd coincidence,' he said.

For different reasons, none of them wanted to be reminded of their college years. Hugh always felt left out when his friends reminisced about St Warburgs. It meant nothing to Roddy or Robin either, Fred realised. He quickly changed the subject.

'Anybody else seen the pig?'

'I've seen a pig,' replied Charlotte, and glared at her husband.

'Yes, I went down earlier,' Roddy said, quickly. 'It's behind the kitchen garden. Every castle should have a pig.'

There was an awkward silence. Roddy, Charlotte and Heather looked meaningfully at Hugh. He failed to notice.

'In my country we have many goats,' pointed out Alberto, helpfully.

'Alberto comes from Puerto Rico,' explained Roddy, kindly, to Freya. She loathed being patronised and did not grace him with a smile.

'No!' replied Alberto imperiously. 'Not Puerto Rico! Costa Rica!' He almost stamped his feet in frustration. 'I come from a beautiful country! We have jungles. One quarter of Costa Rica is national park. Biodiversidad! But Puerto Rico?' He sneered. 'Puerto Rico is just a colony of the gringos. They have parties', he added. 'They invented salsa,' he almost spat. 'But we have no army! We are the Switzerland of Latin America.'

'Only not as rich,' added Robin, hurriedly. 'He's from a favela you know,' he said, proudly. 'A place called Triángulo. He danced his way to freedom.'

Everyone stared in fascination.

'Is true. I was spotted by a Venezuelan choreographer,' said Alberto. 'He took me to Vegas to dance with Bette Midler at Caesar's Palace.'

'That sounds lovely,' said Polly, tactfully.

'Was not lovely,' said Alberto, with a dramatic sigh. 'The choreographer abandoned me in Caracas.'

'I got some of those for Christmas,' said Freya, spotting her chance to join the grown-ups' conversation. 'But I prefer the recorder.'

Alberto looked at her in dismay and flounced out of the room.

'Blimey!' said Roddy. 'So highly strung!'

'He's probably going to make biscuits,' said Robin, apologetically. 'He turns to cooking at times of emotional turmoil. The man's a genius in the kitchen.'

'Talking about Central America,' said Heather, sensing an opening. 'Did I tell you about the time there was a coup in El Salvador? Luckily, I was only next door, in Honduras, god only knows why…'. As several people drifted away, she found herself talking to Roddy, who seemed fascinated to hear more. He steered her over to an armchair and sat on the arm, gazing into her eyes, as she highlighted several key features of recent Central American politics, pronouncing every name in an exaggerated Spanish accent – NICK-A-RA-WA. In the background, Freya stood fingering her recorder silently, waiting for her opportunity to serenade her new friend.

Hugh was looking nearly as awkward as he felt. Standing on the fringe of the group, he sipped a beer which was too chilled for him. He had gone off Heather completely since they had had their little tête-à-tête. He hated feeling so subservient to someone from the Mainstream Media. Polly tried to ask him about his van, but in his embarrassment he only managed to stammer monosyllables, so she gave up, and wandered over to talk to Charlotte. Hugh edged to the side of the room and glanced over the books on the shelves, which seemed to be a job lot from a junk shop. Lots of S.P.B. Mais and Dennis Wheatley. Did anyone read any of this stuff anymore? They were for show really, he thought.

On her way to fetch another cocktail, Heather gave him an encouraging smile. He scowled at her, and then felt bad about it. She wasn't so awful. Even though he felt totally manipulated and hated himself for it. He wasn't stupid enough not to notice the effect that her open-necked white shirt and tight Levis had on him. He checked his jacket pocket for the torch.

Roddy wandered over to him, Martini glass in hand, able to look dashing in any outfit, which was just as well, given the limitations of the fancy dress store.

'Hugh, old boy,' he said, jovially. 'You know you look jolly shifty, lurking over here.'

'Not really one for parties,' replied Hugh, honestly.

'Get that drink down you and lighten up. A minor bit of burglary never hurt anyone.'

'The precedents aren't so good,' said Hugh, thinking of *The Hobbit* for some reason.

'Tis a far, far better thing you do,' replied Roddy, smoothly. He has no idea he was quoting Charles Dickens, thought Hugh. Roddy turned and glanced significantly at Heather.

'We will all be very grateful.'

Hugh sighed. He'd never liked Roddy.

'Yeah, yeah. Don't worry. Consider it done.'

He abruptly turned his back on Roddy and studied a battered copy of the *Natural History of Selbourne*.

Over at the entrance to the drawing room, Alberto had returned to Robin's side. Fred was not far away and Alberto had decided that he was safe for now. No one would dare make a move in front of a crowd. And now a significant announcement was about to be made.

'Ladies!' Robin smiled at Freya. 'Gentlemen! Dinner is served!'

'Oh, good,' said Heather, loudly. 'I'm starving.'

Charlotte shook her head. 'That'll be the alcohol on an empty stomach. It's really not good for you.'

'Stuff and nonsense!' said Roddy, boisterously illus-trating his wife's caution. He gave Hugh a random pat on the shoulder as he passed. Hugh ignored him. The word 'starving' only reminded Polly of the many foodbanks in her Borough. She wasn't sure that either Roddy's politics or Heather's journalism would do much to help food poverty, at home or abroad. She sighed, and wandered after the others.

As people drifted into the dining room, Fred tried to implement a seating plan, from his place at the end of the walnut table.

'So, why don't we have... Polly next to me... Heather on the other side... Oh, Alberto next to me? OK then. After that, Heather, then Roderick perhaps... Robin next to Polly? Then... Freya, do you want to sit next to your mum? No? Perhaps next to Robin? Be careful, he might psychoanalyse you! Only joking, love. Right, and then Sonia, then Freya... and then Hugh... Is that all of us? Oh Lottie, nice to see you, can you take the chair by Hugh? Great. Perfect.'

Everyone sat down and started talking to a neighbour. Fred sighed. He hoped it wasn't going to be like herding cats all weekend.

Charlotte leaned across the table to talk to Sonia.

'Are you enjoying the book?' she asked.

'Yes, as far as I've got,' said Sonia. 'He starts with the accident, which I think is good. *In media res*, as it were...'

'I always think writing a book is like having a baby,' said Charlotte. 'You gestate the bloody thing for nine months, then it occupies your entire attention for years while you're writing it, then it sets off into the world, free from your control, and vulnerable to anyone who cares to criticise it...'

'I wouldn't exactly know,' said Sonia, shortly. 'I suppose in your analogy, I'm just the midwife.' She turned to Freya and tried to engage her in a conversation about what she liked to read. Charlotte stared at her in surprise. No need to be quite so sniffy, she thought.

People had seemed to enjoy the roast vegetable soup, thought Robin, as the meal continued. Though they probably hadn't even noticed that the bread was homemade sourdough. That meat loaf for the main course was perhaps a bit too old-school for a celebration dinner. But at least he'd scored a hit with the nut loaf. And the roast veggies were perfect with that balsamic glaze. Although it was a bit too obvious, perhaps? At least he'd made it all, not bought it in.

Alberto started collecting dinner plates. Now, the pudding had better hit the spot.... Dishes were passed around, and there was appreciative silence.

'This whip thing is fantastic, Alberto!' said Fred, a few moments later. 'What would you call it in English?'

'A fool?' suggested Charlotte. Her husband looked up.

'It's called syllabub. Completely Georgian! It's just the sort of thing they would have eaten when the house was built,' explained Robin. 'We thought it was in keeping.'

'In Costa Rica, of course, we have the best puddings in the world!' said Alberto, proudly.

'I think you'll find it's only actually a pudding if it's got flour in it,' said Hugh. 'It hasn't got flour in it, has it?'

'No,' said Robin, shortly. 'But it's still a f—' He stopped himself. 'I think we can still call it a pudding, Hugh.'

'You know nothing about puddings!' Alberto snapped at Hugh. 'This is *buenazo*!'

'We can all drink to that!' said Fred, diplomatically. 'Now, everyone, shall we raise a glass to the chefs?'

People stopped in mid-flow and dutifully raised and clinked. Alberto beamed an orthodontically dazzling smile at Fred, and the suspended conversations resumed their undulating flow towards the sea of inebriation.

The candles down the centre of the walnut table winked at the guests from the cut glass bowls and the crystal glasses. The artisanal candles were certainly not the emergency items provided by the Trust, but came from a mislaid box that Fred's assistant had found left over from a probate case the previous month. No point in leaving them in store.

Sonia was talking to Robin, who was seated next to her.

'So, how do you know Fred again?'

'I met him in Cambridge,' replied Robin. 'He was doing his law conversion course after St Warburgs and his accident, I was training to be a clinical psychologist, we shared a house on Mill Road. Played a lot of pool in the Duke of Argyll pub.'

Sonia looked around to see if anyone was listening to them and then turned back to Robin and spoke in a lower voice:

'You're a mental health professional, so can you cast light on his... Thing?'

'His "thing"?' queried Robin, cautiously.

'You know, if he sees a woman's naked flesh – shock – vomit – pass out – whatever. That "thing".'

'Well...' said Robin, cautiously. 'It's not my place to diagnose, of course. Very unprofessional. But speaking generally, traffic accidents are obviously terribly traumatic. Many students get very emotionally strung out after Finals. Add it all together, and sometimes these things can mark you. Psychosexual problems are more common than you'd think. Recalcitrant when combined with Post Traumatic Stress Syndrome.'

'But it's pretty dramatic, isn't it?' said Sonia. 'Vomiting when you see female flesh?'

'Yes,' said Robin. 'But then remember John Ruskin…'

'Who?'

'The Victorian art critic. Apparently, when he finally got married, and it was, you know, the time to consummate the marriage, he was horrified to discover that his bride had, err, pubic hair.'

'I beg your pardon?' said Sonia, wondering if anyone had written a novel about this yet.

'Well, he'd seen a lot of nude females in art, and of course, they never had pubic hair. But his bird had a bush, as it were.'

'And he couldn't cope with it?'

'No,' said Robin. 'As far as I remember, the wife, Effy, left Ruskin on the grounds of non-consummation. But the pubes thing may be a myth.'

'Oh, that's sad,' said Sonia. 'To be unable to do something so natural and joyous. Of course, in Fred's case it was all because of that terrible accident.'

'As I say, it's not professional to diagnose someone at a distance, and certainly not to discuss a case with someone else. But mix together trauma, stress and paralysis and it all gets very complicated.'

'Oh, I am sure of that,' agreed Sonia, with feeling. 'You know poor Fred and Roddy's mother was called Effy? Euphemia, I mean?'

'Yes, that she was. I never met her.'

'Odd coincidence,' said Sonia.

As a friend, Sonia thought it was sad. As an agent, it was gold dust. She could picture Fred on the daytime TV sofa. Or beside it, rather. Sonia turned to Robin again.

'You've never thought of writing yourself, I suppose?'

Robin shook his head.

'I don't approve of clinicians mistaking their clients for material to use as part of their literary career. Now, if you don't mind, I think I'm needed in the kitchen.'

After a moment, Robin returned from the kitchen with a tray of biscuits and cheese.

'All English!'

Alberto came back to the table fortified with a bottle of Port and another of Madeira, and a slight sneer.

'Here you are, colonial types! The drinks of Portugal, like milords adore!'

He sat back down next to Fred, and put his arm around his shoulder. 'A digestif, Frederick?'

'I'll make coffee,' said Sonia. 'Anyone else for decaff?'

Hugh felt now might be the right time to slip out for ten minutes. If it were done, 'tis best 'twere done quickly, he thought, then lambasted himself for falling into Shakespearean like the others. Roddy caught his eye and nodded to him significantly. He bloody hated being an accomplice of that stupid jerk. But a confiding smile from Heather compensated. Now glowing, not glowering, he slipped quietly down the corridor, past the kitchen where it looked as if Sonia was putting the coffee on. He thought this might give him at least ten minutes grace. He'd go up the back stairs.

Chapter 14

As Hugh flashed the torch around, he first saw the double bed which dominated Sonia's bedroom. There was an odd gadget lying on the counterpane. Was that a vibrator? he thought, in shock. And there was a tube of KY Jelly oozing slime! Too much information!

Hugh averted his eyes and looked around for the manuscript. He could hear the rumble of voices from the dining room below, as well as the faint strains of 'Frère Jacques'. Freya had obviously trapped a victim. He just hoped someone was keeping Sonia talking. Then he saw a bulging folder on the bedside table. Sonia must have been reading it in bed, he thought.

He first went to the window. He noticed approvingly that it was a proper sash window, and he opened it carefully so it didn't squeak. He could see in the dark that there were bins to the right. Maybe he could just dump everything there... although it would be better to destroy it, wouldn't it? That's what he'd promised Heather. He took the folder, and holding it to his chest, pulled his jacket closed around it. Now for the memory stick... It must be still in Fred's room, back on the ground floor. Thank goodness Fred didn't trust the Cloud.

Not that he did himself, come to that. But then, he was unlikely to write anything longer than a shopping list.

Looking around the bedroom, Hugh wondered whether the right thing to do was to mess it up. So it looked like there'd been a burglary. An outside job, he corrected himself. Leave the window open… tip open the case. But at that moment, he heard someone coming up the stairs. He froze.

The footsteps were coming nearer. He waited, heart beating loudly. He hoped it wasn't Sonia. The steps passed the door. After a few more minutes, Hugh opened the bedroom door a crack, and listened carefully for a moment. The hubbub was continuing in the dining room below. He quietly left the bedroom, shut the door and crept away.

Now all that Hugh had to do was to go down to Fred's room and locate the memory stick. Then he had to slip away and feed everything to the pig. He quietly slipped down the stairs. This burglary business was not his style. Covert operations sounded exciting. Poaching, that could be fun. But he wasn't keen on trespassing into people's bedrooms. As he tiptoed down the corridor to Fred's room, he heard people talking to each other in the kitchen. Their voices were so carrying, he thought. That was some consolation at a moment like this.

Opening Fred's bedroom door, Hugh looked first at the bedside table; no memory stick. He crossed quickly to the antique dressing table and opened the drawer. It squeaked badly. Needed some linseed oil. His own furniture never squeaked. With growing desperation, he rummaged with his left hand. Nothing. Nor under the socks, pants or anywhere in the chest of drawers. The problem with wheelchairs was that they glided so quietly that you could never hear them coming.

He didn't want to be found like a sneak-thief in his old friend's bedroom.

He tried to put himself into Fred's shoes. Where would he hide a precious memory stick? Shoes! Hugh turned to the windowsill where several pairs of shoes were neatly lined up, ready for their owner. He tipped up a pristine Caterpillar boot (they lasted so much longer if you never walked in them) and bingo! There was the memory stick. He popped it into his jacket pocket. Job done. He congratulated himself for remembering to pick up the manuscript again, and quietly tiptoed out of the bedroom.

Fred was still safely playing Mine Host in the dining room. Heather was in an armchair near the fireplace, her grin fixed, with a small child equally fixed in place in front of her, warbling a familiar tune. Sonia was talking to Charlotte over their coffees. Hugh edged closer to the front door. No sign of Humphrey, thankfully.

'Are you leaving us already?' Hugh nearly jumped out of his skin. But it was only Polly, coming down from the upper landing.

'Hello,' he said. 'Just going for a breath of air.'

'Freya says she likes you,' said Polly, smiling at him encouragingly.

'Oh...' He fumbled for words. 'That's nice. Good.'

Hugh hoped she wouldn't notice the folder. Then an idea came to him.

'I could, you know, take her on a walk tomorrow, if you like. Around the estate. See what we can spot... wildlife, you know?'

'That would be so kind! After all, you know what you're looking at, and I don't.'

'OK, I will,' he said, resolutely. It would probably be OK, he thought. Hugh edged closer to the front door.

'What's so urgent?' asked Polly. She looked at him quizzically. 'Are you up to something? An assignation?'

'No, err… just stretching my legs,' said Hugh, trying to look nonchalant.

'I might come and join you,' replied Polly, who felt relaxed and happy after a few drinks. 'Have a look at the stars. You can probably point out the constellations, can't you?'

'Yes… most of them… but I'd rather you didn't,' said Hugh, quickly. 'Join me, I mean. Don't mean to be rude… I'd just prefer to be alone, on this occasion'.

He hated himself for saying it, particularly to her. But he didn't see that he had much of a choice, given the bulge inside his jacket.

'Fine,' said Polly, feeling unaccountably hurt. 'Well, see you later then.'

'Yes…' Now he felt bad. Had he been terribly impolite? He tried to placate her. 'I really will take Freya for that walk tomorrow! And teach her a new tune or two!'

'OK,' she said, shortly, and wandered back into the dining room.

Feeling guiltier than ever, Hugh strode to the big oak door of the hall, opened it as quietly as he could, and then ran, ducking down, on the gravel path around the building.

At that moment, Freya was the only one of the party who was looking out of the windows. Heather had said she had a headache, and no one else seemed keen to hear her play. In truth, Freya was spying through a crack in the shutters. She was keeping quiet, partly to avoid being sent to bed, and partly to practice her spy craft. The evening had been frustratingly dull, and she felt it was time she expanded her repertoire. So she was the only one who saw Hugh sneaking past at speed. Freya wondered what he was up to. He seemed to have something bulky under his coat – he was definitely up to no good. Finally! Freya thought. A real mystery! Just in time. The weekend at last had possibilities.

Chapter 15

After coffee, Heather slipped out of the front door and made her way over to the statue. This time, not even Freya noticed. She looked about her. She was on her own, and it was blessedly quiet. She pulled her phone out of her pocket, frowning at how the bulge ruined the line of her clothes. Flicking her hair aside, she put it to her ear for a transatlantic call. Clancy was on speed-dial.

'Honey? It's me. I'm in Suffolk... It's a part of England... Yes, that England... No, just as expected... No one interesting... although I do appear to have a seven-year-old stalker. How's things in LA? All day with the lawyers? You poor thing... Don't let her screw you!'

And after that, it turned out to be a rather one sided conversation, as Clancy's divorce grievances were in pressing need of an audience.

'So what made you want to be a writer?'

The others were in the drawing room, relaxing over after-dinner drinks. Sonia was talking to Fred as she dried the dinner service that he was washing in the sink. A minor spat had broken out earlier between Hugh, who had vetoed use of the dishwasher on ecological grounds, and Robin, who thought that a dishwasher used less energy than hot water. Partly to distract from the squabble, Fred had insisted on taking his turn after the meal.

'Well, I'm very good at Scrabble, you know...'

'Really? Not sure that being able to spell IMBROGLIO or knowing that LI is a Chinese measurement of distance are the usual qualifications for an author,' said Sonia.

'No, I can quite see that,' said Fred, hurriedly. 'But I like choosing the right word. And I hear a lot of stories, being a lawyer. I love listening to clients.'

'Good dialogue is a very important skill.'

'I hope you're not saying I'm a hopeless writer?' said Fred, anxiously. 'And anyway,' he added thoughtfully, 'IMBROGLIO is a nine-letter word, and I doubt you could make it in Scrabble.'

'Good to know,' said Sonia. 'So far, the memoir looks heartwarming. I've only read about half of it so far. You tell the story of the crash with compassion, and I think the reader will be fascinated.'

'Thank goodness for that,' said Fred, who had had a moment of panic about his literary abilities.

'But you're pretty bad at washing up,' said Sonia, passing a serving bowl back to him. 'You've missed this gunk entirely.'

'Oops! I thought it was the ceramic pattern,' said Fred.

Alberto came into the little scullery, bearing glasses. He looked surprised to see Sonia standing next to Fred. His eyes narrowed, and there was a moment of tension.

'Hello, Alberto,' said Fred. 'Everything OK? Enjoying yourself?'

'First rate,' muttered Alberto. He turned to Sonia suspiciously. 'Speak to me!'

'Excuse me?' said Sonia in surprise. 'What about? Is there a problem?'

'No problem at all!' said Alberto, breaking into a broad smile. 'You are perfectly fine. You are not one of them'. He turned on his heel and strode out of the kitchen. There was a moment of silence after he left as the two friends looked at each other in surprise.

'What on earth was that about?' said Sonia, laughing. 'What am I not one of? Is he looking for St Warburgs graduates?'

'Absolutely no idea,' said Fred, shrugging his shoulders. 'He's a lovely man, and I am so pleased for Robin, but Alberto has been following me around like a puppy.'

'Perhaps he fancies you?' said Sonia.

'Fancies me?' said Fred in surprise. 'I very much doubt it.'

'Never any interest from those quarters?' said his friend, drying a saucepan.

'Well, once or twice, there were guys who wanted to... you know... mother me... Friends of Robin's.'

'But you weren't tempted?'

'Not at all. I mean, don't get me wrong. Gay people are great, some of my best friends, etcetera...'

'Just not your style?'

'No. I don't like being mothered, regardless of gender.'

There was a pause, as Fred pulled the plug out of the sink and dried his hands.

'Look, Fred,' said Sonia. 'I'm going to do my very best by your manuscript. Believe me. But whether or not it gets picked up, I hope it doesn't affect our friendship.'

'Of course it won't!'

'It just feels a bit like mixing business with pleasure,' admitted Sonia.

'If I have to hear some home truths, I'd rather it was from you,' said Fred, who felt less brave than he sounded.

'Publishing is a lottery, and even if you have the best written story, it might not be flavour of the month.'

'I know,' said Fred, looking resolute. 'Well, just do what you can.'

'You can rely on me for that!' said Sonia. 'And I promise not to mother you,' she added.

'If this doesn't work, I could always try again with a novel,' Fred said. 'I just need a good idea. My clients always have great stories. Certainly, those accused of crimes do. No doubt they make up at least half of the details. Unfortunately, I never know which half.'

'Best if you can discard the boring bits,' said Sonia. 'Anyway, I'm off to bed. I'm yawning like someone with a clockwork jaw, and it's not yet ten.'

In the sitting room, Robin was still listening patiently to Roderick explaining at some length how former Labour voters in Red Wall constituencies could be brought back to their old allegiances. After that, Robin had a pressing need for sleep, but couldn't find Alberto anywhere. Finally, he thought of trying outside, given that it was so mild, and spotted a silhouette by the ha-ha. He tiptoed closer. It was Alberto glued to his ubiquitous iPhone. Robin's Spanish wasn't brilliant, but he understood a few words:

'You do it so well.'

'I love that.'

'Tasty, tasty!'

'Sweetie! Oh, darling!'

He didn't like what he was hearing one little bit, so he retreated, heart thumping. That's what you got for eavesdropping, he thought. But when Alberto came upstairs a few minutes later, he flung his arms around Robin, and suggested they have a bath. Robin looked at him suspiciously. It was as if nothing was going on at all. Could he really be such a good actor?

Chapter 16

As the chimes of midnight rang from the grandfather clock in the hall, everything appeared to be going well at Threepwood. Most of the guests had retired to bed. Alberto and Robin were in the bathroom on the top landing, sharing the huge Victorian tub. Despite it being of larger than average proportions, they had to entwine their legs and still only just fitted together. Robin quietly intoned *The Owl and the Pussycat* to his lover. The two did not linger on the question of which of them was which voyager in the pea green craft, because other intimacies obtruded. Afterwards, they disembarked from the claw-foot bath, and began to towel each other dry. Tying himself into his enormous white towel, Robin felt like a Roman emperor. That surely excused his girth, and his incipient baldness. Leaning over, he pulled the chain to drain the bath. A few minutes later there was a shriek from the floor below, followed by a shout. Alberto and Robin looked at each other in surprise.

'What on earth was that?' said Robin. They both listened, craning their heads. There were no further screams.

It did not sound like Fred. It's not something we need worry about,' sniffed Alberto. 'Let's go to bed?' he added, significantly.

'Oh goody,' said Robin. 'I'll race you.' And with that, the two of them retreated to their room, oblivious to the continuing noises from downstairs.

On the floor below, Roddy had turned on the bedside light, and leapt out of the covers. Charlotte had vacated the bed with equal speed, grabbing her dressing gown from the chair. They were now both standing next to their bed, in perplexed fury. As they watched, water poured through the ceiling in a steady flood. It felt like being inside a chillingly-accurate simulation of an Amazonian rain forest. Much of the deluge seemed to be falling precisely on their bed, but there were random cascades in other parts of the room too.

'Bloody hell!' said Roddy. 'A pipe must have burst! That's all we need!' Being rained on, while under a roof, seemed to him a particularly unjust indignity.

'I feel like Noah,' retorted Charlotte, as she dragged her weekend bag to a table of apparent safety amidst the rapidly filling swamp that was their bedroom.

At that moment, the light went out.

'Noooo!' said Charlotte, with feeling.

'Probably fused,' said Roddy. 'All this water wouldn't help the ancient electrics.'

'What do we do now?' Charlotte asked, helplessly.

'Shout for help?' suggested Roddy. 'Or feel our way out?' In the dark, he edged his way around the corner of the room to the door. Opening it, he found the landing not quite pitch black, thanks to the light of the moon filtering through the overhead cupola. He edged his way to the staircase, and promptly fell down the first half-flight with a crash.

'Damn and blast!' he exclaimed, angrily. He began to rearrange his nightwear.

Hearing unaccustomed noises and intense swearing, Sonia and then Polly each attempted to turn their own bedside lights on, only to find them uncooperative. Heather decided she would only be the intrepid trailblazer if an actual video camera was involved. Doors opened on landings. Voices were heard. Questions were asked, with increasing urgency. Points of order were mooted. Meanwhile, Fred wheeled out into the downstairs hall below. He tried to discover what was happening up the stairs which he could not ascend. He was not the only person to feel impotent. It was only five minutes past midnight, but chaos had descended on Threepwood Hall.

The front door creaked open, and a narrow shaft of light punctured the entrance hall. Fred recoiled instinctively against the intrusion of a stranger. But it was only Hugh come in from his van, dressed in ancient pyjamas, what looked like the dressing gown that he had taken to boarding school and a night cap. Fred thought he looked like Badger in E. H. Shepherd's illustration to *The Wind in the Willows*.

'Hullo, everyone! I heard noises, wondered what was going on,' said Hugh. He shone his torch around the stairs and then to the upstairs landing. 'Oh, you're all up, are you? Is this a game that everyone can play? Sardines?'

He couldn't see the scowls, but they were evident in the silence that followed his jovial greeting.

'Not really the best time for jokes, Hugh,' said Fred, from the hall. 'It looks like we've lost power for the night. But look on the bright side everyone,' he called up the stairs. 'No harm done!'

'It's pitch black and freezing cold, we can't even turn on the lights. There is quite literally no bright side!' muttered Roddy from the stairs.

'We've had a flood, Hugh,' called Charlotte, in explanation.

'And now the lights must have fused,' added Sonia, from the first floor landing.

'Let me go and have a look at the fuse box,' said Hugh, swinging the torch around the line of people craning their necks at him. 'I noticed it down in the cellar when I arrived.'

'You know where the fuse box is?' called Polly, in surprise. 'How on earth would you know that?'

'I always like to look at a building closely from top to bottom. Put it this way, it doesn't surprise me in the least that the plumbing turns out to be a bit dodgy. Original lead piping, you see.' He poked at the wallpaper enquiringly, and made a hole in the plasterwork.

'Would you mind checking out that fuse box right away and talking after?' came Roddy's voice. 'Only it's a bit dark on this landing...'

'Sorry. Just a mo...' Hugh strode off towards the basement door, and gingerly descended the stone stairs. Fred could him talking away to himself as he examined the fuse box. A moment later, all the lights went on again. There was a ragged cheer. Then they flickered and went off again, and everyone groaned. Finally, they went on, and stayed on. There was a rumble from the boiler and a round of applause from the guests. They heard steps returning from the basement.

'Sorry about that. I had to improvise some fuse wire out of an old Kit Kat wrapper I found in my pocket,' explained Hugh. 'It's a bit dodgy, but it should last the weekend... Although it could start a fire,' he added, thoughtfully.

'Could we request you to keep eating chocolate bars then?' called down Sonia. 'In case it happens again.'

'Is there a fire alarm here?' asked Charlotte, suddenly anxious. Beside her, Polly quietly drew her attention to the telltale shapes on each ceiling. Sonia gestured weakly at the chaos and went back to bed.

At this point, Alberto belatedly came out of the room on the top floor, dressed only in Calvin Kleins, and ran down the stairs to stand next to Fred, who smiled weakly at him. Heather, Robin and Freya now seemed to be the only ones who hadn't come out to see what was up. Alberto gazed defiantly around him.

'Was it just a Latino thing to be so attentive?' wondered Fred. He hoped Alberto didn't have a thing for him. That would be really unfortunate. This was not the time for Heather to get the wrong impression.

'Right, good night again, everyone,' said Polly firmly, and drifted off back to her bedroom. Roddy and Charlotte remained on the landing, with Alberto still standing protectively next to Fred and Hugh hovering in the hall.

'We've still got the not insignificant problem that our bedroom is now a swamp,' said Roddy.

'Swamps are an important part of biodiversity,' mused Hugh.

'But not a helpful part of the human sleep process,' stated Roddy, firmly.

'You really can't sleep in the bed?' asked Fred.

'Not being a muskrat, no,' said Roddy, folding his arms in disgust.

'The name muskrat is a misnomer of course,' said Hugh, thoughtfully. 'It's from an Algonquian word, originally, but the muskrat is not actually a member of the rat family.'

'How utterly inappropriate, then,' said Charlotte, glaring at Roddy.

'OK, well we can dry things out in the morning but for tonight, obviously Roderick and Charlotte will have to find a new bed, jointly or separately,' said Fred, thinking aloud. 'I am a single in a double myself. I suppose I could swap? Perhaps you could share Heather's room, Lottie...'

'There's also room for another one in my van,' said Hugh. 'Been done before.'

'I could always join Hugh and you two could have my bed. Although I think clambering into the van might be a bit difficult for me,' reflected Fred.

'Wouldn't hear of it!' said Charlotte. 'We're not going to turn you out. You're our host.'

'I could go in the van myself,' said Roddy. 'I'd rather not wake up Heather again unless we have to,' he said, gallantly.

'I suppose you *could* join me in the van', said Hugh, rather regretting he'd made the offer. 'But you'll have to bring your own pillow,' he added.

'But Charlotte, you're not going to feel comfortable about sharing with me, are you?' said Fred, with concern. 'I mean, of course we are family, but still?'

'Worry not, Fred, as long as you don't sleep naked or snore like a pig, it doesn't matter to me in the slightest. Might be quite an improvement on the first Mr Twistleton. I am however not going to sleep alongside Hugh, who I hardly know from Adam. The only other option is wake up Heather again, which my husband seems strangely opposed to.'

With that, Charlotte walked down the corridor to get into Fred's bed. Alberto glared at the departing back of the potential murderess, while Fred looked at his brother helplessly and shrugged.

'Don't worry, bro,' said Roddy. 'You'll hardly notice she's there, if my experience is anything to go by.' He had a sudden thought. 'Hey folks, the only thing is, nobody is to breathe a word about this. I don't want the papers to know, or anything like that.'

'Oh, come off it, Roddy,' said Hugh. 'Nobody's going to think you're gay just because you bunk up with another bloke in an emergency.'

'That's the least of my worries!' replied Roddy, with a quick glance at Alberto. 'It would be positively brilliant for my political career if I gave people the impression that I was bisexual,' he said. 'No, what I mean is, Lottie is my wife, and she now appears to be sharing a bed with my own brother. If we're not careful, it could very well turn into one of those salacious three-in-a-bed sex stories in a red top tabloid, and that wouldn't wash at all well with the Party.'

Alberto could think of nothing worse than being accused of sexual relations with either Roddy or Charlotte.

'That's true, "Christian falls from grace" stories always do well,' mused Fred. 'Not that I buy any tabloids myself, of course,' he added, hurriedly. 'But my secretary Mrs Tuzinckiewich does.'

'Why have you got a Polish secretary?' asked Hugh, with interest.

'If you want anything done quickly in East Anglia, you have to get an Eastern European on the job, whether it's harvesting Brussel sprouts or sitting on reception, at least if they arrived before Brexit. Her English is brilliant. But then so was Conrad's.'

'Did you know it was actually his third language?' said Hugh.

'Amazing!' replied Fred. 'I always remember Two-Gin-Kay-Wits otherwise I wouldn't have a hope of remembering her name. Please don't ask me to spell it. Her husband was the first man to ski the Chilterns from one end to another.'

'Look,' said Roddy. 'I'm loving this discussion, but do you think we could all go to bed now?'

Fred and Hugh looked at each other in surprise.

'Tell me about Mr Tuzinckiewich's *langlaufing* over break-fast then,' said Hugh, turning towards the door.

'It's absolutely true, and I'll explain tomorrow,' said Fred. 'That's why we call him the Ski Pole in the office,' he added. 'Good night.'

Alberto wasn't happy about Charlotte sharing Fred's bed. He was sure he'd correctly identified their voices earlier, and he was suspicious about what she and her husband might be up to. He shot the bolts emphatically, and returned upstairs.

Moments later, the clock quietly announced half past twelve to an oblivious world. Snores gently reverberated across the upper landings. Back in his room, Fred thought it was rather nice to have a bed companion for a change, although a goodnight kiss might be inappropriate in the circumstances. Turned away from him, Charlotte murmured incoherently to herself. Fred carefully arranged himself on the other side of the bed, so as not to come into contact with his sister-in-law. Within moments, he too was asleep, only to have a series of anxiety dreams featuring orgies to which he was not invited. There followed a nightmare about a Belgian rabbit reporter doorstepping his home with persistent questions about adultery.

Chapter 17

Fred woke, in his strange bed, to an even less familiar sensation. He was lying on his back, warm and comfortable, gazing at the ceiling. Nuzzled against his shoulder, her hair against his chin, was a woman. It was rather pleasant. Tentatively, he stroked her head with his free hand. She burrowed closer in, and flung an arm around him. He froze, hardly daring to breathe for fear of waking her. They held on to each other, like floundering swimmers grasping a buoyancy aid. Charlotte's steady inhalations and exhalations continued, and he lay still, trying to ignore his throbbing head. Then the rhythm of her breathing changed, and he sensed her gradually surfacing. He closed his eyes, pretending to be asleep himself. Famous authors almost certainly woke up in bed with other people's wives all the time, he thought.

Charlotte didn't alter her posture at first, so he wasn't sure whether she had even opened her eyes. Then with a sigh, she gave him a squeeze around the shoulders, kissed him tenderly on the cheek, and turned to get out of bed. He listened as she gathered her dressing gown about her, tiptoed to the door and opened it. As he opened his eyes, he saw her standing there, gazing at him. She put one finger to her lips and was gone.

Was that a salute, a kiss or a warning? He might have had a sense of loss, were it not for the newly wakened pug staring resentfully at him.

He folded Humphrey in his arms and let out a long sigh, not least because his head hurt. Sure, nothing whatsoever had happened. Yes, it may have been his sister-in-law, but that was the longest and most intimate encounter with a woman that he had had for nearly twenty years. Certainly, a nice way to wake up on your birthday, although possibly not quite the right way, all things considered. But a start. Heather was not the only fish in the sea. Although perhaps it was time to make his move, not least to avoid misunderstandings.

After he had showered and dressed, the first woman he saw was Sonia, who was on Kitchen Patrol. She'd volunteered for the early breakfast shift because she was off alcohol. As Fred came into the kitchen, she smiled warmly at him. He groaned.

'Morning has broken!' she said, with the perkiness that only the recommended eight-hour sleep can afford. Fred took a big slurp from the cup of black coffee she passed him.

'With enough coffee and some painkillers, we might just be able to put it together again,' he muttered.

Sonia brought a glass of water and paracetamol from the First Aid box in the kitchen.

'Are you ready for some initial feedback?' she asked him.

'Hit me with it,' he said, suddenly more awake.

'At first sight, I think it's very good,' she said. 'Much better than I'd feared when you gave it to me.'

'Oh, that's great,' he said. 'I think...'

'Of course, you'll need a good editor,' she said. 'There are things you'll want to cut out and things we will want to hear more about... I'd like to see more of you in it.'

'But it's all about me,' he said, in confusion.

'Yes, but we need to hear your feelings! And you will need a strong narrative arc.'

'I guess I'll have to work on that,' said Fred, who would have paid good money to learn how the story would turn out.

'Although, I was rather surprised to discover how funny it was...' she continued.

'Funny?'

'Yes. Your voice is terrific!' she pronounced.

'Great!' he said, thinking that he must he'd achieved that entirely accidently. Though he might be on his way at last. Life begins at forty and all that. He would be clapping in glee if his fingers weren't crossed.

Alberto came down the stairs, smilingly. He kissed Sonia and the top of Fred's head.

'Now, Alberto, have you had crumpets yet?' asked Sonia. 'They're about as English as you can get, and I'm afraid I haven't got any lovely Sri Lankan breakfast for you.'

'Crum-pets? We didn't have those in Costa Rica,' he replied.

'Don't forget, he has a very sweet tooth,' said Robin, coming into the room. Sonia brought the honey from the sideboard.

'Crumpets are generally eaten with honey, marmalade or jam,' she explained, handing Alberto a teaspoon.

'Or cheese,' added Fred. 'Or marmite.' Alberto looked at him blankly. Fred felt it was far too early in the day to explain marmite.

'The one big advantage that crumpets have over toast,' explained Robin to his beloved, as he took the next pair out of the toaster, 'is three-dimensional butter.' He dabbed a hot crumpet liberally with butter and bit into it with a satisfied sigh. Alberto looked around the table, before experimenting more cautiously.

Sonia kept them supplied with a continuous flow of toast, eggs and 'bacon for those who eat it'. Which now seemed to include, to her mother's alarm, Freya. Polly glared at her daughter.

'Please don't tell Georgie!' she hissed. 'Or I'm in the doghouse.'

'What happens at Threepwood, stays at Threepwood,' said Charlotte, meaningfully.

'Let's take Humphrey for a walk!' squeaked Freya in excitement, remembering their canine companion. Hearing his name, Humphrey got to his feet.

'Maybe in a bit,' said Polly. 'Give me a moment to have breakfast first. And shouldn't we wait for Hugh?'

That Saturday morning, the day of the big dinner, conversation around the breakfast table at Threepwood Hall was all of waistcoats and stocks, not to mention smocks, and whether an ordinary shirt was adequate, if you left the collar up, versus the merits of the dress shirt. At the other end of the walnut table, an indignant conversation about sleep disturbance and floods was continuing.

Neither Alberto nor Robin seemed quite to comprehend the devastation their inundation had caused. They promised, with some reluctance, to restrict themselves to a shower next time. Charlotte had hung out the sheets next to the boiler, and Hugh had helped by putting the mattress on its side to dry out. Probably if they just turned it over, it would be fine for that evening, he suggested. After breakfast, Polly went upstairs and taped a sign to the bath taps stating that they were not to be turned on in any circumstances. People were too delicate to draw attention to Charlotte's bed-hopping. Nor did Fred mention it.

Heather was failing to attain the companionate warmth that was expected of her by her new fans. When Freya brandished her recorder expectantly, she reacted in horror, and held her head in her hands until the little girl went away with a pout. Then Heather complained, again, about the mobile phone reception. Finally she asked Fred pointedly when it might be her turn to read his manuscript. He said he was flattered by all the interest in his memoir, but that Sonia was still reading it. Heather seemed satisfied.

'Sonia's still reading Fred's book,' she said to Hugh.

'What?' he replied blankly. Mornings were never his best time.

'Sonia's. Still. Reading. Fred's. Manuscript,' said Heather, gesturing upstairs.

'Excellent,' said Hugh, getting her drift at last. 'She must like it?' he added after a few seconds. Heather rolled her eyes. Accomplices were so dim these days.

'Hoping so,' said Fred, wheeling past. 'Hoping so!'

Roddy, when he emerged from the van, complained about having a sore back, monopolized the coffee pot and issued periodic complaints about the non-availability of weekend papers. Fred, somewhat reluctantly, went out into the yard. Alberto trailed after him, but Fred vehemently insisted he did not need help. Fred got in his car, stowed his wheelchair, drove down to the local store at the other end of the village and unstowed his wheelchair, to the immense curiosity of a passing seven-year-old. Fred pulled himself up the step, negotiated the narrow aisle of the mini market, and bought a selection of papers covering the political spectrum. He then reversed out of the shop with a bump, slung the papers on the back seat, slid into the front passenger seat, laboriously stowed his chair again, slid into the driver's seat, and was back in the dining room within twenty minutes. It was quite a workout. Nobody appreciated what a hassle it was just to go to the shops if you used a wheelchair. And Fred had found there was always an unhelpful audience, to enjoy the added drama when you dropped something, or fell out of the car. Clearly these rural villages had a dearth of entertainment for small boys.

Aside from Alberto, who had stood by the front door like a shadow as Fred got into the car, nobody had even noticed that he'd left. Roddy, Charlotte, Heather and Hugh were gathered at one end of the table, no doubt gossiping about old times, Fred thought rather jealously, although he had overheard something about a pig. Was that a reference to dinner? Having relieved Fred of his newspapers, his friends now set upon their favourite reading matter with cries of delight, and called for more coffee and tea. Everyone seemed content, which was the main thing. Silence reigned.

Bored with the everlasting breakfast, and having failed to serenade Heather again, Freya scowled in frustration. She then beseeched her mother; couldn't she just go off on her own around the garden with Humphrey? Hearing her pleas, Hugh reminded her of his offer to make her a bow and arrow, an offer which nothing could top for a seven-year-old. The two of them disappeared outside in the direction of the copse, the dog tagging along behind them, leaving Polly sinking gratefully into a comfortable chair in the sitting room with the books pages from the paper, supplemented with literary gossip from Sonia. It was almost relaxing.

Freya and Hugh began their entertainment by throwing sticks for Humphrey, several of which he dutifully returned. Soon he tired of his role as entertainer, having concluded after considerable experimentation that sticks were inedible, and returned to his main priority, which was finding somewhere to sleep.

Hugh had already produced a ball of string from the van, and showed Freya his jackknife, although to her chagrin he would not let her test how well it cut. They now went off in search of suitable archery material. It was a large garden with many original features, including a clump of pampas grass beyond the formal rose garden. This quickly generated some arrows, which could be very agreeably sharpened with the knife. As they roamed, Hugh told Freya all he could remember about the history of the English longbow. He even summarised the main stages of the battle of Agincourt, supplemented by poorly remembered but enthusiastically rendered extracts from *Henry V.* Freya seemed to soak up all available information in a most gratifying manner, he thought. For some reason, he didn't feel at all shy with the child.

It was the dramatist Chekhov who had observed, as Fred had learned on one of his writing courses, that, if in the first act, you have hung a pistol on the wall, then in the next act you must expect it to be fired. As if to prove this dictum, the contented scene back at the Hall was now disturbed by unexpected drama. Fred, having remembered that Heather was keen to read his memoir, asked if Sonia would go up to her room to fetch it. She came back and asked her new author for a quiet word in the corridor. Following a furiously whispered conflab, Fred re-entered the dining room dramatically, followed by his erstwhile agent.

'It's missing!' he said, in an urgent voice. 'It's gone!' His tone became increasingly panicked.

'It was on the table by the bed!' said Sonia, indignantly. It wasn't as if she'd mislaid it by accident. She'd never once lost a manuscript.

'What's missing?' asked Robin, looking up from the Saturday property pages.

'My book! *Wheels of Misfortune*! A huge pile of paper, in a folder… Sonia had it. Has someone taken it to read?'

For one moment, Fred was suddenly very hopeful that there had just been a silly mistake. What's yours is mine, sort of thing, he thought. Somebody had obviously just taken it to read. Fred's vantage point meant he could gaze around the faces of all his friends in the dining room and sitting room. All those present looked at each other in surprise. They shook their heads in a choreographed apologetic wave.

Not that everyone could look Fred directly in the eyes. It was like an Am Dram adaptation of an Agatha Christie novel, thought Sonia, immediately suspicious. After all, she'd actually read the memoir. She knew that more than one of them had a motivation. Here was literary gossip in the making.

'You've written a book?' said Alberto, as impressed as he was oblivious. Surely this couldn't be the reason that the others had wanted to assassinate Fred. Was it one of those murder mystery weekends? He gazed pointedly at Robin.

'Well, I've certainly not got it,' said Roddy, grasping for anything that he could say with complete honesty. 'I've not even seen it!'

'If someone had wanted to have a read of it, that's fine,' said Fred. 'Really. You just had ask me.'

'I did want to read it,' said Heather. 'But of course, I don't have it,' she added, slowly and with emphasis.

'Well, where could it be?' Fred didn't trust anyone right now. No random burgler would have swiped a pile of paper.

'I have no idea,' Heather said, with almost total honesty. 'I never touched it'

Fred wheeled hurriedly back to his own room to check something. He returned with a look of incredulity on his face. The horror was deepening and he now felt sick to his stomach.

'My memory stick has disappeared as well!'

'Where did you keep it?' asked Polly, patiently.

'Well, I think I left it in the machine, actually,' admitted Fred. 'Which was obviously a mistake. I should have secured it in the office safe. But after lunch yesterday, I remembered that great story about Heather and the prawns...'

'Oh hell, Fred, you weren't going to tell the story of the prawns!' Heather almost snarled and clenched her fists.

'Well, you have to admit, it's a corker.'

'Not from my perspective...' growled Heather.

'Anyway,' said Fred, recollecting himself. 'Everything's gone. My memory stick has definitely gone. Sonia says she can't find my manuscript anywhere in her room. It's about 80,000 words. 200 pages of print-out. It's taken months. More than a year, in fact. It wasn't finished of course, I was polishing...' He looked apologetically at Sonia. 'But I thought... maybe new authors always think this... but I hoped it was pretty good.'

Sonia nodded, and said, slowly and carefully, 'What I read of it was good. Funny... out of the ordinary... It showed very definite promise!'

Fred beamed for a moment, before realising that Sonia was using the past tense.

'It was publishable! Even allowing for my inexperience, and all of that, someone might have published it!'

Sonia nodded, reassuringly. She really had felt it had something, something that publishers were looking for. Trauma! Lust! A disabled person who could write! Fred's story seemed to have everything.

'Maybe they will,' said Polly, optimistically. 'A bit of editing is all...'

'They well might,' said Fred, 'but not if I can't FIND the bloody thing... I haven't got another copy!' He looked around the room glaring. Quailing broke out, and more than a bit of blenching. At least one guest even felt remorse.

'We'll find it!' said Polly, decisively.

'My whole manuscript!' said Fred, dismayed. 'Everything, gone! All that work!' Alberto looked at him sympathetically. Fred groaned. Memories of all those late nights and dull weekends were flooding back. What a waste! But worse than that: what a humiliation! To have come so near, and to have failed again. It was beginning to be the story of his life.

No relationship. No kids. Now, not even a book! When it came down to it, what did he have to show for the last forty years? Almost nothing, except a winner's medal from the Sudbury Wheelchair Marathon, and second place in the East Anglian Solicitor of the Year contest.

Heather, Roddy and Charlotte avoided looking at each other. Charlotte, in particular, looked white. She sat huddled in her chair next to the coffee table in the sitting room, nursing a cold cup of tea, rocking slightly. Polly looked at her closely. Sonia meanwhile wondered what Miss Marple would have done next. She gazed around the table. She had her suspicions, and a shrewd understanding of human nature, well-honed by her study of literature.

Alberto found the whole interaction fascinating, as well as slightly chilling. He could tell something was up. It must be his Latin intuition. Maybe even his Bribri heritage. He turned to his boyfriend, who shrugged. Who could tell what was happening with these people? At least no violence seemed to have been committed. But perhaps it was only a matter of time.

Roddy glanced out of the window at the parkland, wearing a fixed expression on his face that he hoped conveyed both innocence and concern, blended with a touch of outrage. He had been trying to perfect this particular look for those times when he might have to support constituents who had been the victims of terrorist incidents or perhaps extreme travel disruption. He wasn't absolutely sure he'd got it right yet. He really needed a mirror to check.

Heather looked at him in sympathy.

'Are you OK, Roddy? You look a bit like Matt Hancock... Was it something you ate? There's a bathroom through that door in the hall...'

'I'm fine, Heather.' He assumed the hang-dog expression that came most easily to him, and gave a thumbs up. 'Thanks, though.'

Roddy went over and patted his brother's back solicitously.

'You've probably just mislaid it... put it somewhere safe and forgotten.'

Fred looked at him as if he had just announced he'd voted for Brexit.

'No, Roderick. It's definitely been stolen. And unless anyone else is also missing a worthless item of great sentimental importance, then it's an inside job.'

Everyone busily studied the parquet flooring. Charlotte stifled a sob. Fred looked at her closely. You could never tell what the problem was with Lottie. He looked at Sonia. She was looking at Charlotte closely. So was Polly. Half the guests were looking around suspiciously, and the other half just looked suspicious.

Fred glared at the room.

'It's one of you. It has to be!'

Polly shook her head and frowned.

'Couldn't it have been an outside job?'

'Well, why the hell didn't they take the laptop then? And the sash window is still latched shut.' Fred stared stonily at his companions. 'No, it was definitely someone here.'

'None of your friends would do that, Fred,' said Polly, gently. 'We're here to celebrate your birthday! We love you...'

'That's what I thought, Polly,' said Fred. 'But I was obviously wrong.'

Sonia mentally ticked off the group on her fingers. Polly was either innocent or a brilliant actor. Charlotte looked as if her conscience was troubling her, but that was usual for her. Sonia wouldn't trust Roddy as far as she could throw him, but perhaps that was because he was a political hack. Heather had no ethics at all, but she seemed unlikely to get her hands dirty.

At that moment, Freya ran into the sitting room. She appeared to have a long bow across her back, and was holding half a dozen arrows in her hand. Mud spattered her leggings and top. Thankfully the proto-Maid Marian had long forgotten her recorder. Hugh followed her into the sitting room, looking rather pleased with himself.

'Not made a bow for years,' he told the room. 'But it's rather good actually.'

'I made an arrow stick into the tree!' said Freya with excited pride. 'It went "boing!" Just like on Robin Hood!'

'That's lovely, darling,' said Polly. 'But please don't shoot anything with a pulse.'

'Where's the dog?' asked Fred, suddenly alarmed.

'We didn't shoot him!' said Freya. 'Although he did try to eat one of my arrows.'

'We tied him up outside the kitchen,' said Hugh. 'He was a bit muddy, so I felt it was better he didn't come inside.'

'You felt right!' said Charlotte. Grateful for any excuse to leave the room, she headed out with thoughts of a bucket of hot water and a damp cloth from the scullery. After a decade as a mother, she now cleaned up compulsively.

'Thanks, Lottie,' called Fred. 'Give him a chew or something to keep him happy for a bit.' Fred was now sunk in despondency. It almost felt like when he first woke up to find himself paralysed. First, a nightmare, then a period of disbelief, and then finally a wave of suicidal depression. He didn't need Robin to explain the five stages of bereavement.

'Fred's lost his book,' said Roddy meaningfully to Hugh. 'None of us have seen it. Have you?'

'Freya, you haven't been using Fred's manuscript for drawing, have you?' enquired Polly. Freya shook her head and brandished the bow. At least her alibi was sound.

Alberto decided Roddy needed someone keeping a close eye on him. His voice was definitely one of the ones he'd heard the previous day. Alberto came from a culture where 'politician' was a synonym for 'criminal'.

'Oh. That's bad,' said Hugh, who sounded almost as wooden as Roddy, but at least had no political aspirations. 'I think I'll have my shower now, if that's OK with everyone?' He disappeared back to the van to get his towel.

Polly gazed after his disappearing back, deep in thought. Hugh was always pretty abrupt, but that was evasive even for him, she felt. And then she remembered their odd exchange the previous night.

'Time to take Mummy outside and show her your archery skills,' she said to her daughter, firmly.

Chapter 18

Moments later, Freya was fitting a notched arrow to her string with exaggerated care. Polly was looking around at the windows of the hall flanking the pillars of the main entrance. The shutters on each side were rather a pleasing shade of sky blue. The Trust must get through such a lot of Farrow and Ball paint, she thought, it was a wonder there wasn't an advertising flyer in each bedroom. Polly looked back at her child, now fully transformed into a medieval archer, rather than a secret service agent or a troubadour.

'Now, make sure you shoot away from the house!'

'Yes, Mum. Look! Look!'

Polly watched as the arrow sped with impressive velocity towards the ha-ha, thankfully coming to earth just before it. Her daughter cast her a glance of pride. Polly nodded in approval.

'Very good, darling. Hugh has been so nice to help you with that. But again, please don't tell Mummy Georgie. And if you do mention it, remember, it's nothing to do with me, all right?'

Freya nodded. No bacon, no archery. She was good at secrets.

'I like Hugh. He knows all the outdoors stuff! He said we might be able to make a den tomorrow!'

'Just make sure you don't lose your arrows. By the way, Freya… I wanted to ask. Did you see Hugh doing outdoors stuff last night?'

Freya paused, and thought hard. Was she being an archer now, or a secret service agent? Or a secret service archer? Did it count as treachery if you told things to your mum? Surely not.

'Freya?'

Faced with the stern face of her mother, Freya thought that sharing information was likely to be her best strategy. Mums had all sorts of powers that more junior agents lacked, in her experience. Like being gated.

'I did see him sort of creeping past the windows last night,' she admitted.

'Really?'

'Yes. As if he was practising… like being a spy.'

'And when was it that he was practising being a spy?'

'After dinner. He was holding something under his jacket. It looked suspicious.'

'You've done well, Freya. I might even give you a promotion. Or a medal.'

Her daughter swelled with pride. 'Could you give me a gadget?'

'What?'

'I mean, like a watch that tells the time in different parts of the world. Or those glasses where you can see behind you? Spies always have gadgets.'

'Let's see, darling. Maybe after we leave, on the way home, we can investigate new gadgets.'

'Yeah!' Agent Freya jumped up in excitement.

'Now I've just got to do an advanced interrogation...'

Her daughter looked at her in confusion.

'Nothing you need to worry about. It's Mummy Agent business. Why don't you go and see if Robin or Alberto would like to play another game with you? Or listen to "Frère Jacques" again?'

Freya gathered up her arrows in preparation for a new companion.

'I meant an inside game,' said Polly, meaningfully. 'I don't think the boys want to get hot and bothered outside.'

'Yes, Mum,' grumbled Freya. On her way back into the house, she hid her weapons under Hugh's van. They'd be fine there until the next time she needed them.

Five minutes later, having checked that Freya and Alberto were safely, if somewhat heatedly, playing Beggar My Neighbour, Polly went back outside to the van. She knocked on the window. After a moment, it slid back. Hugh looked out.

'Oh, it's you,' he said, nervously, and went to open the door of the van.

Polly looked at him standing above her in the entrance.

'You're wearing a SKIRT!' she said with incredulity.

'It's a sarong,' Hugh replied, defensively.

'I wouldn't have thought it's your thing,' said Polly.

'It's a SARONG,' Hugh said again, more firmly. 'Preferred nightwear, and indeed daywear, of most men on the Indian subcontinent. It's something I picked up in Sri Lanka. Very comfortable.'

'OK!' said Polly. 'We'll say no more.'

'If it helps, think of it as a kilt. A batik kilt. Anyway, it's not a great time, I was just getting dressed after my shower...'

Ignoring him, Polly climbed into the van, as he edged backwards, holding up his sarong. She slammed the door behind her and turned to face him.

'Now. What's going on? You're meant to be his best friend!'

Hugh's face went as red as raspberry ice cream, and then he started stammering.

'I don't know what you are talking about!' he said, quickly. 'Why are you accusing me? Of whatever it was...' he added, hastily.

'See!' She almost spat the word out. 'You know exactly what I'm talking about!'

Hugh gazed at the ceiling. The van was far too cosy to have this sort of confrontation. It was bad energy. Polly glared at him.

'I'm 100 per cent sure you've got something to do with it.'

'What? Why would you think that?' he replied. 'About whatever it is,' he added, as an afterthought.

'Well, you were looking shifty in the hall last night, and then Freya saw you creeping around outside... You were definitely up to something after dinner!'

Hugh felt the game was probably up, but thought his best tactic might be to say absolutely nothing. You have a right to remain silent etcetera. Maybe she'd just go away. There was a pause. Polly looked thoughtful.

'But I just can't work out why Fred's memoir would be of any concern to you...'

She sat down on the bench seat. As she glanced out of the van, she saw Heather walk past, Afghan homespun woollen scarf around her shoulders, stick in hand, looking as if she was going to walk from Sudbury to Samarkand.

Polly had a sudden thought.

'Heather put you up to it, didn't she?'

She stared sternly at Hugh. He looked at the floor, avoiding catching her eye. But his face had now gone beetroot. She thought she had probably hit a nerve.

'Worried about her image, was she? If she said jump in the lake, you'd bloody do it, wouldn't you?'

Hugh's head dropped further down on his shoulders, and he said nothing. Polly almost stamped on the floor in fury. Men should just take responsibility for themselves.

'Pathetic! I thought better of you. You know, I actually liked you. You've certainly been very kind to Freya and me. But you're led by your dick, like every guy who ever existed. And now you've betrayed your best friend.'

He shook his head in protest. But Polly had summed it up. It would serve him right if she hated him forever (which he realised would really bother him), and if Fred never spoke to him again, which would be worse. It wasn't as if he had many friends, certainly not ones he'd had for twenty-five years, and he couldn't afford to lose one. Family members barely tolerated him as it was.

As he wriggled, Polly glared at him.

'Well, this is where it stops.'

'What do you mean?' asked Hugh, in a small voice. He had never found angry women easy to deal with. Not since the business with his mother and the milk pan.

'You're going to tell him what you've done.'

He looked at her aghast.

'I can't do that!'

'If you don't, then I will...' said Polly, folding her arms across her chest.

'You wouldn't do that, would you?'

'Give me one reason why not? It's his bloody birthday weekend, he's paid for all of this, and this is how you repay him. Shameful, I call it!'

Hugh scrambled for a justification.

'Well, he was wrong to write about private stuff, you know, without permission. Consent and all that,' he said, weakly.

'He's not a newspaper! And I'm sure he wasn't saying anything that was untrue.'

'But has he any right to reveal secrets?' asked Hugh, scrabbling for a defence.

'What "secrets"?'

'Well, you know. About Charlotte, for instance. She comes out very badly from the revelations... Among others... Apparently...'

'Well, I remember Lottie from college, and I'd say so do about five hundred other people, so it's not exactly a secret, is it?'

Hugh shook his head, feeling more and more like a small boy who'd let the side down. Polly snorted.

'Public domain, I'd call it. Very public. Embarrassing maybe, but hardly libellous. Barely news at all.'

She remembered something more important than debating the past.

'Anyway, where did you put the manuscript? And the memory stick?' She looked around the van. 'Have you hidden it in here?'

She started opening cupboards. She couldn't help noticing that everything was very neat. On any other day, she would have been charmed.

Hugh leapt up to stop her. 'It's not here. I promise!'

'Where, then?'

'I, err, I… well…' He took a deep breath. 'Actually, I fed it to the pig.'

'The pig?' Polly stared at him in disbelief. 'Did I hear you say "the pig"?'

'I thought it was for the best.'

'You blithering idiot!' She grabbed him by the arm. 'Now, come with me!'

She flung open the door to the van and jumped down.

He followed her obediently in his sarong and flip-flops. She marched him off down to the pigsty, occasionally whacking his bare legs with a whippy stick she had plucked from a convenient hedge. He felt he now could appreciate exactly the mindset of a cow on its way to the abattoir.

When they reached the sty, they could see no sign of the pig. The little fellow had retired to the little shelter, perhaps. The pig-woman was nowhere to be seen either, thankfully. But then neither was the manuscript.

'So what happened here last night?' Polly had folded her arms again in that intimidating way. 'Tell me exactly…'

'Well, I sort of… pitched the manuscript into the feed thing, that tray… Some of it went all over the floor, actually…'

'And what about the memory stick?'

'Oh, that was much more successful,' he said, proudly. 'I called him, you see, the pig, and then when he opened his mouth to, you know, grunt, I managed to just lob the stick in…'

For a moment he felt rather pleased with himself, and then suddenly realised that was probably not the best impression to convey. He stopped smiling. Polly was glaring at him. He felt like someone who'd brought sausage rolls to a vegan picnic.

'You did what?' she said, outraged.

'Well, we'd agreed that we'd feed everything to the pig!' he said.

'You fed the pig a little wedge of plastic and electronics?' She stared at Hugh in disbelief.

'Yes,' he admitted. It did sound rather stupid, when it came to it.

'Hardly appetising!'

'No, I suppose not.'

'Did you hear it crunch?'

'No, I don't think so. Though I didn't hang around, frankly.'

Polly poked around the sty with her stick, leaning over the railings. No sign of the manuscript at all. But surely, the pig couldn't have eaten it all so quickly?

'Obviously keen on contemporary writing!' said Hugh, again forgetting that joviality was the wrong note to strike.

Polly glared at him viciously, as if she was a cannibal who'd been dieting, and he was the dinner. He felt that further jokes might be out of place in the circumstances.

'Look, please don't tell Fred,' begged Hugh. 'What's done is done.'

'Well, the manuscript is certainly gone. But we don't know about the memory stick…'

The small, black, pot-bellied pig chose this moment to emerge, blinking, into the light.

'There's still a chance…'

Hugh followed Polly's glance. He shook his head doubtfully.

'I'm not sure a memory stick could survive a pig's stomach. They probably have several of them. There'd be all sorts of acid in there!'

'Well, you don't know… They're pretty robust those memory sticks. As long as he swallowed it, rather than chewing it, I would imagine it would come out the other end within twenty-four hours…'

'Well, I'm not standing here waiting for the pig to shit!' protested Hugh. 'I don't know how I would explain my sudden interest in poo to his keeper!'

'No, you're right. That would be too difficult. She probably cleans it all up.' He nodded in agreement.

'Which is why you're going to steal the pig!' she announced, with finality.

'What!'

'Yes. As soon as it's all quiet. When everyone is changing for dinner would be the best time. You are going to come back here… you could put a collar or a rope around it or something… and then we, I mean you, are going to remove this pig!'

'No!' he yelped. 'Impossible!'

'Either that, or we go straight to Fred now?' she threatened.

'I can't do that!' he said, aghast.

'Exactly. Now that you've embarked on a life of crime, you need to keep your hand in with this larceny business. You don't want to get out of practice. By next week you'll probably be mugging pensioners or something. Thankfully, I'll be far from here.'

'Where would I even put a pig?' he said, in disbelief.

'In your van, of course! He's a miniature pig, after all. I'd think it would be quite a nice sty for him. A home from home. Good and warm. He'll need a leg up. But I am sure he would manage. Seeing how cosy you've made it.'

'But the smell! The… the… pig shit! I have to sleep in there!' Hugh felt horrified at the thought of his lovely nest being desecrated by livestock. Polly shrugged her shoulders.

'Pig poo's what you're there for, Sunny Jim. You will be clearing it up. You just need to collect his mess and poke around...' She handed her stick to him. 'You can even use this lovely poo stick that I prepared earlier.'

Like a deflated paddling pool, he subsided without protest. She relented a little.

'Look, it'll probably only be overnight... if you check, the memory stick might even come out in the poo before nightfall and then you wouldn't have to do all this. I'm sure nobody will miss the business pages of the papers. Bung a few sheets of newspaper down, give it a bowl of water, wait for the memory stick to come out the back end. No worse than having a dog. Pigs are rather cleverer, apparently.' She smiled at him, benignly. 'And then you could even be the one who announces to poor old Fred that you've found his memory stick. Happy ending. Everyone goes home cheerful. He'll be like a pig in shit!' She laughed more uproariously than Hugh thought was justifiable in the circumstances. 'Now that's really funny!'

Chapter 19

As it turned out, it was fortuitous that mobile signal scarcity had driven both Roddy and Robin into unusual proximity beside the Wally Smithson statue later that morning. Seeing them there, Heather went back inside for her camera, and took a rather nice long-range shot, with the two of them like bookends, and the Suffolk countryside rolling on in the background.

Polly had decided to take advantage of the sunshine to take a gentle jog, leaving her daughter to serenade Heather. Polly had set herself the task of circling the stately home via the fields that surrounded it. This appeared a bit more challenging than merely running the perimeter path around the gardens. Having changed into bright blue trainers, cycle shorts, a bright red singlet and a yellow cap, she had already nearly come a cropper, getting over a fence. Not seeing the electrified cable, she had stung her ankle as she swung her foot to the ground.

'Yeow!' she yelped, and rubbed her leg. That zap had hurt like hell. A red welt was already rising, and the skin felt hot to the touch. Thankfully she had not put any weight to the fence. She turned, saw there was a proper gate on the other side of the field, and started jogging towards it.

Disturbed by the shout, one of the bullocks started ambling over to investigate. With her blue, red and yellow garb, Polly was a magnet for bovine attention. As is the way of cattle, others followed behind the first. They saw Polly jogging across the field, and picked up some speed in her wake. Polly was oblivious to the danger, having been born and brought up in urban postcodes.

At that point, Roddy looked up from his emails and saw what was going on. There was every chance, at the current rate of progress, that the single-minded cattle would reach multi-coloured Polly before she reached the gate. He yelled. She ignored him, as in all honesty most women did, so he yelled again, this time with Robin to add decibels to his entreaty.

Polly now heard and looked across at the two men, who both stood on the top of the ha-ha, waving their arms and gesticulating, as if age had not been kind to one third of Village People. She looked behind her, only to see the lumbering mass of cows, and performed a pantomime double-take. It was obvious that she could not get over the opposite gate in time. She hesitated for a second, and then doubled back on herself, running full tilt down the field towards the ha-ha. It took a moment for the cattle to realise that the rainbow streak had now changed course. Bullock crowd control followed for a few seconds. Then the collective herd-mind asserted the new direction of travel. This delay was all the advantage that Polly needed to widen the gap between her and the chasing cattle.

'Come on, Polly!' shouted Roddy, in encouragement.

'You can do it!' yelled Robin, as the hooves began to drum ominously on the dry earth. Both men jumped up and down and waved their sweaters to try and scare off the bullocks. Cattle are inveterately curious beasts, and not easily deterred by knitwear. Polly was panting and wheezing now. Roddy and Robin willed her on.

'How on earth will she climb up?' asked Roddy in alarm. The ha-ha was a sheer wall of about six or seven foot, he thought.

'Give me a hand!' yelled the psychologist, throwing himself on the ground and reaching down.

Roddy hesitated briefly, and sighed. He was wearing his new Hugo Boss shirt. Nobody ever realised what it cost to be noble. Brushing what dirt he could aside, he stretched out. Now the two men lay on the top of the ha-ha, legs splayed for anchorage, and stretched out their arms towards the field below. Polly arrived, fearfully sweaty, at the bottom of the wall. She raised her arms above her head desperately and tried to connect with the dangling hands. After a second of fumbling, both men managed to grasp one of Polly's hands, and clasped tight.

'Lift!' bellowed Robin, and they gradually pulled her up. Their faces reddened with the challenge of lifting an adult woman into the air. She walked her way up the wall to assist their efforts. Just as the grunting beasts reached the bottom of the ha-ha, Roddy and Robin managed to drag Polly onto the solid ground of the lawn. All three collapsed on their backs, wheezing. There was a moment of wordless recovery. Next to the ha-ha, the herd of twenty bullocks churned, several of them rubbing their backs against the ancient bricks of the wall.

'Risky business, trying to outrun livestock,' panted Robin.

'Thank god you guys were here,' muttered Polly, as she got her breath back. 'I might have been a goner otherwise.'

'Prominent social worker trampled to death by brutes,' suggested Roddy. 'Not the most promising of obituaries.'

'I'm such an idiot,' said Polly. 'I was out with Fred and Humphrey yesterday, and I remember thinking how cattle don't like dogs, I even remembered that story about the farmer crushed against a wall by his own bullocks. Don't they kill several dozen people a year? And yet I try to run through that field! What a prat.'

'I think they're asking to be eaten, frankly,' said Roddy.

'Mince!' Robin called over to the bullocks.

'We'd better warn the others to avoid all fields with cattle in,' said Polly. 'But please, let's not tell Freya. She'll have nightmares.'

'It would have ruined Fred's birthday if you'd been hurt,' said Roddy.

'It's bad enough that he's mislaid his book,' said Robin. 'Such an awful blow!'

'Perhaps he needs counselling?' asked Roddy, as sincerely as he was able.

'What do you know about the book, Roddy?' asked Polly, suddenly suspicious of his tone.

'Me?' asked Roddy, in surprise. 'Not a thing! Nothing whatsoever!'

'Do you know what's in it?' she asked.

'Yes! I mean, no... I mean,' he spelled out carefully, 'I haven't read it *as such*. But I have a... general idea.' Roddy gazed at Polly as sincerely as he could. 'I'm sure it will turn up.'

'Let's hope so,' said Robin. 'Alberto's very worried about it.'

'We all are,' said Polly, ominously.

Roddy wandered off with a casual wave. That was a close shave, he thought.

'The thing with the bullocks only added to the drama,' said Robin. 'Let's not try that again. Leave it to Pamplona?'

'Agreed,' said Polly, and Robin departed to see where Alberto had got to.

She had learned her lesson. As she stood alone next to the ornamental rose garden, Polly pondered the frisson that it had been, in her moment of greatest peril, to be so firmly gripped. It was a dozen years since a man had last held her hand, and it was a strangely enjoyable sensation. Put it down to sheer relief, she concluded.

Chapter 20

For this fortieth birthday weekend, Fred had hatched a plan, and he wasn't willing to give up on it, regardless of missing manuscripts. His literary career would just have to be put on hold for three hours. Heather had been the woman of his soft-focused dreams for far too long, he said to himself. Less soft-focused than unfocused. There would never be a better moment for his femme fatale to transition to the status of de facto. She had a soft spot for him. He just knew it. She only needed to see him at his most masculine and fascinating, which he hoped meant while wielding the paddle of a kayak and demonstrating the delights of rural Suffolk. A sport that made no call on the legs was ideal for the paraplegic, after all. He had kayaked the Norfolk Broads, from the Bure to the Yare. He was fit and familiar with the terrain, and knew lots of local colour. His upper body would take them along the River Stour, and Constable country would surely do the rest.

To this romantic end, he had packed his inflatable kayak in the boot of his car, with the rigid in reserve on the roof rack, and scheduled the outing for the Saturday afternoon of his birthday gathering. The long-range forecast had been anxiously observed. As long as the weather continued fair, then a couple of hours along a bucolic English river should see her as putty in his impressively muscular hands.

The previous day, he had canvassed the others for kayaking interest. Fred felt that he needed a couple of friends as cover for his amorous intentions. At first, no one seemed willing, but by the evening Robin and Alberto had volunteered to accompany him, which was odd but pleasing. A couple, and a gay one at that, would mean no competition. More worryingly, Roderick, who seemed to be tailing Heather in an alarming fashion, given that he was a married man and that his louche manner was hardly alluring, said he would come along for the ride, assuming he had finished his conference call by then. To the great relief of the house party, he was parking up in a nearby lay-by for these. Most importantly, Heather herself had been cajoled into participation, although with an absence of eagerness that her host found disappointing. Was this a signal that she wasn't interested after all? He'd thought that a foreign correspondent would be more intrepid.

'Outdoors, Fred? Really? This is England! It's still only May! Nettles for days and industrial effluent by the gallon. Drizzle most likely. Hardly appealing,' she grumbled.

'Do come, Heather!' he begged. 'A birthday treat! I'm sure the landscape will grow on you. It's almost sunny. And at least there's no bilharzia!'

'I suppose it's better than continuous recorder serenades,' said Heather, checking that Polly and Freya were not in earshot. She had grown weary of having a seven-year-old troubadour with a limited repertoire invading her personal space.

Fred's calculation was that as soon as they embarked, his practised paddle work would put clear water between his craft and the others. The rest were likely to be such amateurs that he would surely shine by comparison. And then he could edge the boat into a quiet backwater, where he and Heather could watch kingfishers together and lie in wait for an otter, while he murmured his much-rehearsed sweet nothings into her shapely and receptive ears.

Inflating the kayak was easy, thanks to the electric pump. He had shown Robin and Alberto how to lift the other, rigid, double kayak down off the roof rack. Roddy had obligingly said that it was better for him to watch from the bank. No doubt he would take a stroll, or catch up on his emails. The others were strapped into life jackets, and then they were all out on the water together.

Within a few minutes, Fred relaxed. He was in his element. He knew he was as good as any non-disabled person when it came to kayaking – or even better. Nobody could tower over him. And at this moment, with sun glinting off the water, a light breeze, with no sounds aside from the woodpigeon cooing in the trees, he and Heather were as close as they had been for years.

Fred called out a few instructions to Robin – Alberto already seemed adept with the paddle. Heather seemed to be enjoying it so far. The two kayaks glided away, leaving still water between them. The strokes of the blades dipping in, one side and then the other, were rhythmical, soothing… the sun shone cooperatively down… it was quiet… the only murmur was the river itself. Would 'limpid' be the right word?

Before they had even turned the first bend a shriek from Heather destroyed the idyll.

'My bum's getting wet!'

Fred turned to check. There seemed to be more than a splash of water at the back of the kayak.

'I think it's OK. I'll paddle more carefully.'

'No, it's getting worse, Fred! It's bloody cold!' He reached out to give the hull a squeeze. It seemed alarmingly flaccid. But he'd certainly pumped enough. He frowned. This might be bad news.

'Drat, there might be a slow puncture. We'd better turn back.'

The problem with turning inflatable kayaks was that it was like searching the Land Registry. Nothing happened quickly. He dug in his blade and backed them around. Even within the minute that it took to aim for the landing stage, he could feel that there was less air in the hull.

'Paddle faster!' she shrieked.

'We're OK, Heather' he replied, as calmly as he could. 'It's not deep. There aren't any crocodiles in East Anglia!'

'I'm not scared, you idiot. I'm wet!'

Stung, Fred put his head down and paddled hard. Within two minutes they were alongside the bank. By this time, Heather was up to her navel in water. She grabbed the mooring ring, and vaulted ashore with surprising agility.

'Damn! Blast! It's sodding freezing!'

Fred pulled himself carefully onto the concrete jetty and dragged the kayak after them. He squeezed along the gunwales until the puncture revealed itself in bubbles.

'That's the trouble with these inflatables,' he remarked, with frustration. 'Very convenient, but you pull them over one sharp stone and you've got a problem like this. I'll mend it when I get back next week.'

Meanwhile, Heather jogged on the spot in an attempt to warm up. Nice bottom, thought Fred to himself. Albeit a bit damp.

Alberto and Robin had spotted their maritime mishap, and were now alongside the bank. It was obvious what had happened.

'Fred, this is your weekend. We can swap boats,' said Robin.

'Oh, would you? Are you sure? That's very kind,' said Fred, delightedly. He turned to Heather, who was still hopping up and down from one foot to another, trying to get warm.

'Hey, Heather, we can go out again in the rigid hull!'

She looked at him as if he'd proposed raw slugs for the evening's hors d'oeuvre.

'You are surely joking?'

'Really?' said Fred, in surprise. 'It's turned out quite sunny. I wanted to show you a kingfisher. Maybe an otter, if we're lucky?'

'There's no way, I'm afraid, Fred. All I want to do now is just want to get back to the Hall and have a hot bath. Sitting in three inches of cold water for the rest of the day is my exact idea of hell.'

'She's otterly against it, bro,' remarked Roddy, who had walked briskly back along the towpath and now popped up rather too smartly for Fred's liking. Fred felt as deflated as his kayak.

From the bankside, towering over his seated form, his friends looked down at him kindly.

'It was worth a try, Fred. It would probably have been great fun, but perhaps another year?' Heather shrugged her shoulders.

'Wait, what about the others?' Fred turned to Robin and Alberto, who had now moored alongside the jetty. 'What would you like to do?'

The kayaking plan having sprung a leak, perhaps he could rescue the situation by proposing a game of Scrabble back at Threepwood. He was pretty good at that too, and he could envisage himself and Heather wrapped in towels with a mug of cocoa and a busy board. He'd been known to get a seven letter on a triple word score.

'Alberto has taken to paddling like a duck to water,' said Robin, proudly. 'He's so versatile.'

Alberto swung his blade alluringly, and beamed an orthodontically-perfected smile.

'Fred, why don't you swap with me, and go out with Alberto?' suggested Robin. He thought his friend would be quite safe with his boyfriend to look out for him. 'It is your special treat after all. You can show him all your favourite places.'

'Yes, that's a great idea, Freddy!' said Roddy, eagerly. 'That way you get your birthday outing, and nobody need get a wet butt!'

'Well, that wasn't quite the plan…' said Fred weakly, thinking that he could imagine little worse than being a tour guide for an over-enthusiastic Latino while his lecherous brother told tall tales to the woman of his dreams in front of a cosy fire back at the Hall.

'Go on, Fred,' said Roddy. 'Now you're just being polite!'

Robin scrambled ashore.

'In you go, Fred. Alberto's easy. He doesn't mind where he goes.'

Cursing inside, Fred allowed himself to be guided down into the double kayak. He couldn't see how he could get out of this one without being rude to Alberto.

'Heather, I'll take you back to Threepwood,' said Roddy. 'Luckily, I brought my own car. We can get you out of those wet clothes.'

As he heard this, Fred's heart sank.

'I'll hop in the back, then,' said Robin, 'and Fred, even though it's your birthday, I don't want you seducing my boyfriend now!' He winked at Alberto: '*Adiós, chico amante*! Everyone's completely safe!'

Alberto blew a noisy kiss back, and turned to the matter in hand.

'*Vámonos!*' he said, and with a firm stroke of his paddle, sent them downstream into the current.

'See you later!' called Fred, weakly, as he saw Roderick put his arm around Heather's shoulders and lead her off to the car. Robin followed them, alert for conspiracy.

'Bastard!' muttered Fred, under his breath, following up with other choice expletives.

'What's that, Fred?' replied Alberto. 'Faster?!'

Chapter 21

Within minutes, the kayak was out of sight of the jetty, Alberto's eager strokes driving them forward down the river. On each bank, there was an apparent jungle of bushes and trees, with the occasional flash of a bird. Wild orchids and other flowers poked through the undergrowth. Butterflies were making merry with the spring blossom. Dragonflies prowled like attentive biplanes, all scarlet and blue in the haze. It could have been a perfect afternoon, after all. Fred mentally cursed his bad luck. Alberto was just pleased to have his host under his watchful eye.

'Fred?' said Alberto, a few minutes later.

'Yes, Alberto,' said Fred, still irritated.

'Do you have frogs in England?'

'Yes, we do.'

'In Costa Rica we have 190 species of frogs.'

'Really? That's… impressive. We have about three, I think.' He wasn't sure he needed a natural history lesson.

'Let me tell you about them, Fred…' Not much choice about the lesson. Alberto did not stop to draw breath.

'We have the flying leaf frog. The red-eyed leaf frog. The blue-sided leaf frog. The blue-sided leaf frog is found only in

Costa Rica,' he pointed out, proudly. 'There are many other sorts of leaf frog...'

'Yes...' said Fred, weakly.

'Then there are the tree frogs. They live in trees,' Alberto explained.

'I can imagine...' replied Fred.

'Then there is the ghost glass frog, Fred.'

'Does it live in a glass?' said Fred, vacantly.

'No, Fred!' giggled Alberto. 'It lives in the jungle! There are no glasses in the jungle! Then there's the common rain frog.'

'Is the rain common or is the frog common?' asked Fred, doing his best to show willing.

'What? No, both rain and frog are common in the jungle. Much rainings, many frogs. There are a few more frogs whose name I have forgotten.'

'That's a bit of a relief, actually,' admitted Fred.

'But I must also tell you about the poison frogs! The blue jeans poison dart frog. No, before you ask, it doesn't wear jeans!' Alberto chuckled at his own joke before continuing: 'The Caribbean striped poison dart frog...'

'Ah, yes, the poison dart frogs,' said Fred, knowingly.

'These frogs, you see, Fred, are all very, verrry beautiful. They have bright colours. Red and green. Like jewels. But the beauty is lethal, Fred. Do you understand? The point of the beauty, is to tell other creatures that these frogs can kill!' Alberto felt that in the animal kingdom, he had found the perfect metaphor. Heather was just a rather well-groomed frog in human form. So far, he had failed to convey this metaphor to Fred.

'Killer frogs?' queried Fred, to whom this was an unexpected surprise. He knew Australia was rife with homicidal spiders and sharks and snakes and even birds, and had made a point of avoiding that continent. But Latin America had seemed a more benign destination, always excepting the piranha fish. And the fascist dictators. He'd heard that one of those had been found in Devon. Fish, not dictator. Killer frogs were new to him.

'Yes!' continued Alberto. 'These are the frogs of death. Dangerous! Woah! Some of the most venomous creatures you ever meet! You know what neurotoxin is?'

'Sort of…' admitted Fred, interested despite himself, as he continued paddling. He noted that Alberto was resting his paddle on the kayak and gesticulating at the river as his explanations became ever more passionate.

'Well, it's a toxin, yes, a poison, which affects the nerves,' declaimed Alberto at the dragon flies. Causes paralysis, heart attack and death. Remember Indians with poison arrows and blow pipes? All from frogs. Killer frogs!'

'Maybe we shouldn't mention this to Freya?' suggested Fred. 'She might want some for her arrows.'

Alberto ignored him.

'In order to… to… intensify the poison, the Indians heat up the frogs over a fire.'

'Heat them up? You mean, toast them?' This seemed far-fetched to Fred. He idly wondered if you could put a frog in a toaster. Only if it was dead already, of course. Either way, it would make a terrible mess.

'I see,' said Fred politely, puzzled at the ingenuity with which either God or natural selection had engineered Creation. 'Thank you. If I should ever find myself in Costa Rica, this will be invaluable information. Shall we turn around now?'

Fred dug in his paddle without seeking agreement and started turning the kayak. They had now sped down the river, aided by wind and current, for nearly half an hour. It would take much longer going back up-river. For the next ten minutes, Fred and Alberto paddled rhythmically along. Alberto was satisfied that his metaphor had been perfectly clear.

Sweat was trickling down Fred's back. It was harder work than he had thought. They were making slow progress. If only they had begun by going upstream and then paddled back down. As it was, they'd headed off in the wrong direction, and were now fighting both the current and the wind. He began to worry about getting home and preparing for dinner. And he couldn't help thinking about Heather. And Roderick.

'Fred, this weekend is your special time, isn't it?' said Alberto, after a while.

'Yes...' panted Fred. He hoped Alberto would not stop padding again. In fact, he wished Alberto would just shut up.

'I feel that this journey we are taking...'

'Well, it's an outing really,' said Fred. 'Some people might call it an excursion, perhaps.' He thought to himself that he would call it a total disaster.

'Myself, I would call it a journey,' said Alberto, decisively. 'A journey on the water of frogs. I feel these things, Fred.' He beat his chest proudly with a fist. 'I contain the spirit of the Indians.'

'The spirit of the Indians?' enquired Fred. 'Incas you mean? Or Aztecs or Mayans or whatever...' he added, as an afterthought. He didn't want to offend the man. Which were the ones who had gone in for human sacrifice? He felt momentarily anxious.

'No! The Bribri. My ancestors on my mother's side. So, now I want to share with you a story...'

'That's very kind, Alberto,' interrupted Fred, 'only it's a bit of an effort to paddle and hear at the same time. Maybe it could wait till we get back?'

'No,' insisted Alberto, firmly. 'It cannot wait.'

'OK,' said Fred, weakly.

'It is the story of the river. It is about the frogs I mention. The poison frogs. You see, this toxin is also important drug for my mother's people. The shamans.'

'Really? Shamanic? I thought you said it killed you? Paralysis and heart attack, you said.'

'Hush, Fred. I tell you a different story. No more symbolic.'

'Fair enough. But can you paddle at the same time?' Fred thought that 'shambolic' would be a better description of his day than 'symbolic'. 'Talk and paddle together, yes?'

Alberto ignored him. As he looked over his shoulder, Fred saw that he had his eyes closed, and the paddle across his knees. Alberto began intoning. Fred kept paddling. This excursion was becoming more nightmareish by the minute. Roderick was probably ensconced at the end of Heather's bath by now. He ground his teeth in fury.

'At night, the shaman goes into the jungle and he can speak the language of the frog, and the frog answers!' continued Alberto. 'Then he scrapes the toxin off the frog. And this is called Kambo. We are inviting the spirit of this beautiful Kambo into our body to purify us.'

'To purify?' panted Fred.

'Yes. You stab your arm and then rub in the toxin. You can eat, you can drink, but this is best.'

'Wow. Stab? Sounds risky. Then what?'

'Your throat feels really dry. There's like a burning in your ears and a burning in your... in your private parts. Your face feels numb. You weep. Your face feels strange. You cough. You spit.'

'To be honest, it's not sounding great, Alberto.'

Alberto ignored his interruption.

'You swell up, your eyes go puffy, your throat constricts. You're all croaky. Fred, It's like you become a frog yourself.'

'You become a frog? For real?'

'Partly. And it's good for your skin. So smooth afterwards. Exfoliation, but more spiritual than... than cosmetic. Things change after Kambo,' intoned Alberto, mysteriously. Alberto opened his eyes and smiled at Fred. 'There are many people who would say it has benefits like medicine.'

'If it doesn't kill you,' pointed out Fred.

'This very rarely happens.'

'Good to know.'

'It is a very powerful story of my mother's people, the Bribri of Costa Rica.'

'Thank you, Alberto.'

'We have shared this. On our special journey. Just to remember: beautiful things can be dangerous too.'

'Yes, I appreciate that. Do you think you could manage to do some more paddling now, Alberto? Only, we're really not making much progress here.'

'I will paddle now,' intoned the Costa Rican.

'Thank you, Alberto,'

Alberto turned round and whispered in Fred's ear, 'Remember the Kambo.'

'Yes, I will,' said Fred, paddling as hard as he could.

'Please do not share this story.'

'I'm – totally – OK – with – keeping it – between – ourselves.'

'We share the Kambo!' With a triumphant finish, Alberto turned and dug in his blade once more.

'Marvellous!' groaned Fred, feeling that hallucinogenic amphibians might be as good as it got this weekend.

Chapter 22

Back at the hall, the rest of Fred's guests had been lingering over their cups of coffee on the terrace after lunch. Sonia had deployed one of her herbal tea bags. The missing manuscript was at the forefront of everyone's minds, whether or not it was spoken of. Opinions were as finely divided as they had been on Brexit: half of them wished the memoir to be reinstated, and half devoutly hoped that it was a thing of the past and they could now look forward to the sunny uplands.

Over on the lawn, Freya was playing with Humphrey, throwing a ball which he would occasionally catch and retrieve in order to humour her. Neither of them had an opinion on Memoirgate, or Brexit for that matter.

'Freya's great, Polly,' said Charlotte. 'You must be very proud of her.'

'She's at a lovely age,' said Polly. 'Soaking up knowledge like a sponge, but still with that openness and imagination.'

'I would have loved to have had a daughter,' said Charlotte, wistfully.

'Well, it's not too late!'

'I know. To be honest, and I feel a little bit disloyal about saying this, I'm not entirely sure that Roddy has been the best dad for the boys. He's a bit selfish. He's so obsessed with his career. But don't leave it too long, Sonia! You fall off the fertility cliff after forty.'

'That ticking clock is so sexist!' said Polly. 'Men can carry on impregnating any woman they can get their hands on, well into old age. Especially if they're Prime Ministers.'

Sonia nodded vehemently. This difference felt so unfair.

'I do wonder about Heather,' said Charlotte. 'She shows no signs of settling down.'

'She's no better than Roddy,' said Polly. 'Eyes fixed on her media profile. She should do what we did,' she continued. 'Find a cooperative gay man and a turkey baster.'

'You don't mean literally?' asked Charlotte, in horror.

'Quite literally,' said Polly. She didn't add that the best way to get your basal body temperature was to put a thermometer into your vagina. She didn't think that Charlotte was ready for that information. But how else could you know when ovulation had occurred?

'I think I'd want to actually sleep with him,' said Charlotte, firmly. 'The sperm donor, I mean. When baby-making is separated from the love, I think it must feel a bit… clinical.' She wondered for a moment whether her sleeping with her own sperm source had ensured that baby-making was closely connected to love. Best not go there, she thought.

'Well, I might have, to be honest,' admitted Polly. 'There's nothing romantic about a pipette from Boots. But Georgina wasn't having any of it. Hence the donation.'

'If I was in, say, Heather's position, I'd just go off the pill, find an eligible man and do the deed,' said Sonia. 'No need to mention fertility at all.'

'I still feel uncomfortable about it,' said Charlotte. 'Fairly sure it's not something I can reconcile with my beliefs… Not that I am judging you, Polly, I don't mean to be rude. But I'm not endorsing Sonia's idea either. Morally wrong. Totally exploitative of the bloke. And think about the poor child!' said Charlotte, firmly.

'Although there's actually quite a lot of unnatural reproduction in The Bible, isn't there?' said Sonia. 'Take Abraham and Sarah. She was well past menopause, by the sound of things. Then you've got the Immaculate Conception, and then Gabriel announcing to Mary that she was up the duff while still being a virgin. God was quite clearly the original fertility specialist.'

'You must have gone to some very alternative Bible classes!' called Robin, who had come out to the garden, dragging a heavy wooden box behind him.

'Perhaps a bit unorthodox, but whatever gets you through,' said Polly, casting a conspiratorial smile at Sonia. She felt they were both on the same side, whether it came to conception, or manuscripts.

'Anyway folks, I found this in the entrance hall. Guess what? Croquet! I think we should play,' said Robin. 'This lawn is obviously just the place for it.'

'Shame you didn't find the manuscript!' said Sonia.

'That's most mysterious' said Robin. 'But it's definitely not in the box.'

'A different sort of ball game,' said Sonia. 'Not sure this one's for me either.'

'Oh, do play!' said Charlotte. 'We need to start getting into role for this evening.'

'Robin probably won't let us off the hook until we agree,' muttered Polly, gloomily. 'Even though we'd be better off searching for Fred's book.'

At this moment, Freya emerged from the shrubbery, dragging Hugh by the hand.

'Hello, darling! Thank you so much, Hugh,' said Polly. 'Please don't feel you have to entertain her all weekend. Freya, would you like to play croquet? Lay off Hugh for a bit?'

'Don't know how!' said Freya, a bit cross at being told to leave her new friend alone.

'Robin will teach us,' said her mother. 'And then maybe we should help Uncle Fred find his book?'

'This lawn seems a bit uneven,' said Sonia. 'Maybe it's sunk over the years?'

'At least there's grass,' said Robin. 'We English always take our lawns for granted. If you're in Asia or Africa, you don't have anything like this.'

'Have you ever played croquet overseas?' asked Polly, trying to catch Robin out. He did tend to pontificate about everything, just because he was the only one there with a doctorate.

'I did once get into a croquet competition in a hotel in Tanzania,' he replied, defensively.

'Not sure I've heard of a croquet hustler before,' said Charlotte.

'You mock. But I did once think of writing a book about croquet. For example, Which characters from Shakespeare would have excelled with the wooden balls?'

'I'm not sure I want to play this game,' said Charlotte, while making mental notes for her next article in *Country Life*.

'Did they have croquet in the Tudor period?' asked Polly. 'I'd have thought it was more of a Victorian thing?'

'There was a huge craze for it in the 1860s. But the English had been whacking balls about with mallets since the seventeenth century. They called it pall-mall. Hence the London street.'

'Ah. Should I ever find myself trapped in a pub quiz, my success is now assured,' said Charlotte, sarcastically. Robin was continuing unabashed:

'The key innovation was the croquet stroke itself...'

'Ah, you mean where you use your ball to bash another ball to kingdom come?' asked Hugh.

'Yes. It's quite the most diabolical aspect of the game,' said Robin, with relish.

'Don't remind me,' said Hugh. 'My father is a croquet demon. I remember as a ten-year-old, playing my dad. Sometimes, I only used to get one turn at the start, and then I watched, completely impotently, as he went on to beat me.'

'Sounds like child abuse,' said Polly.

'I was frequently reduced to fits of purple rage.'

'Exactly!' said Robin. 'Character forming. I have a theory that it wasn't the playing field of Eton, it was the croquet lawns of England where the stiff upper lip came into being.'

'Well, it didn't do much for my self-esteem,' said Hugh. 'So I'll sit this one out, if you don't mind.' He felt it was best if he kept a low profile for the rest of the weekend.

'I'll play, if you're short of a player,' said Sonia, joining them on the lawn. It was the safest form of exercise, she thought.

'You're only saying that because you missed Robin's peroration,' said Polly.

While they'd been talking, Robin had pushed the six hoops and two stakes into the ground carefully, as Freya watched him in fascination. She now picked up a mallet and trying to swing it around her head like a weapon.

'Careful, Freya!' said her mother. 'It's not a toy.'

'Well, it is a toy,' said Hugh. 'Just, not that sort of toy.'

'Is it like Quidditch?' asked Freya.

'Almost exactly,' said Sonia. 'Only without broomsticks, or a Snitch.'

'Well, it's certainly going through hoops,' said Hugh. 'But no magic whatsoever. Basically, Quidditch without the good bits.'

'You're in danger of sounding like a misery!' replied Polly. Hugh shrugged. Freya giggled. She quite liked it when people wound up her mother.

With the red, yellow, black and blue wooden globes all lined up on the line, it was time to start. Robin, Sonia, Polly and Charlotte all took the first shot together. By common consent, it was agreed that Freya should get next hit. She swung the mallet like a mace, and manage to connect with the blue ball she was sharing with her mother. It advanced a few yards.

Charlotte took her shot, and then it was Robin's turn. He went through his hoop and started taking Charlotte's ball around with him.

'Here we go,' said Hugh. 'Exactly as I warned you. The rest of you might as well sit the rest of the game out with me...'

'So where do you imagine the book can have gone to?' Sonia asked Charlotte. Hugh stared into the shrubbery.

'I bet it's still somewhere in the grounds,' said Robin, as he used his ball to knock Charlotte's ball through the first hoop. She was beginning to feel picked on. And she didn't like how the conversation was going, either.

'After all, I can see no earthly reason why anyone would want it!' said Robin.

'Well, I wanted it!' said Sonia, indignantly. 'I bet lots of people would have enjoyed reading it.'

'We're not doing so well,' Polly pointed out to Freya, who jumped up and down in excitement.

'It's all very mysterious...' pondered Robin. Charlotte wondered if he was talking about the theft or the croquet.

'Ssssh,' said Charlotte, as Sonia concentrated on her shot. She knocked her yellow ball through the hoop. With her bonus shot, she hit herself backwards, so that her ball just kissed Robin's ball.

'Ha!' Sonia said, with satisfaction.

'Is that good, Mummy?' asked Freya.

'You villain!' exclaimed Robin. 'You wouldn't dare!'

'Watch me!' said Sonia. 'I've been well schooled! Anil taught me all I know. And he's a product of the Raj.'

She placed her ball carefully against the psychologist's.

'I want his ball to go as far as possible from my ball or your ball,' she explained to Freya.

Freya nodded very seriously. She was quick to learn the evil ways of adults. They were all the same. One night, it was Hugh creeping about. Then the next day it was Sonia being vicious.

'I think I understand, Aunty Sonia.'

'It's not strictly allowed, you know, Sonia,' said Robin, weakly. But ganging up against him was clearly permitted. Thank goodness his boyfriend wasn't there to see.

With the two balls kissing, Sonia put her foot on her own ball and drew back her mallet. With a smart 'crack', she whacked her ball so hard that the impact sent Robin's flying to the opposite corner of the green. Everyone looked to see where it would go. But standing on one leg, on grass that was slightly damp, and balancing to swing and hit, and twisting to watch the balls fly across the court, was too much for Sonia's balance. Simultaneous with the follow-through of her shot, she wobbled, slipped and then fell with a thud. Her fall was broken by the croquet hoop, which was driven into her side by the weight of her body.

'Owww!' she howled, and lay doubled up in pain on the grass. 'Damn, damn, damn, damn, damn!'

'Oh no!' exclaimed Freya, running up from where she'd been standing. She flung himself down and rested her head on Sonia's lap. 'Are you broken? Do you need some new swear words?'

'Just bruised,' said Sonia, struggling to sit up. 'That'll teach me to try and be too clever for my own good. Sugar, sugar, shit. Excuse my language, dear Freya.'

Freya gazed at her with renewed respect.

'Sorry for swearing,' added Sonia. 'It is really very naughty. So please don't copy me. Sorry, Mummy,' she said, as Polly came up to her.

'I think the grass must be a bit damp still,' said Charlotte, anxiously. 'Is there anything we can do? I think I might have some arnica somewhere.'

'I'm not sure,' said Sonia, wincing and rubbing her hip. 'I bruised my side a lot. The hoop bashed me. I must have tripped over it.'

'You certainly came down to earth with a crash' said Polly, with concern, 'You'll have a dreadful bruise.'

'At least you're not bleeding, Aunty Sonia!' said Freya, helpfully. Sonia looked at her in horror.

'Oh god! I hope not!' she said, moving stiffly and trying out her range of movement. 'I might retire wounded. Go and have a lie down.'

'Do you want a shoulder?' offered Hugh, gallantly. Polly had been glaring at him, so he thought he'd better offer.

'No, I think I'll manage,' said Sonia, rubbing her side. 'Better just rest with my feet up. But thanks... and let's not mention this to Anil.'

She looked desolate, as if she'd just witnessed a well-tipped client being beaten at an awards ceremony. She hobbled off back to the house.

'Well!' said Charlotte. 'That was unexpectedly dramatic. Poor Sonia! I hope she's OK?'

'It must have hurt a lot more than it looked,' said Polly gazing after the departing figure. 'Maybe one of us should go after her? To check if everything's fine?'

'First, can we play some more?' said Freya, with all the callous indifference of the young.

'As long as you can promise me no violence and no nastiness!' Robin said to Freya. 'We can finish the round just as a practice game. Maybe Hugh could take Sonia's ball?'

'Fine,' said Hugh. It seemed the least he could do in the circumstances. Polly was not sure whether it was best to stay helping Freya, or go after Sonia. Perhaps she should be rubbing on ointment or massaging or something?

'I do need the practice,' Freya said to Charlotte, solemnly.

'Why don't you go and see if Sonia's OK?' Hugh suggested to Polly. 'I'll keep an eye on Freya.'

'Well, if you're sure?' Polly said. 'She can be very persistant.'

He wasn't so bad really, thought Polly. And she did want to search Charlotte and Roddy's room while everyone was otherwise engaged. Heather's too. It might be time for her Harriet Vane impression. After all, it seemed impossible for that tiny pig to eat an entire manuscript.

Polly quietly headed off, as Hugh continued talking to her daughter.

'Maybe if you like playing, we could make you a small mallet later?' he said to Freya. 'I remember my dad got a log, drilled a hole in the top and put in a broom handle, and that was my mallet. I could do that for you too, if you like.'

'Oh, yes please!' said Freya. 'I'd really like that. I think I might be a croquet champion when I grow up,' she said, very seriously. She obviously wasn't bothered about her mother returning to the house, thought Hugh. He quite liked being *in loco parentis*. At least for brief periods. Brief quiet periods.

'As long as you can be patient,' said Charlotte. 'Are you any good at that?' she asked, coming down to Freya's level. Freya shrugged. She hated it when adults did that. And Aunty Charlotte's tone wasn't at all welcome. Robin gave her a warning glare.

'Just try not to trip yourself up,' said Hugh, casting an anxious eye in the direction of the house. But he had no time to worry about that. It was his shot at it.

Chapter 23

Heather had extricated herself from Roddy's clumsy clutches, and gone to her room. She waved abstractly as Polly passed her on the landing. So far, things were going Heather's way. Her charms were intact plus the manuscript had obviously been successfully stolen by Hugh. She had a most agreeable hot bath, and then lay on her bed, swathed in an acceptably fluffy towel. She hadn't bothered with period costume for the evening. She thought that the suit in her bag would be quite glamorous enough for these surroundings. Her phone had downloaded twenty-four hours-worth of emails and news-papers on the drive home from the kayak trip, so there was plenty of doom-scrolling to do first. She felt a professional duty to keep up to date on which global conflict was about to become media-worthy. Yemen? Gaza? Ukraine? They all required a different outfit.

As soon as she looked at the CNN and Fox News headlines, she discovered a story about Clancy that had just broken in the US press, but not yet been covered in Britain. She sat up in shock. The scandal seemed already to have hit peak pundit on the breakfast shows. The crudity of the Kiss 'n' Tell left her horrified. She had felt inured against all bad publicity, but not this. Being caught with a stripper was awful in itself but the details of his proclivities that were emerging were tackier still. It was all sickening,

As she stood there, her face still wrinkled up in a way which would play havoc with her complexion, she opened her emails. Sure enough, there were a stream of messages from Clancy protesting his complete innocence. Mistaken identity, blah blah blah, trust, blah blah blah, outrageous media stalking, blah blah blah. Plenty of *Stand By Your Man*, but not very much *Don't Take Your Love To Town*, or Sunset Strip in his case.

She looked again at the news coverage. Clearly, Clancy's ex-wife had hit pay dirt. The press was eager for her side of the story, and having not yet signed the non-disclosure agreement, she was letting rip. Ouch! Clancy was not coming out of it well. His sexual foibles would not be good reading for the Bible belt, let alone for the Latino Catholic vote. You would have to be a sitting President to get away with that sort of thing.

Heather paced the room, clutching at her towel for security. She calculated rapidly. The ex-wife did not know her name, thank god, and the media had no idea of who Clancy was dating. After all, she and Clancy usually holed up in hotels, not houses, and they weren't stupid enough to show themselves in restaurants and nightclubs. It wasn't hard to fly under the radar if you had no intention of being a news headline. But now Clancy was in trouble. Deep trouble. Trouble so deep that it would take several years of good behaviour and expensive public relations to clean up his image and restore his name. If ever. It had worked for Hugh Grant, but he was much cuter than Clancy. Plus he was in that Paddington movie.

Heather didn't need to be involved with a scandal, she felt, and she had no time to waste. Her clock was ticking, her reputation was ratings gold, and her time was now. She was quite realistic about the brevity of beautiful women's careers in news media. Life was like that: it could change in an instant, as easily as someone changing a TV channel. Sure, she could have been in a Transatlantic Power Couple. But perhaps her future was as part of a Great British Power Couple. That could play really well. She could see herself as a regular presenter of the One Show.

Clancy was on his own now. And, excitingly, so was she. She turned off her phone. It felt oddly liberating. She reached for her moisturiser.

Arriving back at Threepwood Hall, cold, damp and deeply unwilling to countenance further discussion of hallucinogenic frogs, Fred sent Alberto off skipping happily in the direction of Robin, with a reminder to remember to shower rather than bathe. It was 5 p.m., and nearly time to change for the birthday dinner and prepare for drinks. The sitting room was quite empty, but the great table in the dining room was already laid for the meal. The croquet-playing contingent had discovered teamwork. He didn't know it, but Polly was taking the opportunity to quietly ferret through Roddy and Charlotte's luggage, while Freya was reading to Charlotte on the terrace. There was no sign of Heather or Roddy.

Rather relieved at not having to engage with his friends, Fred thought he might go and say hello to the pig for ten minutes, before changing his clothes. He felt rather flat, and it was pleasant communing with the pig. He went and collected

Humphrey, who had been sleeping happily in the bedroom after the excitement of the croquet game. Once the dog had wolfed down some kibble (about the only wolfing he was capable of), Fred attached his lead and wheeled out of the back door.

As usual, Humphrey insisted on inspecting every clump of flowers or tree thoroughly, and then vigorously asserted his preference for escaping the constraints of the lead in favour of more intimate inter-species engagements with the squirrels and rabbits who scampered about the sward. When Fred refused to allow him to pursue his instincts, he sat down firmly and barked instead. The balmy evening was riven by a grumpy pug demanding his rights. It wasn't what Fred needed. Having lost his life's work and a lifelong fantasy, he was taking no nonsense from a dog.

At this point the French doors opened behind him, and Roddy appeared on the terrace, as welcome as a new zit on a date night. He wandered down to his younger brother's side, looking particularly airbrushed. Occasionally, Fred deeply resented his brother's pulchritude, and this was one of these times. Roderick, of course, was completely oblivious.

'Hi, Fred!' he called. 'Hello, Humphrey! Everything OK?'

'Not completely OK, Roderick, no,' retorted Fred. 'Just the small matter of my life's work being stolen. Anyway. Where's Heather?'

'She's not reappeared since her bath' said Roddy, who felt it was better not to talk about the book. 'I was trying to do some reading. Except it turned into forty winks,' he admitted.

Fred looked at him suspiciously. Damn, thought Roddy. He should never have mentioned reading.

'You know, I had been hoping to have some time alone with Heather this weekend,' said Fred, grumpily. 'Only, you keep on loitering around like her shadow or something.'

'I don't think I do,' said Roddy, defensively.

'Well, it looks like that to me,' said his brother. There was a difficult pause. Roddy bent down and scratched Humphrey's ears.

'Do you think you've got any chance with Heather?' he said at last.

'Why? Has she said anything?'

'No,' admitted Roddy. 'But she hasn't exactly glowed about you either. She was furious about getting wet this afternoon. I think you might be barking up the wrong tree.'

'You'd think a foreign correspondent could cope with a bit of cold water.'

'Well, it's her weekend off. I think it was kind of her to come, myself.'

'Kind? Kind?!' Fred retorted, taking great exception. 'I'm not a charity case! I'm one of her oldest friends!'

'No need to be touchy!' said Roddy.

'Anyway,' said Fred, 'you're a married man, so I don't know what you think you're doing…'

'To be fair, Frederick, you can probably hear the writing on the wall for my marriage as well as I can…'

'I think you're pretty unfair to Lottie. She's a sweet person. It's not her fault she's, well… a bit too fish-positive.'

'Well, you must admit, she's changed a fair amount since we first got married.'

'So have you!'

'Possibly. But the Godsquad thing… that column… Frankly, it's a bit of a bore. It's not me! I'm in a different place, going forward…'

'Well, don't make it so obvious! And for god's sake, leave Heather alone. It's beginning to look ridiculous. And so humiliating for Lottie.'

With that, Fred pushed his wheels angrily, and jerked Humphrey's lead. Nothing was working out right. He pulled his pug away, just as Humphrey was directing a long hard stare towards the local rabbit community, who were clever enough to recognise a leash when they spotted one. Suddenly docile as a carriage dog, Humphrey trotted behind the chair until they reached the pigsty.

Roddy was left standing on the terrace, contemplating his options in life. His father had died ten years ago, and his mother now had galloping dementia. With no parents to guide him, he had only a younger brother to discuss life choices with. He was through with that! A brother, he now reminded himself, who knew nothing of married life, nor how people drifted apart, let alone the pall of once-urgent romances. He and Charlotte hadn't had sex in months. His wife was not the woman he'd thought she was. Worse, she was not the woman she thought she was, for god's sake! His brooding resentment turned to irritation. If there was a cat to be kicked in the vicinity, he would certainly have kicked it. He was sick of being told what was good for him! Birthday or no birthday, it was time he cut loose. Once he was selected as a parliamentary candidate, it would be too late to make big changes in his personal life. It was now or never.

Down on the farm, Fred and Humphrey found the small black Vietnamese pig snuffling happily in his trough. Humphrey put his front paws up on the bars of the pen and gazed with interest. Pig pellets did not appear to be quite as exciting as dog food, but nevertheless, food was food. Humphrey was willing, in most circumstances, to hoover up almost anything. Vin Pong looked around at his visitor, as if to say, 'just got to finish this excellent scran, be with you in a minute, my dear fellow.' Humphrey seemed willing to wait, looking up at Fred to check that they weren't leaving in a hurry.

Fred stroked his dog's neck absently, scratching his folds of skin, as he gazed around the little farmyard. As well as the pig, there seemed to be chickens. Across from the coop, Fred could see that the kitchen garden was being prepared for more planting. A crop of – what, broad beans? – appeared nearly ready for harvesting. A bed of early potatoes had just been earthed up. Garlic bulbs had already flowered, but still shook their pom poms in sentry duty down the main aisles of the garden. Did a garden have aisles? Lines? Files?

'Hello, Fred!'

Reverie interrupted, he swung around in his chair. It was Nel. Fred was delighted to see her. She had been the unconscious motivation for his stroll. He needed to forget about the book, for now. At least someone was pleased to see him. He felt guilty that his faithful fantasy of Heather was besmirched by even the most tenuous, inchoate attraction to someone he'd only just met. So silly! Shame at his own shallowness fought genuine warmth at Nel's appearance. She smiled at him. Warmth won.

'How is your house party going?' she said. 'Any dramas?'

A chill blast of memory hit him like the shower in a Northumberland Youth Hostel.

'I was going to tell you. Someone's nicked my manuscript! I'd call that a disaster.'

'What?' She was astonished. 'You're joking!'

Her reaction was gratifying.

'Do you remember, I told you about my dream of becoming a writer? I was making good progress, had a book, basically. Well, I don't now!'

'No! But it was surely on your computer?'

'Memory stick. Also stolen. Nightmare!'

'Why? Was it going to be a bestseller?' She giggled. He didn't look amused. She resumed serious. 'Who? Not one of these friends who are with you?'

'Reckon so.' He frowned.

'You must feel awful!' she said.

'Absolutely I do!' he said.

'Who do you suspect?'

'Could be several of them.' Unable to pace, Fred wheeled up and down in agitation.

'My own brother. His wife. Heather, the war reporter. None of them have been exactly delighted about me writing a memoir. The only one who I don't suspect is my school-friend Hugh, who wouldn't even notice if I wrote about him. And Polly, I can't see her being bothered either. But who knows? It could be you!'

'No,' said Nel, slowly. 'It couldn't be me... I've not even been inside the Hall yet. Let alone featured in your memoir. What does the manuscript look like?'

'The usual. Hundreds of double-spaced pages. In a sort of buff folder. No doubt it's self-indulgent crap.'

'I'll look out for it,' she said. 'Might be in any of these bins around here. Have you looked in the composters?'

'No, but that's a good idea. I'd be grateful if you'd check. And you're coming tonight?'

She paused and frowned. Fred looked at her beseechingly.

'Go on, you must. There's a place laid for you. It would all just feel better with a pal.'

He realised how odd it was to treat this woman, who he didn't know well, as an ally amidst this group of his oldest friends. Odd but somehow natural.

'Well…' She made a decision. 'A party would certainly brighten up my container-based existence. It gets boring living out here with only a spoiled pig for company.'

'Much like married life, so far as I can see. Where do you bathe?'

Fred immediately realised that he might have crossed a line and blushed.

'I don't mean to be personal.'

'In the river.' She gazed at him neutrally.

'Really?' Now he was surprised. 'Must be pretty cold. Heather complained bitterly when she got wet during our kayak outing.'

'You don't mess about on a river without getting wet! Take me next time,' said Nel.

'I just got stuck in a boat with Alberto for an hour, which has left my head ringing… far too much shamanism for one weekend,' said Fred.

'Anyway, I was pulling your leg. Am I allowed to say that, by the way? What I meant was, there's a shower in the stable block.'

Fred didn't care if people said the wrong thing from time to time, and wasn't so stroppy as to make a fuss about it. He went for 'walks', even though he couldn't. He knew his blind pal 'saw the point', although he never, literally, would. But Fred didn't call people 'idiots' or 'mad' anymore.

'Shamanism has always involved a suspension of disbelief too far for me,' said Nel. 'Although they do have amazing knowledge of the environment.'

'A bit too amazing, to be honest. This one was trying to interest me in hallucinogenic frogs.'

She laughed raucously. For the first time that afternoon, Fred permitted himself a smile. Nel bent down to tickle Humphrey's chin, then looked at his owner again.

'I forgot to say happy birthday! How does it feel to be forty? A milestone? Or the beginning of the end? Tell me the worst, because my big four-oh is looming quicker than I'd hoped.'

'Oh, it's not so bad,' mused Fred. 'Once you go through a near-death experience, everything else is a bonus. It even makes it hard to feel that terrible when your entire life's work is stolen. A close shave puts everything into perspective. But I had thought it would be nice to be surrounded by my friends.'

'I think that's the bit I am dreading most.'

'Understandable. The plan is much better than the reality. Especially as at least one of these people is not a friend at all. Possibly several of them. They might just be the wrong friends. I had thought these people were good folk, however rarely I see them anymore. Who was I kidding?'

'I'm impressed you even have eight close friends. Not sure I do. Perhaps good friends are the ones you remember from better times, but now see rarely?' said Nel.

'Maybe. You've shared so much of life with them. This guy Hugh, for example. We were at school together more than twenty years ago. We've both changed. We don't really have much in common anymore. He doesn't have a career, as such. Drifts through life playing his fiddle and doing things with wood...'

'Sounds rather good to me!'

'Well, it's an insecure sort of existence. But at least he has no incentive to steal my book. Here we all are, nothing in common anymore, as our cohort slides downwards to the grave.'

'Oh, charming! I was hoping we are only half way there...'

'Well, if we're spared,' said Fred.

'You are gloomy today.'

'John Donne wrote that "We are all born in close prison, and all our life is going out to the place of execution,"' said Fred.

'I love that you know things like that.'

'Like what?' said Fred, rather pleased.

'Well, you can probably quote reams of English literature.'

'It's always easier to quote others than to come up with something original yourself.'

'Also true.'

'At least, according to Oscar Wilde,' Fred smiled at her.

'Clever dick!'

'You know stuff too,' said Fred. 'Birds and bees and pigs and stuff.'

'I reckon between us we'd rock your average pub quiz.'

'I've never actually done a pub quiz,' admitted Fred.

'Perhaps we should start. Sport might be a weak spot?'

'Most of popular culture has passed me by too. And I think we'd need my pal Robin. He knows all sorts of trivia.' He smiled. He liked the idea of a shared enterprise with Nel.

'Putting pub quizzes aside for the moment,' she said, 'if I do come to your party, this will give me a chance to suss out your guests...'

'Suss out?'

'At least one of them is plainly a thief. If we are to work out who, then two heads are better than one.'

'Like with quiz questions?'

'Exactly. Sitting down here on my own, night after night, you get to read a lot of crime novels...'

'Agatha Christie?'

'I hope I'm a touch more dashing than Miss Marple!'

'Well, if you can solve this mystery...'

'Leave it to me. I was quite keen to see the memoir myself. But don't expect miracles. I may have read Dorothy L. Sayers, but I'm strictly a folding camping chair detective.'

'Well, I am so pleased you're coming,' said Fred. 'After a grotty day, it will brighten up my evening.'

He beamed at her. She smiled back. Mostly, she met metaphorical or literal pigs. Things were looking up when she met a well-bred male of her own species.

'Anyway,' he added, 'I had better go back and change. I only came to walk the dog and check on you. See you in an hour or so!'

She waved him off, checked her porcine charge for the last time that day, and strolled back to her container to transmute either into stylish Regency lady, or zombie. It was a close call as to which would be easier.

No sooner had the two of them walked away in separate directions, when there was a rustle in the bushes. A tall bespectacled figure in a shabby parka first looked both ways to check whether the coast was clear. After overhearing the recent conversation, he was far from gruntled to be labelled an insecure drifter by his friend. And being called a traitor by Polly was too close to the truth to feel comfortable. Nevertheless, he pulled a length of cord from his pocket, and fashioned a lasso.

'Here pig, pig, pig!' Hugh called through the bars. 'I've got a treat for you!'

There was a rustling inside. Hugh held out a handful of nuts and raisins from his snacking cannister. Vin Pong shuffled forward, suspiciously. Tousle-headed figures in spectacles were unfamiliar to him. But this visitor appeared to be offering food, which was never knowingly spurned. Vin Pong put his head through the bars to have a sniff, and a moment later, Hugh felt a pig's tongue scooping treats off his outstretched palm. It was ticklish. With his other hand, he dropped the noose over Vin Pong's head and jerked it tight. The pot-bellied pig, sensing that it was suddenly restrained, instinctively ducked away. But the knot held – rough but firm. Hugh quietly unlatched and slid back the gate. He was quite pleased with himself. He obviously had a talent for burglary.

'Here pig, pig, pig,' he whispered. 'Come with me, Mr Pongy!' He threaded the leash out through the bars. Hugh reached into his pocket for another handful of nuts and raisins, which he held enticingly in front of Vin Pong's nose. The animal shuffled into a walk. He'd obviously go anywhere for food. So far, so good, thought Hugh. As long as he managed to avoid the rest of the house party on the stroll to his van, all would be well.

Feeling that the porker was dawdling somewhat, he gave Vin Pong a gentle flick on the rump with the stick which Polly had given him. Vin Pong cast him a resentful glance, but moved a little faster. Man and pig stepped up their stately pace towards the backyard where Hugh's Luton was parked.

Chapter 24

The moment of the big celebration had arrived. Silence had fallen over Threepwood Hall for the previous hour, as petticoats had been arranged and cravats been tied. Now it was time for the grand reveal. It was like a cross between Bake Off and Bridgerton. As Fred waited at the bottom of the staircase in his wheelchair, thinking suspicious thoughts about each of them, one by one his guests emerged and descended the great sweep of the stairs. It was not entirely unlike the grand ball at Netherfield, as described by Jane Austen, but rewritten by Agatha Christie.

Fred couldn't help but be delighted with the efforts that his friends had made. He clapped enthusiastically as each of them appeared and came to join him. He had previously arranged a tray of glasses on the hall table, each filled to the top with champagne, courtesy of Heather's gift case of Moët. Fred found it hard to be miserable for long. He had learned resilience over the past twenty years. That evening at Threepwood Hall was far from a police line-up, even though he suspected that at least one of the guests must have been the criminal.

First to emerge were Roddy and Charlotte. They looked terrific, albeit slightly awkward, and ideally costumed had it been a reception at Versailles with Louis XIV. Fred decided not to mention the anachronism. Privately he suspected Jane Austen might have been scornful. Charlotte was far from her comfort zone, but with every passing moment she seemed to relax a little more, and swell proudly into the sweep of her skirts and the lace of her bodice. Booted-and-suited, Roderick was a vast improvement on the polyester Labour apparatchik, indeed he was positively dashing, although he was reluctant to be photographed in case the image came back to haunt him. The loveless couple descended the stairs carefully, and without glancing at each other, to join the rest of the guests. Heather appeared as herself, in a business suit, high boots, and beautifully made-up.

'Sorry I'm from the wrong century!' she said, apologetically, to Fred. 'A few glasses of champagne, and no one will care!'

'It's quite OK,' said Fred. 'You have bigger fish to fry than fancy dress!' Her peck on the cheek arose barely a frisson.

Next to come down the stairs were Robin and Alberto, who looked as smart as everyone had anticipated. Robin was quite the peacock in a sapphire blue brocade waistcoat and cravat. Alberto looked, as always, as if he had just come from a fashion shoot, very much the twenty-first century Beau Brummel, in a grey velvet smoking jacket and thigh-length riding boots.

'You look amazing, Alberto!' said Charlotte. 'So stylish!' Their guest preened. After having made such an effort, it was a relief to be appreciated, thought Alberto. He patted his pocket to check that his mobile phone was not disturbing the cut of his jacket. He had an assignation on the ha-ha in twenty minutes.

More understated was Polly. Her slight figure suited the high-waisted empire line dress she had chosen, and her hair was in a mob-cap. It looked as if Jane Austen herself had stepped off a banknote to join the party. Polly had found the internet to be full of Regency costume tips and had done her best. At her side, Freya, as promised, was wearing a blue party dress, which was the closest she thought she'd get to Grace Holloway, Doctor Who's twenty-first century assistant in search of Mary Shelley. Nobody recognised the allusion, but everyone thought she looked most charming.

Fred took Polly's hand and kissed it warmly, and then had to kiss Freya's hand gallantly as well. People found themselves to be speaking in arch Regency prose, as if their garments had infected their very diction with self-consciousness. It was that sort of an evening. When she appeared, Sonia looked very suitable in a plain but elegant Empire line dress, wearing long gloves. She was subdued, accepting Fred's compliments with quiet grace and moving on into the sitting room.

A knock came at the great door. For a moment, Fred thought that if this were a film then it would be Hercule Poirot, here to track down the missing manuscript. When he went to answer the door, it wasn't David Suchet, or even Kenneth Branagh. Instead Fred found Nel standing there, unrecognisable in what appeared to be a lacy black dress, with a scooped neckline, and a flowing skirt. Around her shoulders was a shawl. She was even wearing make-up. She smiled nervously at her host.

'You look wonderful!' said Fred, in frank astonishment. 'Such a difference from an hour ago!'

They kissed cheeks and she gave him a supportive squeeze. This was a much better movie than a Poirot. Nel smiled at Fred, gratefully.

'Just don't look too closely!' she said. 'Basically, it's a swimsuit paired with an old shower curtain. It's a shame I have a tattoo. Quite clearly, it's the only thing letting down my Bridgerton impression. If you'd look at me only in right profile, it would probably be for the best.'

'Well, I think it's ingenious. It's certainly a huge improvement on the boiler suit,' said Fred, with feeling.

'That's because the boiler suit is intended to repel male attention,' said Nel, smiling.

'Whereas this ensemble isn't?' asked Fred.

A close observer might have seen the seasoned ethologist blush.

'Put it this way, if I had a fan, I'd be fluttering it now.'

Behind Nel hovered Hugh, looking like Oscar Wilde's thinner and less louche brother. A smart pair of dress trousers – Oxfam Ipswich he assured everyone loudly – was paired with a corduroy jacket. Around his neck was a silk scarf.

'Thanks for making the effort, Hugh,' said Fred. 'You look entirely right for the evening.'

'Well, if you say so,' said his friend. 'I was worried I was more Northanger Abbey than Nethercote.'

'Any marriage plot in a storm,' replied Fred.

Having thronged around the champagne, taken the obligatory group shots and selfies, and then fanned out into the sitting room, the party now broke up, most of the men drinking at the table, women relaxing into armchairs, pulled up close to others to continue an earlier conversation. The Gotan Project rumbled away in the background, largely ignored. Hugh even started reading something, standing close up the bookshelves. Fred had given up worrying about his old friend.

Out of the corner of his eye, Fred could see Polly wandering over to Nel. She clearly had a mission, although she was trying not to make it too obvious. She picked her way between the occasional tables, pushed aside the footstool and reached Nel's sofa, where she sat down very close to her. That was interesting. His best friend and his new friend. This was probably the first time they'd properly met.

He'd have preferred to have joined that conversation, but he'd become trapped in a one-sided dialogue with Alberto, which seemed to be something about patenting dessert recipes. Fred's knowledge of intellectual property was limited to what he'd picked up in college. But Alberto did not seem to need anything by way of response. He was trying out his ideas on Fred, so all that was required was the occasional nod and a solicitous expression, rather than a solicitor's expertise. Fred's wandering mind toyed between the three apparently divergent meanings of 'solicit'. He often seemed to be the audience for other people's obsessions. Alberto prattled on about his enthusiasm. Matters hobby-horsical. Fred thought perhaps he should put him in touch with a more appropriate lawyer, one of his old friends from college who'd headed towards the City rather than the livestock mart.

At the other side of the drawing room, under the ornate mirror, he could see Polly nodding in agreement, and then Nel laughing at something she'd said. Nel had a great laugh, an infectious guffaw as if she found the whole world entertaining, which it was of course, once you thought about it. She was wearing such a ridiculous outfit, half Regency, half mermaid. Her shawl kept slipping and she kept hitching it up. Polly could have been Jane Austen herself, observing and recording. He could see two pairs of shoulders shaking with the joke. Fred felt somehow excluded. For a moment, he thought with panic that Polly might be making a move on Nel. Surely not. He glanced over again. The body language seemed to signal agreement, not flirtation. Not that he should be worried, anyway. Polly deserved to meet someone nice. He thought he would like to be able to make someone laugh like that. Laughter was important.

At that moment, Polly turned and saw him staring at them. She caught his eye and smiled. She gave him a thumbs up. Now what on earth did that mean? Great party? Good outfit? Or go for it? He wished he knew. And realised with a jolt that it rather mattered to him. But here he was, stuck with a budding Costa Rican dessert entrepreneur. Fred was saved from further legal niceties by the dinner gong. The party thronged through to the dining room, fuelled by champagne and an eagerness to consume venison – and nut loaf.

'Let's get the seating organised,' said Charlotte, taking control. 'Could it work to have carnivores this end and vegetarians that end? That would help us serve up the right nosh to the right people.'

Freya looked anxious.

'I think you're this end, Freya darling,' said Sonia. 'With the lettuce munchers.'

Freya replied with all the seriousness of a seven-year-old to whom consistency mattered.

'But I want to sit with Hugh. And he told me that if a car hits a pheasant, he'll eat it, so he can't be veggie, can he?'

'I think we can make an exception for Hugh,' said Polly, coming to the rescue. 'If he's willing to forgo his meat for an evening. I'll slip you some beast-flesh later,' she added to him. 'It's the least I can do if you're prepared to eat with my sprog.'

Hugh blushed as a red as the beetroot salad that awaited him. She raised an eyebrow and smiled knowingly.

'There's an offer I can't refuse,' said Hugh. He was beginning to rather like Polly. They seemed to have weathered the social embarrassment of pig stealing. They were now bonded in criminality, the Bonnie and Clyde of Constable country. He felt that he might have got on with Jane Austen, had she had the chance to encounter him.

At last, everyone got seated. As he unfolded his napkin, Fred could hear fragments of conversation. At a moment like this, he enjoyed orchestrating the gathering more than leading it, overhearing strange meetings. Nel smoothed her skirt down next to Freya and got underway with a serious pig conversation. Alberto seemed to be talking to Polly and Sonia about venture capital. Robin appeared to be counselling Charlotte. As Fred had feared, Roderick and Heather were huddled together at the far end of the table. He couldn't help a frown. But looking up and down the table, at least most people seemed to be happy. He tapped a glass.

'Great efforts, everyone! Thank you. You look fabulous, as I knew you would. Makes my job more difficult. I'll have a think and award the prize after the main course. Now, can we raise a glass to our much-loved mum and dad?' said Fred. 'Missed now as much as ever.'

'To Effy and David!' said Roddy. Everyone murmured in support and glasses were chinked together and downed. Polly started handing around bowls of vivid purple soup.

'It's vegan,' she called. 'Inner-city beetroot from my own allotment. Hence the blood on my hands.' She brandished her scarlet-stained hands like a murderer. 'Although there's sour cream to add if you prefer, along with the chives, of course. You'll get real blood in the second course, thanks to Hugh.'

Fred felt it was time to build bridges with his brother. He called across the table to Roderick.

'Do you remember those camping holidays? In the dormobile? Hugh's van must have felt very familiar last night.'

'I do remember you read "The Voyage of the Dawn Treader" and decided you wanted to be Reepicheep the mouse,' replied his brother. 'You had Mum make you a cloak and Dad came up with a wooden rapier. Even though it was against their pacifist principles.'

Everyone laughed. Fred was not sure he entirely enjoyed his childhood quirks being revealed. It was all part of the cut-and-thrust of brotherhood, he supposed. At least Roderick hadn't mentioned his sew-on tail.

'They certainly wouldn't have approved of your bow and arrow, Freya,' said Nel.

'And don't forget there was that time you ate sheep droppings,' said Roderick, turning to Fred with another memory.

'Yeugh!' said Freya, sticking out her tongue.

'I did not!' retorted Fred, flushing as red as his handkerchief.

'Yup, you did,' said Roddy, insistently. 'Somewhere near Alston I think. You were crawling around on the moor, and then Mum noticed that you were picking up and eating sheep poop. Probably thought they were smarties.'

'I got smarties in my vagina once,' said Sonia. Everyone around the table stopped mid-conversation and stared at her in astonishment. She'd been quiet up to this point. 'It was at my brother's birthday party, I was only about three. My dad was working at the WHO in Copenhagen, I think. I must have had too few clothes and too many sweeties. I announced to the world that I had smarties in my vagina. And they never let me forget it. My parents always used the right anatomical terms,' she said, by way of explanation.

Roddy wasn't sure how to take this revelation. Did it show a refreshing willingness to disclose or an alarming lack of dignity? He decided to respond with a knowing but slightly superior chortle.

A memory came back to Fred.

'Well I remember a certain person going off to take a leak in privacy, and nearly getting bitten on the balls by an adder!'

Everyone laughed.

'Sounds terrifying!' said Charlotte. 'I hate snakes.'

'Fred's exaggerating,' said Roddy, in embarrassment. 'But he's right, I did hide behind a huge gorse bush to have a wee on one of our picnics in country Durham, near Stanhope or somewhere. I didn't notice an adder was basking in the sun until I nearly peed on it.'

'It's also true that you howled in shock, and everyone came running. You hadn't even put your willy away,' Fred added.

'My genitalia were never at risk,' said Roddy, firmly.

'Thank goodness for small mercies,' said his brother.

Roddy decided not to speculate about whether Fred was casting aspersions on his manhood. He was bigger than that.

'What is "wee"? And "willy"?' asked Alberto, and Freya delighted in explaining English nursery terminology to the Costa Rican, who very seriously practised his new words.

'Hugh?' called Fred across the table.

As Fred and Hugh compared notes on schoolboy humiliations, Alberto tried out his new words on Robin, who beamed at him. Sonia offered the equivalent words in Sinhala, and Alberto explained what Costa Rican children might say in their place. Robin started giving them a lecture on child development, but stopped when his boyfriend and Sonia started teasing him. Fred smiled at him.

'Don't be defensive. Laugh at yourself! It comes from a place of love.'

'Not so easy,' said the psychologist, but smiled just the same.

'When you are disabled, you have to laugh at the world and yourself. Otherwise you would be consumed with anger or shame. So much goes wrong and so many moments are ridiculous.'

'As they say in Sri Lanka, "What to do?"' said Sonia.

'Does that mean the same as "shit happens"?' asked Fred, at which Freya giggled and Polly frowned.

'I do want to do a wee,' said Freya to her mother in Sinhala, and then translated it for her benefit into Spanish, and eventually English. By the time she'd understood her child's meaning, it was the pause between courses and an ideal time for a break. On her way to the bathroom, Freya talked to her mother about families.

'So, Mummy, I could have had a daddy and a mummy rather than a mum and a mummy?'

'Well, yes you could. But then it would have been Mummy G and someone, or me and someone. You couldn't have had both me and Georgie.'

'I would be sad about that,' said Freya. 'I do love my mum and my mummy.' Polly gave her a squeeze and gathered up her party dress as she hopped on the loo. 'But I would quite like to have a daddy,' added Freya.

'Darling, I am not sure you will ever have a daddy. But you will always have two mummies who love you very, very much'.

'Most of the other children in my class have a mummy and a daddy,' pointed out Freya. 'Although sometimes their daddies are in prison,' she added.

'I am sorry if it's difficult to be different at school,' said Polly, as Freya hopped down and she took her place.

'I don't mind,' said Freya, pulling up her knickers. 'I tell them why it's better to have two mummies and two houses. Did you ever have a boyfriend?'

'I did once or twice. A long time ago.'

'Didn't you like it?'

'No, not really.' As she readjusted her dress, Polly thought back to her brief relationship with Fred, and then to her seduction of her third year tutor. That had been the big mistake. That was probably where it all went wrong. This was one story that she had no intention of sharing with her daughter.

'You see, darling, it's just that I wasn't very good at it,' said Polly, putting her daughter's hands under the taps and washing them. Freya seemed to accept this line of argument. 'I found it much easier to be myself with another woman.'

'Would you ever have a boyfriend again? You don't have a girlfriend at the moment,' said Freya, in a rather calculating fashion.

'I suppose it's not impossible,' said Polly. 'I wouldn't rule it out completely.'

'Mummy G does!'

'She does indeed' said Freya, between gritted teeth.

'See,' Freya said triumphantly, as they arrived back in the dining room. 'I might end up with a daddy after all!'

'Is everything all right?' asked Nel, seeing mother and daughter deep in intense conversation as they returned from the bathroom.

'No, everything's fine,' said Polly. 'It's just that Freya is having a heteronormative moment.'

'Mum, what's heteronormative?' asked Freya, as she slung her Doctor Who Assistant legs under the table.

'I'll explain it when we're on the way home,' said her mother, reminding herself you could never have a private joke in front of a seven-year-old.

The main course was venison, courtesy of Hugh. He'd run into a muntjac deer in the Home Counties, and it had died in the collision, or so he said. He felt that made it fair game (everyone groaned at that one). Apparently, he'd slid the dead animal onto a tarpaulin, and pulled it into the back of the Luton. He had then gutted, skinned, hung and butchered the buck himself, he explained proudly. Luckily, there were plenty of survivalist clips on YouTube to explain the details of these procedures. His neighbours were not ready for quite that level of detail, particularly as he was seated at the vegetarian end of the table. Freya, of course, was delighted.

'What did you do with the antlers?'

'I don't think muntjac deer have those big heads of horns, Freya. This one certainly didn't.'

'Shame! You could have worn them!'

'Not if I was coming to a Jane Austen party! That's more of a shaman thing.'

Of course, the concept of shamanism then had to be explained to Freya, which was quite complicated, but Hugh managed it with the aid of several forks and the water jug. Polly was most impressed.

Once they had eaten their roast venison – or nut roast – Charlotte tapped her glass.

'Everyone, I have an announcement...' She beamed at everyone from the end nearest the kitchen. 'We have a surprise dessert tonight...'

'Oh, yum,' said Roddy. 'I love surprises. Especially sweet ones.'

'We had planned to revive one of the boys' favourites from the 1970s...'

There was a groan from Fred's end of the table.

'Not banana custard... you know I just hated that.'

'No, not banana custard, Freddy darling... but we did begin a search for Bird's Angel Delight.'

'Not vegan!' called Polly.

'We have Vegan Dream for you folks, don't worry. Anyway, in the end none of that was necessary. Because we have in our midst a Celebrity Chef...'

Murmurs of disbelief chorused up and down the shiny walnut wood table.

'... who I am now in a position to "out" for the very first time in the history of catering. Would Alberto, chef-patron of the Eulalie brand, bringing us the famous desserts of Costa Rica, please step forward!'

With a round of applause, Alberto stood up, and bowed tightly from the waist to all points of the room. He smiled at his boyfriend, who was staring open mouthed.

Eulalie brand? Costa Rican catering? What was all this? Then it wasn't another man! thought Robin in total relief. Even during this celebration dinner, he'd noted Alberto slipping away for ten minutes. But it sounded as if he was competing with a ready-made artisanal-food business! Which was probably totally on trend! You couldn't be a two-timing tart *and* sell boutique cake at Herne Hill Farmers' Market! Robin sat back cheerfully. He could rest happy. They might even get rich, via YouTube or Instagram or something. And even if that was too good to be true, it was highly likely that Alberto would end up getting plump, which was almost as wonderful. It would give Robin a break from the wearying comparisons of their physiques. His own family, back in the day, had run a small ice cream business. He couldn't wait to tell Alberto about that. He'd be delighted at the connection. Maybe they could dig out some old recipes.

'Dear friends,' Alberto began, 'as I begin this new phase of my life with my darling partner, Robin,' – his boyfriend beamed at him – 'I have long believed that the national dishes of Costa Rica, the most beautiful nation on the planet, deserve to be experienced by a wider audience. I dedicate my business to my mother, Eulalie, who made all these puddings for me many years ago, and gives me her secret recipes today. Tonight, I am pleased to offer you a special dessert, which we call Tres Leches. As you all know, this means, 'three milks'. In your country, it might be called a trifle. But it is no trifle!' He laughed at his own joke and repeated it again for emphasis. 'We have evaporated milk, we have condensed milk and we have whole milk. We soak the sponge. And now you taste this treat from Latin America.'

As he spoke, Charlotte and Polly brought out glass sundae dishes, each with a sprinkle of what looked like hundreds and thousands over a slice of moist cake.

'I am proud to present my signature dish, particularly for my new dear friend, Frederick, whose birthday it is that we are celebrating,' Alberto continued, turning to his host. 'Fred and I shared a trip on the river this afternoon. We feel bonded, do we not?'

Fred nodded, with some embarrassment. He had tried very hard to put his damp afternoon behind him.

'Fred, as you eat this special dessert, remember our time together!' finished Alberto, with a significant gaze in his direction.

Fred noted with some concern that the hundreds and thousands on his dessert were all red. He wasn't sure that was a good thing. No one else's seemed to be red. Maybe it was just his birthday decoration.

'He even made a soya milk version,' said Polly, in admiration.

'Try it!' said Alberto. And everyone gathered around the table and watched expectantly. Fred dipped his spoon in the dessert. With his eyes closed, he tasted it tentatively. It was cakey and frothy. It was rather nice. Actually, it was very good.

'Delicious!' he called out. Everyone cheered as they dug in. Alberto went back to his place with a satisfied but rather knowing smile. As he passed behind Fred, he whispered:

'Remember the frogs!'

Fred looked up in concern.

'The frogs?'

Barely aware of what he was doing, he had already finished the pudding, which really was very tasty. He took a deep drink from his water glass. He felt a little thirsty, and his head was beginning to spin. Perhaps it was just auto-suggestion.

Chapter 25

At that moment, there was a crash from outside.

'What was that?' said Charlotte, in alarm.

'One of the cars,' said Roddy. 'Sounded like a door.'

'I'll go and check,' said Hugh. 'Back in a mo…'

'Come back quickly,' said Fred, feeling rather light-headed, 'for Lo! I am about to award the Jane Austen prize!'

Hugh got up from the dining table and headed past the kitchen to the back door. From his basket, Humphrey pricked up his ears, wondering if a walk was in the offing, or perhaps even another snack. He got up, ready for anything.

As a result, unbeknownst to Hugh, when he opened the back door, there was a small dog at his heels. When Hugh opened the door, Humphrey shot out with unexpected alacrity.

'Oh hell!' exclaimed Hugh. He turned back to see where the lead was. It was hanging from a hook in the corridor, and so he grabbed it and ran out after the pug.

In the car parking area, he realised he might have bigger worries on his hands than one escaping pet. The door of his Luton was hanging open. He dashed forward to look inside. A flurry of newspapers, some broken household items, some half-eaten fruit, but no pig. It was impressively messy, but he thought it impossible that even the smallest porker could be hiding amidst the chaos. In panic he looked around the outside of the van, and then underneath it. No sight of the fat little fellow. It was still twilight, and as he squinted through his John Lennon glasses around the parking area and the bins, he wondered which path Vin Pong had taken to freedom. He felt like a dozy American marine, foiled once again by the Viet Cong.

Hugh had forgotten Humphrey, who had an acute sense of smell, and an even more acute longing for the companionship of another small mammal. From the undergrowth came a yelp of excitement, followed by a snort of alarm.

Oh bloody botheration, thought Hugh. If the dog bites the pig, we're in real trouble.

But aggression was not an issue for either of the two small hairy beasts. Both confined to close quarters, well fed but bored, and missing their humans, they found themselves in total inter-species agreement that the present situation called for a party.

Vin Pong burst out of the undergrowth, putting on an impressive turn of speed for a pig that was as fat as he was small. He bounced along like a blackberry on legs, squeaking happily. Humphrey panted behind him, making up for his slow start with a masterly showing on the bend. Pig and dog performed several excited circuits of the parking area, coming within a whisker of knocking over a bin, narrowly avoiding running full tilt into Hugh's Luton, but turning and wiggling through a gap every time. Snorts and yelps accompanied what was clearly a vastly enjoyable game of tag. Hugh gazed in amazement, lead in hand, but realised he had scant chance of intercepting either animal. It was hard to tell the difference between hairy pig and rotund pug. He would require, at the very least, a net.

One more circuit of the car park, and the delighted porker identified another entertainment option. The back door to the house was open and it was the work of a moment to dash inside. Close on his wiggly black tail was Humphrey, willing to follow wherever his new friend led him. Coming a distant third in the Threepwood Handicap Stakes was Hugh, wondering how any of this could be explained. For one tempting moment he thought about retreating to the van, but with the blood of fourteen generations of Appletons coursing in his veins, he decided against the weaker course.

Conversation in the dining room halted as the distant sound of tapping trotters and pounding paws came closer. Nails scrabbled on the linoleum of the passage. Guests looked at each other in surprise. With a resounding crash, the gong went flying. Then the dining room door swung open, and the mystery was solved. Without pausing to look, the panting porker sprinted – if that verb could be accurately used of a sweaty, over-excited, Vietnamese pot-bellied pig – between the chairs towards the end of the room. Deploying the quick thinking for which he was renowned throughout East Anglia, Humphrey took the obvious short cut under the table. Within seconds, the two animals were rolling about on the floor under the bay window, snorting. To the casual observer, it might have resembled mortal combat, except that the two were grunting happily as they wriggled. As the guests looked from pig to dog and dog to pig, it wasn't clear which was which. But the three plotters were feeling extremely sheepish. How stupid they had been to trust Hugh! Was the manuscript going to turn up next?

'Vin Pong?' called Nel in shock, pushing back her chair. 'What the soybean dream are you doing here?'

'Humphrey!' croaked Fred in surprise.

Hugh now stood in the doorway, polishing his spectacles, gazing towards the end of the room. 'Isn't it interesting how the two species appear to communicate so well?'

Polly was made of sterner stuff. She'd intervened in actual fights in her time. After all, she was a trained social worker, and had taught courses in women's self-defence. A love-in between a spoiled pig and a pet pug was as nothing. She strode to the end of the room, which was now looking rather a mess, with rugs askew. An arm shot out, followed by a yelp, and she hauled a panting, happy pug out from the melée and held him tightly in her arms.

Sonia pulled a face as she thought of the dry-cleaning bill, particularly if that was a hired dress. The excitement promptly ceased. Vin Pong looked disappointed for a moment, and then sniffed. He had suddenly realised that the detritus of a dozen meals was scattered about the floor. He disappeared under the table and started efficiently hoovering up any scraps he could find. This phase of the evening was considerably preferable to the time he spent being shut up. Intermittent snorts and squeaks of pleasure followed. Guests felt rootling around their feet and looked under the table to follow his progress, mostly with delight.

'He must have broken out of the van,' said Hugh, apologetically, looking in the direction of Polly. She frowned and shook her head. He looked a bit embarrassed. 'I've been meaning to get that lock seen to… I've not really had to shut anybody in it before… should have put the padlock on.'

'But why,' said Nel, fiercely, 'did you feel obliged to shut my pig in your van?' She glared at him.

'I was waiting for him to have a dump,' said Hugh, and then added thoughtfully, 'I wonder if he has? Should have checked.' Polly was pointedly not catching his eye. 'I should really go and clear up the mess.'

'Can I see?' said Freya, jumping down from her chair. She had attended various parties with her mums in recent years, but none of them had previously involved pig-on-dog action. The weekend was getting better and better. And now she definitely had mysteries to resolve. She followed Hugh who was retreating down the corridor, having belatedly recollected that discretion was the better part of valour. He did not want to make the situation for Polly any worse than it currently was, and neither did he have the courage to admit his own role in the proceedings.

'And why exactly was Hugh waiting for my pig to have a dump in his van?'

Nel turned to Fred with a furious expression on her face. It was precision that she was now after. Fred was the one who she felt should surely provide an explanation, in his role as host of the evening. She looked around the room defiantly. People were evidently rapt with interest, but nobody was willing or able to volunteer an answer.

'I have not the faintest idea,' said Fred, sincerely, holding his now-leashed dog, and feeling more than a twinge of guilt, despite his mystification at the turn the evening had taken. He could see why Nel's tone of indignation had wreaked such havoc in his alma mater.

'It's probably just his thing,' said Roddy, helpfully. 'He's always been eccentric.'

'Vin Pong is a pure bred, highly valuable animal belonging to my employer,' said Nel, haughtily. 'And more to the point, he is extremely sensitive. He is not in the least eccentric. And your dog could have hurt him!'

'Not the pig!' retorted Roddy. 'Hugh! Hugh's the one who's a bit hatstand.'

'Oh, Humphrey just wanted to be friends,' said Fred, feeling hot and bothered. 'He's not an aggressive fellow.'

'You're not taking this seriously!' exclaimed Nel. 'I have a very unhappy pig! And apart from anything else, he's my bread and butter.'

'You mean, like a bacon sandwich!' joked Roddy, and got a very dirty look in return from Nel.

'Pongy was only upset because Polly stopped him playing,' said Robin. 'He looked as if he was having great fun.'

Polly, who was now scratching Vin Pong's back under the table, thought this was probably an accurate assessment. No harm seemed to have befallen the pig.

'Like you'd know whether a pig was happy!' retorted Nel.

'He is a psychologist!' said Alberto, springing to the defence of his man. 'He knows the secrets of the mind.'

'Although not the pig mind, presumably,' pointed out Sonia.

'Pigs are generally better than men,' said Charlotte. 'More intelligent, at any rate.'

'I feel like some air,' said Roddy, not happy at the way the conversation was going.

'Let's stretch our legs,' said Heather, quickly taking her cue.

With that, Heather and Roddy left the room.

Fred barely noticed them going. He was feeling rather hot. Tides of indignation from Nel were washing over him, the world was oddly technicoloured and he seemed capable only of smiling benignly, which appeared to infuriate her more.

She reached under the table and seized her pig by the make-shift rope collar, which someone with precisely zero knowledge of porcine husbandry had fastened around him.

'Come with me, Vin Pong!' she said. 'These leftovers are the last thing you should be eating!'

'What's wrong with them?' chorused Polly and Alberto, who had high opinions of the food on offer.

'But I was about to award the Jane Austen prize!' said Fred, blithely.

'Keep your effing prize! This has been a complete waste of an evening!' And with that, Nel stomped out of the dining room, shedding tears of indignation and betrayal in her wake.

'Wow!' said Robin. 'She's quite something.'

'Well, you could see why she didn't last long at College,' said Charlotte, woozily. 'Can't take a prank! Silly girl!'

There was an awkward pause.

'And then there were seven!' said Polly, feeling a bit challenged after all the fizz and other wines. 'If you were thinking of awarding the prize to Nel, Hugh or Freya, we'd better postpone the ceremony... or Heather and Roddy for that matter.'

'Well, I did rather like Nel's outfit...' said Fred, with feeling.

'She looked like a mermaid!' interjected Charlotte. 'Caught in a net!'

'Shome mermaid,' intoned Robin. His Churchill impression sounded more like Sean Connery, which may have been a side effect of the whisky. 'Shome net!'

Fred ignored him, and continued, 'I do think Freya deserves a special prize for putting up with all us adults, AND for explaining the plot line of every Doctor Who episode—'

There was an appreciative round of applause.

'We're all Whovians now,' murmured Robin. It came up surprisingly often in therapy.

'—but the Threepwood Jane Austen Memorial Prize for 2018 is awarded to... Polly!'

'Me?' asked Polly in surprise. 'But I thought you were giving it to one of the others?'

'Well, you're just about my best friend,' said Fred, gallantly. 'You've always been there for me, ever since the crash. And your outfit is smashing!'

'Polly!' chorused his friends. She was a popular winner.

'Here is a copy of a book about all the mysteries in Jane Austen,' finished Fred, fishing a wrapped volume from the pouch beneath his chair. 'I was going to read it myself, but I realised I would first have to reread all the novels, and by the time I finished them, I didn't really have the stamina to read this as well.'

'Save it for your fiftieth!' called Charlotte. 'We'll be back!'

'I do hope so,' said Fred. 'The whole pig/dog thing was a bit unexpected. So was the flood. And the electrics. And the missing manuscript. It's all been quite an adventure. I don't whether I should blame Hugh for it all, or whether he's been our saviour all along. If he could only locate my book, I'd kiss him.'

'Sorry?' said Hugh, returning to the party, now that he had spotted Nel disappearing down the path and the coast was clear. 'What's my fault? Why would you kiss me?'

'Everything is your fault!' called Polly. 'And what have you done with my daughter?' she added, anxiously.

'She's washing her hands,' said Hugh. 'There was an issue with pig poo.'

'Ah!' said Polly, significantly. 'And did success crown your labours?'

'I think so,' said Hugh. 'But I'd rather you did the announcement.'

'What announcement?' asked Fred. 'I really don't think I can cope with any more excitement.'

'It's your memory stick,' said Polly. 'We've found it!'

'I found it!' said Special Agent Freya returning to the dining room. 'It was me!'

'Really?' said Fred, in stupefaction. The walls now appeared to be moving towards him. 'How absolutely marvellous! I'd completely given it up for dead.'

'It may yet have expired,' said Hugh. 'We haven't tried it. And it's certainly a bit damp. Not to say smelly.'

'Which must mean it might not work anymore,' said Charlotte, hopefully.

'Let's leave it on the radiator for a bit,' said Sonia, anxiously. 'And try it later.'

'Safe return. No questions asked,' slurred Fred, smiling broadly. 'Although I don't quite understand where it's been.'

'Trust me,' said Hugh. 'You don't want to know.'

Chapter 26

After the dramas of dinner, everyone sat around in the large, ornate sitting room, or the smaller cosy sitting room, reading or playing games. Fred felt so awkward about what had happened with Vin Pong and Humphrey that he did not propose Scrabble, as he had planned. In any case, he was not sure he could focus on the board, let alone the tiles. There was still no sign of Roderick and Heather, so he had no one to squabble with or try to impress, which was actually a huge relief. Fred's head was still reeling, whether from the pig incident, or from the wine he had drunk with dinner. He felt both rather odd and curiously benevolent towards everyone. Perhaps his book would be saved after all! He felt in a forgive-and-forget mood. Mostly forget. He was still a bit anxious about the self-propelled furniture, which he felt was in a threatening mood.

The third of the transatlantic phone calls to be made from Threepwood that day was waiting to be connected. So far, one hope ended in scandal, while the second had a sweeter outcome. Now Sonia was standing outside by the Wally Smithson statue, anxiously clasping her mobile to her ear, hoping that the call would get through to Detroit. Anil would surely have finished his meetings by now. He'd want to know about the croquet lawn. She was so worried that she had done harm taking a tumble over the hoop. There had even been a little blood. It was terrifying. She hoped Anil would understand.

'Hello?' came the disembodied voice.

'Oh darling!' began Sonia, and dissolved into tears of misery. Anil was exactly what she needed, and she felt so much better afterwards, having shared her fears. She went upstairs to lie down and practice her breathing. As Anil had reminded her, this was exactly the right time for Hatha yoga. Nobody noticed her disappearance.

Polly went to put Freya to bed. After her late night on Friday, she was getting fractious and threatening to give a recorder recital, so everyone was rather relieved when Freya reluctantly kissed her new friends goodnight and climbed the stairs, painstakingly slowly. Robin tried to teach Alberto and Hugh a card game, which sounded almost, but not quite, like a game popular in Latin America, while Hugh insisted that he'd got the scoring wrong. This left Fred and Charlotte, sitting beside the tray of drinks, and it was only sensible to have one each solely for sociability reasons. Someone had brought a really rather fine bottle of Islay malt, and then it didn't feel right to stick to only one glass each.

After a while, Charlotte fell silent. Lost in his own swirling thoughts, Fred did not notice at first. He said something to her, got no reply, and then looked at her more closely.

'Are you OK, Charlotte?' She didn't answer. 'Lottie?'

Then she raised her head. Her face was a fist. Screwed up, and resolute, and angry and hurt, all at the same time.

'What's the matter, Lottie?' said Fred, tenderly.

And then it all came out, bit by bit, as he sat with her. How lonely she felt in her marriage. How Roddy was just fixated on politics and had no time for her. How he ogled other women all the time, and she wasn't sure that he was entirely faithful to her. How she'd missed out on having a daughter. That she sometimes even had doubts about God. Not capable of more than listening, Fred sat there, and held her hand, and put his arm around her shoulder, and passed her his handkerchief, and got her a glass of water. Roddy was nowhere to be seen. The other guests saw a weeping Charlotte, and gave them a wide birth. As they passed, they directed a sympathetic smile to Fred. He shrugged his shoulders and gave the time-honoured facial expression for 'What can you do?'.

In the end, he gently disengaged from her, and did his best to rearrange his clothing, and hers. His shoulder was damp, from where she had sobbed against it. She looked at him and smiled weakly, and sniffed, and blew her nose. She offered him his handkerchief back, and he waved it away.

'I think I should go and do some clearing up after dinner,' he said.

'I'll come and give you a hand,' she said, and they went through to the dining room.

Everyone had drifted away from the dinner table. Roddy and Heather still hadn't returned from wherever they'd gone. Fred and Charlotte took the remaining glasses and plates through to the kitchen, put the cheese board in the larder under a wrapping of clingfilm, and began loading the dishwasher. Everything took rather longer than it should have, and every movement was made with exaggerated concentration, but miraculously nothing was broken. Fred had drunk champagne, then wine, then whisky. He had also possibly ingested unknown quantities of amphibian hallucinogens. The room was reeling somewhat, with lighting effects that were distinctly unsettling. He felt hot. Charlotte was unsteady on her feet, and so he sat her down with a big glass of water, and finished loading the dishwasher himself. At least being in a wheelchair meant that you weren't going to fall over. He slid in the soap, pressed the start button, and closed the door. The machine started filling. The noise woke up his sister-in-law.

'All done! S'time to go bed, Fred,' burped Charlotte. 'Tha's good. It rhymes! Time for bed, Fred! Where's your room? Isn't it just past the kitch-kitchen?'

'Turn first right,' said Fred.

'I'm gonna come and tuck you in,' she announced. He frowned at her.

Following him down the corridor, she pushed open the door to his room and turned the light on. The double bed looked like consolation, not accusation. Humphrey slumbered on his bean bag in the corner, paying no heed to the invaders. Fred wheeled in after Charlotte. He must be a lot more drunk than he realised, he thought. His head was spinning and the floor was moving. Or maybe the other way round.

'Now Charlotte, let me get you another glass of water. You've drunk a lot, you know. Wine, whisky... Unsteady on your pins and all that. Us disableds don't have to worry. My wheels keep turning...'

'Oh, I like that. Paralytic but not falling over... Sorry, I don't mean to take the piss, Fred. Blind drunk! Oh, I'm a silly cow...'

'You're not a silly cow, Charlotte.'

'Must be a silly cow or my husband would like me...'

'Maybe it's my brother who's an idiot,' said Fred, who was beginning to think so.

He gazed blearily at his sister-in-law. She hadn't been very pious this weekend, come to think of it. She'd almost lightened up. And she'd been a great help to him from start to finish, in her over-anxious way.

'You're wonderful, Charlotte, tha's what I think,' slurred Fred. His speech was always the first thing to go.

'Thank you, Fred,' said Charlotte, who was now sitting on the double bed, drinking her glass of water obediently. She looked at her brother-in-law. 'You've always been so kind to me.'

'It's easy to be kind,' said Fred, with the terminological gallantry of the inebriated, 'with someone who is… as gorgeous as… as what you is.' Reaching the end of a barely-coherent sentence felt like a triumph, whether or not words were slurred in the process.

'Gorgeous? Do you really think so?' said Charlotte, brightening.

'Oh yes. Very. Fine. Woman.' Fred articulated the words carefully, but his lips did not seem to be getting prompt and precise instructions from his brain.

'Ah, shucks. You're a sweetheart. Come and gissa kiss.'

'One good night kiss, then, Lottie. But then you better go upstairs. Roderick's probably… waiting for you. Will be back soon in any event.'

'Now, c'mere Fred, you lovely man. Oooh, I've got another one: you're legless!' she giggled. 'But so am I!'

'I think that's enough, Lottie,' said Fred, whose frontal cortex had gone in search of his impulse control.

Fred wheeled closer and leaned over, intending only to peck her cheek politely, as he had done hundreds of times before. But as his lips brushed her cheek something happened.

She might have swerved. Or maybe he lurched. Neither were in full control of their actions. But the next moment his mouth was on hers, and she was responding and clasping him to her, almost pulling him out of his chair in her desire, panting and mauling him. His lips seemed to be working fine now and she tasted of whisky. Humphrey stirred in his sleep and whimpered, as well he might.

'Wait a mo!' said Fred. He transferred from chair to bed, and put his arms around Charlotte, who was tottering like the walls of Jericho. Slowly they tipped back, landing heads next to each other on the pillow. Charlotte's eyes were tightly shut.

'Look,' said Fred. 'This is… wrong. You probably…. don't know… what you're doing. You can share the bed… sure,' he mumbled, 'but should stop this… T-shirt.'

Charlotte protested. 'Know what I am doing!'

What she was doing to his nether regions was very pleasant. Fred reached out a hand to stop her. Charlotte opened her eyes and looked at him.

'Where is he? Answer me, Fred!'

'Gone for a walk…'

'With who, Fred?'

'Possibly with, err, Heather.'

'Exactly. He's a selfish shallow man. It's your party and I'll cry if I want to!'

'I think actually the Party is all he's bringing. To the party. As it were.'

'Ezzactly!'

For a woman who had always seemed rather diffident, she seemed to be doing a lot of ordering about. Her hands found her buttons again.

'Don't undress!' he commanded. Her fingers froze. Urgently, Fred fumbled for the light switch and darkness fell over the room.

'Now you can!' said Fred.

She slid out of her dress and was left in her slip. Buttons flew. One landed next to Humphrey's bed and he sniffed it experimentally. A meaty treat perhaps? At second smell, the button didn't seem edible to him.

Meanwhile, Charlotte was holding Fred close to her chest. He had only had time to unbutton his shirt, but he could feel his chest crushing her under the whatever you call it... not a basque, some more simple lingerie. A camisole? He focused on the feel of the lace and the scent behind her ear, trying not to think of the breasts pushed up and together...

His right hand played a piano trill down her stomach...

'Ooooooo,' said Charlotte. He continued with the melody.

'Hmmm!' said Charlotte. 'Nice...'

She smelled so clean, of lavender soap, with a hint of musk.

'Gosh!' thought Fred, he hadn't done this in, what? Twenty years. Since he was about twenty, at any rate. What a great birthday!

Charlotte lay there, moaning quietly to herself as Fred continued his ministrations. It felt good. It felt like a chocolate bar was melting in her mouth, or that she had drunk champagne and the bubbles were fizzing through her veins, or that she was on some roller coaster. It had been such a long time. Someone was loving her.

'Don't stop!' groaned Charlotte.

With that Charlotte howled, her voice modulating, wailing and barking like a wolf.

'Ow ooo argh ragh owwww! Waugh waugh waugggh!'

Her cry was ear-splitting, penetrating, memorable. Unforgettable. Legendary.

Humphrey sat up and looked at her attentively. What was that she had said? Humphrey stood up by his bed and took in a deep breath. He knew his duty.

'Ow ooo argh ragh owww! Waugh! Waugh! Waugggh!'

He threw back his muzzle and gave it his best shot. For a small dog, his bark could be very loud, when he wanted it to be.

The sounds floated through the window and down to the farm yard, where the two collies were chained up in the outside den.

'Ow ooo argh ragh owww! Waugh! Waugh! Waugggh!' they replied.

Their united barks gave the required crescendo added emphasis and vigour. They tried it again. So did Humphrey. The world needed to be informed, urgently. The honour of the entire canine species was at stake. Wolves were abroad.

Charlotte was subsiding back onto the bed, her fingers idly ruffling what was left of Fred's hair after four decades and the hereditary curse of male pattern baldness had taken effect.

The barking had been taken up by Bill, and then by Skip and Jump, and now, more distantly, one by one, all the dogs of Suffolk, and the easterly districts of Cambridgeshire joined in, their ragged canine chorus howling across the Fens.

'Thank you!' said Charlotte, and dozed off. Fred, with a mostly naked woman in his arms, felt that a great weight had lifted from his mind. This time, there had been no psychological impediment. What a great birthday this had been. And so he also fell asleep.

Meanwhile there was the sound of footsteps upstairs because, as Newton's Third Law would suggest, every action has a equal and opposite reaction. Lights went on. The Hall was illuminated.

'What's going on?' asked Sonia, in her heliotrope pyjamas with the old gold stripe.

'Was that really the Howler?' said Polly, in a long and much-laundered nightshirt, wondering what had just happened. 'Sounded very like her!'

'Sounded like the hounds of hell!' said Robin, blinking in the light, as he stood in the doorway. Robin was naked, with a towel round his waist and sweat beading his forehead, Alberto standing behind him.

'Are there wolves in this part of England?' enquired Alberto, nervously. He was clad only in boxer shorts, and Polly noted with interest that his chest was shaved and both his nipples had rings through them. How painful that must be! She clutched her own chest in sympathy.

As Robin stood on the landing, he was also trying to suck in his stomach, which was imperilling the tuck of the towel. Thinking better of it, he retreated back into the bedroom.

There was an alarming rattling at the door. Someone or something was trying to get in. Polly, who had bolted the door before she had gone upstairs with her daughter, tiptoed down the great staircase as quickly and quietly as she could, and slid open the great bolts. This time, when the iron ring on the big oak Hall front door turned, the door slowly creaked open. Two figures tiptoed in, trying not to draw attention to themselves. They had not expected this much pandemonium at Threepwood Hall in the early hours.

Several heads craned over the landing banister and stared at them.

'Roddy!'

'Heather!'

'Where have you been?'

'A walk,' said Roddy, curtly.

'Talking politics,' said Heather, taken by surprise. 'I might well ask what on earth are you all doing up at this hour?'

Now they were in the light, Heather noticed with interest that Roddy's mouth was red with her lipstick. MAC normally didn't leave such a mark.

'Have we missed anything?' asked Roddy, wondering who had organised the welcoming committee. 'Did you hear that awful chorus of dogs barking earlier?'

'Scared the pants off us as we walked up the drive,' said Heather.

'Nothing to see here,' said Polly, hoping that the others would also keep silent.

At that moment, Charlotte tottered down the corridor from Fred's room and into the hall. Her party dress was rumpled and there was a big smile on her face. She ignored the heads learning over at the landing, and the couple by the front door, and almost skipped up the stairs. So much for discretion, thought Polly to herself.

More than one mouth remained open until Charlotte had reached the landing.

'Lottie?' wailed Roddy. Queasy and furious in equal measure, his face looked like a watermelon that had been dropped from a great height.

'Going to bed,' his wife mumbled from the entrance to their room. There was the sound of a door being locked behind her.

With that, the heads disappeared. Each guest slunk back to their room. Roddy cast a hopeful glance at Heather, but she didn't catch his eye, and mounted the stairs.

Roddy looked around, in dismay. It was dark, and cold, and his head was hurting. He had the vacant expression of a man whose brain has just been flushed. In the end, he fetched a rug from the corridor, found the more comfortable of the two sofas in the drawing room, and within moments was also snoring, but far from contentedly. Imbroglio resolution could wait until tomorrow.

'Peace and quiet!' thought Charlotte, from behind her locked bedroom door, and she fell into a deep and contented sleep. Meanwhile, Humphrey shuddered in his slumbers as he dreamt of doggy dinners and piggy pals. His master lay snoring on his own bed, stars still twinkling before his eyes. On his face was a rather satisfied smile.

Chapter 27

Fred woke up with an unfamiliar sense of contentment. It must be having friends gathered round. He lay back, head on the pillow, arms folded behind his head and contemplated the now-familiar ceiling.

Something was tugging at the loose end of a woolly skein of memory and association. He had obviously slept more deeply than usual, he thought. Or drank more… although he didn't even feel very hung-over. What a good result from a fortieth birthday dinner! He felt almost purified. Even his skin felt fresh and soft. Everything seemed clearer. Apart from his memory, which was still wrapped in cotton wool. For the first time in ages, he felt younger than his years.

Dozily, he gazed around the bedroom. The Trust had certainly done a good job with the restoration. This must have been the housekeeper's sitting room or something. Maybe a scullery. People didn't seem to need sculleries these days. What did one do in a scullery anyway? Or larders for that matter, which were presumably places you kept lard, fridge freezers having eliminated that need. Probably dishwashers had something to do with it. Modern properties could do without scullery and larder. Certainly the ones that he'd had to conveyance recently. His eyes slowly tracked around the room, taking in the furniture – brown, the curtains – frankly dull. Although the way that the Trust had found the right door handles, Hugh would definitely approve of.

There seemed to be something hanging off the door handle that seemed out of place. He reached across to the bedside table for his glasses. Yes. It was a pair of knickers. Definitely, women's knickers. Lacy black ones. Was that someone's idea of a joke? Like tying tin cans to the back of the wedding car? Well, he didn't think much of it, if it was.

And then his idle train of thought stopped in its tracks, like a London-bound commuter train when some idiot has instinctively pulled the emergency cord solely because he has failed to get off in time after saying goodbye to an elderly relative.

Those knickers! They must belong to Charlotte. And this was no joke. It was as serious as it could be: Charlotte, the hitherto unimpeachable church-goer for the last dozen years, Charlotte, his sister-in-law, the wife of his only brother. He and Charlotte had been in bed together. Some form of adultery had probably been committed, although the cotton wool inside his skull was unclear on that detail.

His thoughts were briefly derailed into a sliding. Some form of adultery! He'd done something! She, Charlotte, had presumably been naked, he might have gazed upon her flesh, and they'd done *something*, and it had been fun, insofar as he remembered. They'd certainly parted as friends. Maybe he had just been calmer, it being the second night in bed with Charlotte. Perhaps it was the alcohol. Anyway, at last he seemed to have overcome the terrible mental block which had screwed up the whole of his adult life. Two decades of increasingly frustrating erotic connivance might just be at end, he thought. That was certainly a result worth swinging from the chandeliers for. He glanced upwards to check. No chandeliers in this room.

Then from this height of life-changing excitement and relief, he plunged down, like an over-confident gap year student on a bungee rope, into a tropical gorge of despair. He'd certainly been feeling out of his head last night. Alberto must have spiked his milk pudding. Poison dart frogs! Late last night, under the influence of psychoactive substances, going to bed with Lottie had seemed to be a good idea, like a high-calorie snack after a big night out. Two lost souls consoling themselves, with the aid of alcohol and mind-expanding puddings. After all, hadn't Roddy already disappeared off with Heather? Heather! He wasn't sure what he'd ever seen in *her*. No wonder Charlotte had been glum. Her own husband abandoning her like that for a swollen-headed hack who probably didn't even write her own scripts.

And now he'd slept with his brother's wife! Wasn't there something in the Bible about that? Why did he do something so stupid? Couldn't he have tried his chances with Nel? He liked Nel, he liked her a lot. But oh no, he had to go to bed with the only woman staying that weekend who he definitely, absolutely, catechistically should not have slept with. His sister-in-law! Catastrophic! It was practically incest! He and Roderick had vanishingly little in common now, apart from their childhood memories, but regardless of that, cheating on your own brother! Roderick would probably never speak to him again. He dispelled the unworthy thought that this might be a blessed relief, given Roderick's continuing obsession with his electability.

He felt a sudden glimmer of hope. Perhaps nobody knew. Perhaps nobody had noticed Charlotte creeping upstairs afterwards. The two of them had been pretty quiet, hadn't they? And of course, his room was downstairs, while everyone else was upstairs. Perhaps they'd got away with it? There would be no need to tell a soul. He wondered if there was any chance whatsoever of Charlotte keeping their secret... she must be feeling pretty guilty herself right now. And then Fred remembered how many Christmas presents Charlotte had told him about in early December. How his sister-in-law had a tendency to overshare. She definitely couldn't keep a secret. No, this would leak out. Probably over breakfast. It was going to be a total disaster. And just when the weekend had been going to plan. Mostly.

It was like those times at St Wurburgs, when he'd gone into town for a late-night bop. Times when, homeward bound, with half a dozen pints sloshing around his system, he had failed to resist the lure of a kebab from that van that was eternally parked in the marketplace. He could still feel the greasy taste in his mouth. Kebab regret! Kebab regret to the power of ten! He turned over and buried his face in the pillow, groaning weakly to himself. He should have learned: the kebab that seems like a good idea at the time never feels like a wise decision in the morning.

Maybe he could just hide in his bedroom until everyone had left. Except, of course, that he was the host. Not that they deserved to see him. He remembered the lost memoir he'd been trying not to think about. Several of them – at a rough guess, he thought probably Heather and Roderick, maybe even Lottie herself – had conspired to steal his manuscript. It was like Murder on the Orient Express, only he was the victim! They were under his roof and eating his meat! (Well, the Trust's roof and Hugh's roadkill, said the lawyer in him.) He hoped it poisoned them.

And Hugh! Practically his best friend. Certainly, his oldest friend. Could he ever forgive Hugh for being involved with such a treacherous plot? Fred toyed with the idea of never speaking to him again. Whose idea had it been? He wasn't sure he wanted to know the answer to that. It couldn't have been Hugh. Roderick certainly didn't have the gumption to come up with a plan like that. Fred suspected, with a sinking feeling, that it was Heather who was the prime mover. In the cold light of dawn, he knew, with dull certainty, that it was Heather who had betrayed him. Hugh would have been just putty in her hands. Silly boy. He preferred his cotton-wool brain to the cold light of dawning reality.

What about the memory stick? He'd got it back last night, thanks to Polly. Fred slid out of bed and transferred into his chair. Taking off the brakes, he wheeled over to the kicked-aside pile of clothes on the floor and bent down to try and retrieve his waistcoat. Yes, here it was. Memory stick seemed OK. A bit whiffy. Perhaps it had been in a bin? And the plastic seemed a bit marked, as if someone had chewed on it. Well, just so long as it worked. He turned on his laptop, which started up quickly, as if full of unfinished business. He slid the memory stick into the side socket.

But there was no sign of 'Fred Twistleton' in the Finder. To his frustration, the computer refused to recognise the USB stick at all. He took it out and gave the business end a scrape, in case the connection wasn't working. But it didn't work the second time either, or the third. As dead as whatever species of charismatic megafauna had just gone extinct. Perhaps a tech guru might manage something? Drat, drat, drat.

The failed memory stick was a bad blow. He'd spent months writing, he'd harboured hopes of success, of becoming a different person, an author, not a small town solicitor, of realising his early promise. And now he'd lost it all at the last moment. Probably served him right for snogging his brother's wife. Poetic justice, Biblical almost. Although, you could equally say that it served his brother right if he'd stolen the book manuscript. After all the hours he'd spent writing the damn thing. Sonia seeming so optimistic. He'd come this close to becoming the writer that he dreamed of. And now he would have to start from scratch, and climb that mountain again. And the sword of Damocles was hanging over his head. Well, more the ornamental letter-opener of Damocles.

Roderick would have to be faced.

Chapter 28

Sunday morning dawned so bright and sunny, that the overnight dew seemed to vaporize in mere moments. It certainly felt warm enough to have breakfast on the terrace, so the first wave of guests formed a human chain, carting cafetières and tea pots and toast racks outside, as if bravely facing a Middle English humanitarian disaster. Unity was superficial, as normal life was re-emerging on day three. The brighter, better selves that had presented themselves at the first communal lunch had been replaced by the sniping, irritable realities. People who knew a lot about domestic and global politics were becoming just a teensy bit frustrated at being lectured at by others, who only had their gut feelings to guide them. Trained clinicians were rolling their eyes at people who relied on emotional insights derived from *Cosmopolitan*. Social workers did not need to be reminded of prejudices that were almost worthy of the *Daily Mail*. Even Freya, the darling of day one, was now the 'Frère Jacques' fiend of the final morning.

Sonia had come down to breakfast later than her friends, feeling sheepish. Polly and Robin and Heather were on at least their second cup of coffee, and were discussing sheepskin on the terrace, for no obvious reason. There was no sign of Fred, or Charlotte or Roddy. Hugh had already gone off, apparently researching sites for possible den building with Freya.

Sonia made rooibos tea, helped herself to some muesli and then sat on the terrace with the others. She waited for a break in the conversation.

'Hey, everyone,' she began. 'I want to apologise for disappearing last night.'

'No problem,' said Polly.

'I did the vanishing act thing myself,' admitted Heather. Polly rolled her eyes.

Robin waited for Sonia to finish. She seemed to have things to say.

'Only, I've been rather worried for the last few days… you see, Anil and I are trying for a baby…'

The attention of her friends went up a notch, and the background noises went down.

'I've had a couple of false starts…'

'False starts?' queried Heather.

'His Hindu sperm not getting on with my Buddhist eggs, you could say,' said Sonia. 'Miscarriages,' she clarified.

There was a silence. This didn't sound good, thought Polly.

'It gets so damned hard keeping pregnant when you're our age,' said Sonia, clutching a tissue. She looked at Polly as if for confirmation and to Heather as if in warning. 'Anyway, everyone says you're pretty much safe when you reach three months. The milestone was this week. We were about to start celebrating when I came a cropper during the croquet game yesterday…'

'Oh, I remember, you crashed down like a felled tree…' said Polly.

'And hit the hoop! Anyway, last night, during dinner, I noticed that I'd started spotting...'

'Bleeding...' explained Polly sotto voce to Robin, '...in her knickers.'

He frowned. Surely this was not a suitable breakfast conversation? There was such a thing as oversharing. Maybe he should go check on Alberto.

'Anyway,' continued Sonia, 'of course, I was desperately worried that I was losing the pregnancy. I managed to get through to Anil, and then I went off to lie down in a darkened room. Literally.'

'I am so sorry,' began Polly, 'I remember exactly that stress of trying to get pregnant and then stay pregnant. And I started ten years ago. And only managed it once.'

'With a turkey baster,' added Heather. She felt it all sounded like a terrible bother. The struggle to stay pregnant, only to have your offspring pester you for ten years of attention and another ten years of ready cash.

'Well, we've gone traditional so far,' said Sonia. 'IVF was the next option if this didn't work out.'

Robin understood that all this gynaecological detail was indispensable to the continuation of the human race, but thought that he'd made the right decision to focus his career at the opposite end of the human body. He felt squeamish about anything reproductive, which he knew wasn't generous of him. He made an extra effort to look supportive.

'Anyway, folks,' said Sonia, 'so I have a portable ultrasound machine...'

'Wow,' said Polly. 'Things really have changed since my day!'

'Yeah, they're pricy, but so good for reducing anxiety. I checked immediately last night, and you could see the heartbeat, so everything seemed to be OK. I rested checked again just now, and it's still pumping. So we definitely survived my header onto the croquet lawn... and as yesterday was the end of my first trimester... I think we can cautiously announce... I'm pregnant!'

Those last two words felt like an official announcement to the world. Sonia's voice had grown in confidence, and now she smiled at her friends.

Polly whooped supportively, and pumped the air. 'Go sister!'

Polly had only happy memories of her own pregnancy. So much so that she would have signed up for another one, even approaching forty.

Heather smiled wistfully and clapped discreetly. She had once thought she wanted to be in Sonia's position, but now she wasn't so sure. She had been in danger of getting grounded on the shoals of middle-aged regret. But just because you were childless, did not mean you were a failure as a woman. Swinging that door closed with a feeling of liberation, Heather confirmed to herself to the realisation that parenting was not in her future. If she was ever to invest in high-fashion baby clothes, it would have to be for someone else's child.

Robin looked at the women celebrating, and self-consciously stuck two thumbs up and smiled weakly at everyone. Was that sufficient? Alberto came out with his customary cup of black coffee and a sweet bun. Robin whispered the news, and Alberto beamed his 200-watt smile. He flung his arms around Sonia and kissed her warmly on both cheeks.

'This is a wonderful day,' he announced, rather formally. 'I am so very pleased for you. And Anil… *We* are delighted,' he stressed. 'Aren't we?' he added, put his arm around his partner's shoulders. Robin nodded mutely. Alberto had known exactly how to respond. He seemed to have effortlessly made friends with everyone at Threepwood. Perhaps Robin had rather more to learn from Alberto that he had imagined.

Inside the Hall, Charlotte was feeling her way towards the kitchen like the blinded protagonist of a Wilfrid Owen poem, although in this case, she had been the agent of her own destruction. It was as if a Camden bin lorry was reversing its way through her cerebrum, all beeps and grumbles and grinding noises and crashing gears, with men jumping on and off in sequence.

She discovered that it hurt too much to open her eyes. The early summer sunshine mocked her with the cheery insolence of a market trader. She couldn't face company. Standing in the kitchen, she poured herself a pint of warm water. She sat at the kitchen table, sipping until she had finished it. Polly came into the kitchen to fetch more coffee, and saw her old friend. Without breaking stride, she made a cup of sweet, milky tea and passed it to her. Gratefully, Charlotte drank it down, more boldly now. By the time it was finished, she felt she could risk opening her eyes. Polly held out another glass, this time of cloudy fluid. Charlotte looked questioning, but it hurt too much to shake her head.

'Alka-seltzer,' said Polly. 'It might help.' Obediently, Charlotte drank that too.

'Gotta pee,' she said, and left the room.

As she came out of the downstairs bathroom a few minutes later, Fred was outside, waiting to shower. He gave a sheepish grin.

'Hi,' he said, doubtfully.

'Hi!' she replied.

'Are you OK?' he asked.

'Not really,' she answered.

'Emotionally, morally or spiritually?' he asked, with genuine concern.

'Physically,' she replied. 'Hung-over as hell. Divine punishment probably. All the other dimensions – fine. Don't worry. I'm not... worrying. Momentary lapse. I prayed. Forgiven. Forgotten. One-off. Two adults in crisis. Nothing to say.'

Fred nodded in relief, but also with a twinge of regret. Best that way. After all, untangling that particular Slinky of confusion might be a life's work. He went in for his shower and felt a momentary pang. Something could be at the same time impossible and glorious and never to be repeated, like England winning the Rugby World Cup. An improbable memory to privately cherish. But now he had guests to worry about. And he could imagine few more embarrassing things in life than having to explain to an only brother that you came close to sleeping with his wife.

Chapter 29

Half an hour later, Freya's den duly built, Hugh found Fred, looking hungover and confused, sitting in the kitchen with a bowl of muesli and a cup of black coffee. For a moment, he thought of running the other way, but then he decided it was time they went for a walk together. Having had that thought, he couldn't let it go until it happened. He waited quietly until Fred had finished his breakfast, and then stepped forward.

Fred thought Hugh was the last person he wanted to hang out with this particular morning.

'To be honest, Hugh, I don't really feel like it. Not at my best today.'

Hugh looked crestfallen.

'We haven't really had a chance to talk all weekend, Fred!'

'Now isn't the best time.'

'But when, then?'

'Well, later, I suppose.'

'Everyone will be leaving after lunch.'

'Well, before we leave, then.'

'What about now? Surely Humphrey at least needs a walk?'

Fred could see that Hugh was not going to let him get away with this until he'd got whatever it was off his chest. He looked at him and raised his eyebrows.

'I'll give you a push?' offered Hugh.

'OK.'

The two of them set off around the garden, following the stoned paths, but venturing further than Fred had so far done on his own.

'You know I'm blooming cross with you, Hugh.'

'Yes… I'm sorry.'

'How could you do a thing like that?'

'I was weak. And stupid.'

'Bloody weak! And bloody stupid.'

'Yes. We all make mistakes.'

Fred considered for a few moments, in silence.

'Yes. We all make mistakes.'

They wheeled along, not speaking, contemplating their error-strewn lives. How could you possibly get to the age of forty without having some regrets? But perhaps even now it was not too late. Life only half-done, and all that.

'I like your friends, Fred.'

'Thank you, Hugh. I hope by now you consider them your friends too.'

'Yes, mainly.'

'You seem to be getting on very well with Polly.'

'Would you say so?'

'I think so, yes. But don't get mixed up.'

'Meaning?'

'Well, be careful not to confuse the signals, that's all.'

'I always confuse the signals, Fred. That's one of my diffi-culties,' sighed Hugh. 'Although I am guessing you may be guilty of that yourself as well. Anyway, I did want to talk to you about... well, those sorts of issues.'

'Issues?'

'Well, what you'd probably call relationships. Love affairs.'

'What did you want to tell me?' said Fred, guardedly. He didn't think Hugh was quite the role model for successful adult life.

'Well, have I told you my exotic fruit metaphor for human relationships, Fred?'

'No, Hugh. I don't think you have...' Fred felt it was neither the time or the place.

'You see, some people appear pretty unpleasant on the outside... dried up and scaly.'

'Like a prune?' asked Fred.

'More like a lychee, I was thinking...' his friend replied. 'But when you get through the exterior shell, they turn out, well, sweet and juicy...'

'Only with that weird, squeaky texture?'

'I think you're taking the metaphor too far, Fred. Certainly, the lychee type is quite pleasant. Whereas other kinds of people appear delightful when you first encounter them... soft and tasty.'

'A peach perhaps?'

'Or a mango... quite delicious. A very thin peel. And then you realise they are rotten to the core, once you've got stuck in. But by then it's too late. You have a nasty, turpentiney taste in your mouth.'

'I think I see what you mean. What sort of fruit would be perfect, Hugh? In your opinion?'

'What?'

'Well, you don't want a peach or a mango... are you saying you'd prefer a lychee? Or a passion fruit perhaps?'

'A passion fruit?' Hugh stared at him very seriously. 'Hard and completely shrivelled up?'

'But so tasty inside?'

Hugh shook his head. 'No, Fred, not a passion fruit. That's a pleasure, but so brief. For me, it's the pawpaw every time.'

'You're looking for someone sweet and soft... yielding... but orange?'

'You're being too literal again, Fred,' said Hugh, indignantly.

'Well, I think I'd settle for a satsuma, said Fred. Hugh nodded in agreement.

'You know where you are with a satsuma. No surprises.'

Fred thought that Heather would probably fall into the mango category. Often disappointing. Whereas maybe Nel was more like a satsuma. And Charlotte? Perhaps she was a passionfruit after all. Although she came across as wholesome too. Like an apple. A passionfruit disguised as an apple.

Fred waved his friend's hands away from his chair and wheeled forward to look at the view. They had found their way to a rise behind the house, from where they could see everything: the beautiful Regency building, the ornamental gardens bordered by the ha-ha, the kitchen garden and behind it the pigsty. Scattered around the estate they could spot their friends, sitting or walking singly or in pairs around the landscape.

Threepwood was a wonderful place. Hugh stood next to him, silently surveying the skies, noting the birds that soared and banked above the parkland. Fred squeezed his friend's hand in a comradely way.

'Well, this has been very edifying, Hugh. I always learn something from our little conversations. I'll bear your fruit analogy in mind.'

'Satsumas not mangoes, Fred. Just remember that.'

'Good luck finding your pawpaw, Hugh.'

His friend nodded sadly. Hugh could mix a metaphor as well as the next man. But despite his homespun wisdom, he had not the slightest idea how to communicate with a woman. He felt like the unripe nectarine in the fruit bowl of life.

Chapter 30

Feeling sheepish, Roddy emerged on his own onto the terrace an hour after everyone else had breakfasted, rubbing his back. He was not sure how he'd ended up spending one night in a van and another on a sofa, when there had been a perfectly good – if slightly damp – double bed reserved for him all weekend. Armed with his first coffee of the day, he followed the voices and wandered out onto the terrace. Seeing everyone gathered there, he waved in their general direction, and then looked at his wife in particular, as if she had hidden the key to his future somewhere about her person. She held his gaze defiantly. Others on the terrace observed the exchange but looked studiously away or immersed themselves in conversation.

Deciding it was a bigger priority to check his voicemail than to resolve the Northern Ireland hard border of his marriage – after all, there might be an urgent message from his Leader, or his agent, or the press, or indeed anyone that might make him feel like he was someone – Roddy strolled across to the edge of the ha-ha, and took up position, next to the Wally Smithson statue. His fellow guests returned to the discussions that had been paused at Roddy's appearance.

Sitting at the table with a roll-up cigarette, Polly glanced at Charlotte, who was reclining on a sun lounger with a black coffee, looking slightly misty-eyed. Neither of them were taking much notice of Roddy. Polly turned to her daughter, who was jigging from foot to foot, impatient for more entertainment after her den-building foray with Hugh.

'Freya?'

'Yes, Mum?'

'That bow and arrow of yours...'

'Yes, Mum?'

'Is it very powerful?'

'Oh yes, Mum!' said Freya, excitedly. 'I mean, it's not as powerful as a crossbow, but it's pretty good. I shot an arrow across the croquet lawn really, really easily,' she boasted.

'Do you think you could hit the statue from here?'

Freya squinted her eyes. 'The one by the ha-ha?'

'Yes. That really ugly statue by the ha-ha.'

'Oh yeah,' said Freya, scornfully. 'That's easy.'

'Let's see you do it then,' said her mother.

'I might miss...'

'Not a problem.'

'What if I hit Uncle Roddy?'

'Not a problem.'

Charlotte sat up and put her hand to her eyes to squint at her husband in the middle distance.

'Are your arrows sharp, Freya?'

'No, not really.' The child sounded disappointed. 'I don't think they'd hurt anyone.'

'Would you like to earn a fiver?'

'Oh yes, please, Aunty Charlotte!' She beamed wide.

'If you can hit Uncle Roddy on the bum with an arrow, it's yours.'

'Yeah!' said Freya, turning to face her quarry. She screwed up her eyes and concentrated hard. The tip of her tongue poked out of her mouth. With her right hand pulling the string taut against her cheek, she aimed the arrow carefully.

TWANG!

The bow string vibrated.

ZIP!

The arrow sped straight and true across the lawn.

'DAMN!'

As they watched, Roddy leapt in the air, one hand grasping his right buttock.

Because he had his back to them, and because he had been balancing at the top of the brick wall that marked the edge of the ha-ha, the gymnastics he was now attempting were ill-advised. As he teetered on his heels, he realised too late that he was going to fall. Instinctively, his arm shot out and grasped the Smithson statue around its neck, so that he could pull himself back to safety. Or so he hoped.

But not for the first time in his career, momentum proved a false friend. His direction of travel, his weight and his posture meant that, far from pulling himself back onto safe ground, he carried on falling forwards, and inevitably, downwards. As he fell, there was a loud crack, and the above-ground portion of the sculpture parted company with its foundations. Whether the liability for this catastrophic structural failure belonged with the artist, the Trust, or the local-but-Bulgarian builders who had dug the hole and backfilled the cement, would soon be the subject of some complex litigation.

The upshot of Freya's extraordinarily well-aimed arrow was, to Hugh's considerable delight, one controversial contemporary artwork shattered beyond repair, and to Charlotte's guilty pleasure, one promising Prospective Parliamentary Candidate writhing around amidst the cowpats and thistles at the bottom of the wall, broken, but thankfully reparable. Sadly, there were no bullocks in sight. Charlotte offered her abject apologies and said she was too hungover to drive, so Heather gritted her teeth and drove Roddy to Bury St Edmunds A&E in his own car. As far as she was concerned, it was further evidence of what a liability offspring could be.

None of the birthday party were particularly sad to see either Roddy or Heather depart that morning. People were fond of them, but it was the fondness of habitual familiarity, the resigned and intimate knowledge of flawed humanity that binds people together for all their lives, the fondness that is clear seeing about faults, while at the same time being discreetly respectful and forgiving. And as Anil pointed out later, when Sonia updated him on the phone:

'Someone who screws up on such an impressive scale is bound to end up a Cabinet Minister!'

They had always expected Heather to leave them more with a bang than a whimper. In retrospect, Fred realised how foolish he had been to think that their orbits could ever intersect for long. Even if, by some miracle, she had fallen in love with him, she would always have felt embarrassed to have him as her partner. His infatuation was a hangover of student days, when most people were shy and confused, and a rare few mortals, by virtue of their preternatural confidence and determination, seemed almost to be denizens of another world. Now, mostly, they turned out to be narcissists.

Chapter 31

After Roddy had been driven off for urgent medical attention, Polly felt there was something that needed doing. She first checked that Freya was happy, decorating her woodland den with Humphrey. Then she took a wander past the old kitchen garden, down to the pigsty with the bright blue steel container alongside it. It all seemed so familiar by now. There was no one else around. She watched the pig rootling around for a bit, and then she thought she'd risk knocking on the container door. It was Sunday morning, but surely everyone was up by now?

Sure enough, there was a creak, as the door opened. Nel was standing there, in orange neon singlet and polka dot shorts.

'Oh god, I'm so sorry, I didn't realise you were asleep!' said Polly, embarrassed, while mentally questioning this unusual woman's choice of sleepwear.

"I just came back from my jog,' said Nel. She stared at Polly, suspiciously. 'What do you want?'

Nel had decided that the gang at the Hall were not for her. Not after the business with Vin Pong.

'I wanted to explain. If you'll give me five minutes,' said Polly, feeling contrite.

'Hmm!' said Nel. 'Well, as long as it's really brief. I've got some writing up to do, once I've done my chores.'

'Promise it won't take long' said Polly. Nel gestured to the plastic camping chairs beside the bench.

'I'm making coffee anyway,' she said.

Five minutes later, a steaming cafetière was on the bench table, and the two women were sitting opposite each other, expectant with tin cups. Polly did not know where to begin the conversation, and Nel was not about to help her.

'Look, I know you think Fred was responsible for the pig business,' started Polly.

'Oh, I don't care anymore. There's always crap with people,' said Nel. 'That's why I generally opt out.'

'No, don't say that!' replied Polly, almost fiercely. You couldn't be a social worker if you just gave up on people. 'It's not true. The point is, that it wasn't Fred's fault. It was me.'

'You?' said Nel, in astonishment. 'You stole my pig? Whatever for?'

'Well, not just me. It was me and Hugh. It wasn't a jolly jape. We weren't going to keep the pig. We were very careful with him. We just wanted to get the memory stick.'

'The memory stick?' asked Nel, more confused than ever. 'Why would my pig have your memory stick?'

'You see, the others up at the house, well, some of them anyway – Hugh actually – went and pinched Fred's memoir, plus the memory stick that had the data files. Hugh threw the papers into the feed tray, and managed by some lucky fluke to get your pig to eat the memory stick…'

'Without pausing to consider whether plastic and silicon is normally part of a pig's balanced diet!'

'Yes, it was totally stupid. Considering how clever he probably is, he's a total idiot. Occasionally sweet, but doesn't seem to think of the consequences of his actions. Typical man. Anyway, I found out about it... and I care for Fred, you know, a lot, and I wanted to try and sort out the mess, which is why we – I mean Hugh – borrowed the pig. Stupid. But it was my idea. So be cross with me.'

'Because you wanted to sort through pig shit till you got the stick?'

'Yes.'

Nel shook her head in disbelief. 'And did you get it after all that?'

'Yes, amazingly, we did.'

'But it doesn't work, does it?'

'No,' admitted Polly. 'But how did you know that?'

'Call it a wild hunch. For a start, you don't want to get bitten by a pig, even a small one, seeing as they have rather efficient gnashers. Plus very robust digestions. Hydrochloric acid in the stomach and sixty foot of small intestine to navigate. It's a wonder anything came out at the other end at all.'

'Well, it wasn't too chewed up, but it has stopped working. So the whole escapade was for nothing. But at least the pig is OK...'

'No thanks to you two!' said Nel. She thought for a moment. 'But I am glad that Fred had nothing to do with it. I actually liked him, you know...'

'And he likes you!'

'But you and him... you're an item?'

'Us?' replied Polly, in amazement. 'No! Don't get the wrong end of the stick. I care for him like a brother, but there's nothing going on there. We did have a momentary thing. But it was twenty years ago. Nothing since. I promise.'

Nel smiled. 'Well, thanks for that, at least. Now, finish your coffee. Your penance is to help me wash Mr Pongy. Sunday is bath day.'

As the two women splashed and scrubbed the pig – who seemed to accept the attention as no more than his due – they continued talking. After the general pleasantries, Polly cut to the chase: 'So here you are, nearly thiry-eight you said, and on your own…'

'No shit, Sherlock,' said Nel.

'But why? Why maroon yourself out here in rural East Anglia? Why single?'

'I've not always been single. I've not always been here.'

'But you're here now,' pointed out Polly. 'So how did you end up here?'

'Look, I've been burned too many times. Colleagues who stole my data. Friends who turned out to want only one thing. My current boss, who's a total slimeball. Relationships, careers… all that's not worth the candle. I don't need much money. I'm better off alone out here, with my pig and my research studies. If anything goes wrong, there's no one to blame but myself.'

'Five per cent of me thinks you're right. But the other ninety-five per cent thinks you're frightened,' said Polly.

'Not at all!' said Nel. 'I just happen to think you're safer, in the long run, living on Pessimism Island.'

'Well, it must get lonely, alone on your island.'

'Yeah, sometimes. But better than the alternative.'

'I'm guessing that you didn't like the dinner party?' asked Polly.

'I felt like a vegan at a meat auction. Not my scene.'

'Well, you looked brilliant, even if you felt out of place.'

'Yeah!' Nel smiled, proudly. 'It was a great outfit in the end, wasn't it? I was dead pleased with that.'

'Fred couldn't stop looking at you.'

'Really? That's nice.'

'Don't pretend you didn't notice!' laughed Polly. 'And I think a woman with your extensive vocabulary might find a better word than "nice".'

'It made me happy,' admitted Nel, blushing. 'As I said, I liked him. At first.'

'The wheelchair didn't bother you?' asked Polly.

'Nah. Why would it? I'd prefer to look at the person, not that stuff.'

'Me too. That's why I can't understand why some people insist on only being interested in one gender. Seems odd. If you like an individual, then go for it.'

'Don't accept the messages you're given. Make up your own mind.'

'Exactly. Anyway, I am guessing that you've arrived in Fred's life at exactly the right time.' Polly didn't think she should elaborate more.

'Life begins at forty?' suggested Nel.

'Something like that. So, please. Don't rule it out. Don't stay on the Island!'

'Hmm. Let's see if your prince in shining wheelchair can find a way through the thicket of thorns surrounding Sleeping Beauty.'

'At least you're not ruling out a fairy tale ending.'

'I even have my own magic porridge pot.'

Chapter 32

Fred was stripping the bed in his room – not as hard as usual, given the mess that he and Charlotte seemed to have already made of it – when there was an embarrassed throat clearing from the doorway. He turned around to see Alberto, with Robin close behind, urging him forward.

'Oh, hi, guys!' said Fred. 'You're not going already? You should have lunch before you leave us!'

'Ah, well, you know, we are not leaving quite yet. We had definitely planned to stop for lunch, if that's still OK, aren't we Robin?'

His boyfriend nodded, but also frowned at Alberto.

'Of course it's OK!' said Fred. 'Why wouldn't it be? It's been great getting to know you better. I just hope you've coped with meeting everyone.'

'*Verdadero*! We've had a few misunderstandings from time to time, but it has all been lovely, thank you,' said Alberto.

'Alberto has really come to say sorry, haven't you, love?' said Robin.

'Sorry?' Fred was mystified.

'Well, I was a bit naughty,' said Alberto. 'Did you feel strange last night?'

'Yesss…' said Fred, beginning to think he knew which way the conversation was headed.

'You know, I wanted to help,' said Alberto. 'Give you a good birthday evening. So, I sprinkled some of the Kambo powder on the dessert you ate last night. Of course, it would not have the same powerful effect as if you snorted it, but I think it must have made you feel a bit trippy, no?'

'A bit, yes,' conceded Fred.

'Well, I am sorry. Robin, he is very cross with me too,' said Alberto, penitently.

'Drugging people without their consent! It's terrible behaviour. Alberto meant well, but really. I am just so sorry, Fred. Really, I am.'

'You know,' said Fred, 'I'm actually not sorry at all. I don't think I will take up psychedelic drugs, but it was a powerful experience. In fact—' he gestured for them to come in and close the door, '—the thing is, I think the trippy effect might have really helped me. Alberto, you may not know, but for twenty years I have had this terrible blockage… in the bedroom department.'

'I never told him, of course,' said Robin. 'I think that's something only you could explain to someone.'

'Well, I don't need to go into the details,' said Fred. 'The point is, last night, for the first time in my life since I was a student, things went… right… with a woman. Let's not discuss who. But the point is, I didn't vomit, I didn't escape, I didn't screw up… I just… made out, pretty much like a normal person would.'

'That's amazing!' said Robin.

'Way to go, compadre!' said Alberto, relieved.

'You know,' said Robin, thinking further thoughts, 'this is beginning to make total sense. In fact, I am surprised no one had suggested it to you earlier. Maybe because it's quite a new idea in psychology.'

'What?' said Fred.

'Well, they are beginning to use these types of drugs in therapy. For example MDMA – that's Ecstasy to you and me – for people who suffer from Post-Traumatic Stress Disorder. Even LSD, for people who are alcoholics. For some reason, these drugs can reset your mental state or something. The cures can be miraculous. Even though no one understands them.'

'You mean that Alberto may have been ahead of the curve in treatments for sexual neuroses like mine?'

'Sounds like it!' said Robin.

'I thank you,' said Alberto, swelling with pride. He started listing on his fingers, 'Model to the stars; Genius in the bedroom; Prince of desserts; Psycho-sexual therapist. Is there no end to my talents?!'

'Oh, shut up, you big head!' said his boyfriend, lovingly. 'Get your chunky arse out of here and let's pack our bags.'

'No hard feelings necessary,' said Fred. 'In fact, lifelong gratitude may well be in order. Watch this space!'

'Maybe Alberto and I should write it up as a case study,' said Robin, as they left the room. 'No names, obviously.'

'You could call it *The Curious Incident of the Frog in the Night-time*,' Fred called after their retreating backs.

Chapter 33

After an early lunch, people were getting ready to go. A text had come through from Roddy. He'd finally been seen at A&E. The orthopods had set his broken collarbone. Neither he nor Heather was planning to come back, as they both had 'urgent business' in London.

'Good luck to them,' said Charlotte, bitterly. 'They deserve each other. Anyway, she'll ditch him in days. Just wait and see.'

Roddy's Sunday morning would later be written up in the *British Journal of Emergency Medicine*. The doctors at West Suffolk Hospital had thought it was one of the most interesting fractured collarbones they had ever encountered, and felt he would be honoured to contribute to medical science. The patient's own views were not recorded. But having sat for three of those hours in considerable discomfort in the waiting room, Roddy had felt that he would gladly swap becoming a footnote in the history of orthopaedics for a dose of Fentanyl or whatever other opiates were being brandished around hospitals these days.

His brother Fred's Saturday night also made into the *Journal of Clinical Psychology*, as a case report written up by Robin. And once she had calmed down sufficiently, the dining room antics of Humphrey and Vin Pong found their way into *Small Mammal Ethology*, thanks to Nel, under her own name this time. Thus, with three refereed publications, Fred Twistelton's birthday party was responsible for a significant contribution to the subsequent Research Excellence Framework, and ended up forever recorded in the annals of Academe, as well as the Heritage Trust Threepwood Hall logbook.

Back at the Hall, people hung about on the gravel, feeling the tugging ball and chain of everyday duties, but not wanting to part. Goodbyes were said and bags were hefted. Alberto carefully typed everyone's email address in his phone. He felt that Eulalie Costa Rica Dessert marketing could not begin too soon for these sweet-deprived Anglo-Saxons.

Polly edged over towards Hugh, who was standing looking like a lost soul, wanting to leave, but not wanting to end what had turned out to be a surprisingly enjoyable weekend.

'What are you doing next?' she asked him. He blinked at her, as if his spectacles had suddenly stopped working.

'Next? Errrhm. You mean now?' He took off his glasses and polished them, which he considered his options. They were not extensive. 'This afternoon I will meander back to London. There's a church I'd rather like to see on the way. After that, I'll go back to my brother's house in Richmond, park up, and errhm… Wait for another commission, play my fiddle, that sort of thing.'

'I was going to mention commissions. I think I might have a job for you…'

Hugh's heart sank and he responded instantly, 'I'm not stealing anything else!'

'No, no!' Polly laughed. Poor man. What they'd all put him through.

'You're a carpenter aren't you?'

Hugh nodded. 'Yes. Cabinet maker.'

'Well, I need shelves made. Bookshelves. Could you do it?'

'For sure!' said Hugh, in some relief. 'Of course. I mean, depends what you want.'

'What do you specialise in?'

'I generally use reclaimed wood. Style to suit you,' he got into his stride, 'from steam punk to minimalist. I prefer the more ornate designs myself. I don't just put brackets in the wall!'

'Sounds perfect. I want something smart. And after that, I wanted someone to make Freya a new bed. Like a bunk bed? With storage?'

'Oh, that's a great idea,' said Hugh, firing up his imagination. 'Loads of possibilities there. If her archery takes off, I could make one with battlements and a ladder, so it was her castle, with her desk under the bed? Or if she's still really into spying, maybe an MI5 bed with mystery compartments under it?'

'It's up to her, really. But the main thing is that you'll do it? You've got time?'

'Absolutely I have time. That's the one thing I have plenty of.'

'You can park up next to our building, there's a driveway. Use our bathroom. Take as long as you want.'

'It'll be nice to have a couple of projects, and to spend more time with, errhm... Talking with... errhm... you.' He coloured in embarrassment. 'And Freya, of course.'

'She'll be absolutely delighted,' said Polly, unwilling, for now, to follow him into that particular thicket of confusion. 'She seems to really like you.'

Her friends would find it odd that there was an eccentric bloke around the house. But Polly thought it might be just what she needed. After all, she didn't have to sleep with him if she didn't want to. And the main thing was, she felt absolutely and completely safe with this man. He might be a bit unsocialised, but he was thoughtful and kind – when he wasn't stealing manuscripts or pigs to commission – and that counted for a lot.

'Do you think you could give us a lift to the station?' she added. 'I don't fancy trying to hitchhike again, and god knows whether rural Suffolk has buses on Sunday.'

'I can do better than that. I could drive you both home?' suggested Hugh, hopefully. 'That way, I could have a quick look, at your flat, I mean, we could discuss the carpentry jobs.' He added quickly, 'If you're not too tired, that is?'

'Honestly?' she said. 'Door to door would be amazing! Getting some shelves done in the next few weeks would be a dream come true. It's embarrassing to think how long my books have been surviving on a plank-and-brick bookshelf. I'm forty myself in a few months.'

'Exactly! Time to get sorted and settled!' said Hugh. He rather thought it was. He liked this woman, and her sense of the absurd. His life had had a long first act. It was high time to start on the second.

Freya, who had been wandering around the garden with her bow and arrows, checking to see if anything needed fighting, saw her mum standing with Hugh and their bags. She rushed over and flung her arms around Hugh's waist.

'Thank you for making this a savage weekend!' she said, in a tone of passionate seriousness. Polly smiled at her daughter before turning to her new friend.

'Just a minor footnote here, Hugh. "Savage" actually means "good",' explained Polly. 'It's London argot these days. At least, I think that's what she means. Perhaps she just means "savage" as in "savage"? I never really understand my own kid.'

'Like *Stig of the Dump*,' said Hugh. 'Cavemen.'

'I remember reading that! It was one of my favourite books!'

'Mine too. Has Freya read it?'

'Don't think so. We've not got it, and it would be far too masculinist for Georgie.'

'It's in my van.'

'Really?!'

'I've got quite a library.'

She smiled at him.

Meanwhile, Freya was hanging off Polly's arm, swinging to and fro until it felt as if it was coming out of its socket.

'Oh Freya, do stop that! Anyway, no need to say goodbye. Hugh's going to come home with us... I mean, to drive us home!'

'Really?!' Freya's face lit up immediately. That's amazing! Can I play in the back of the van again like before?'

'Sure. You play house as much as you want,' said Hugh.

Hold that thought, Polly said to herself.

'Don't forget, you said we could buy a gadget!' called her daughter, from the back of the van.

Chapter 34

In a companionable silence, but with no further reference to the previous night's activities, Fred and Charlotte had finished cleaning the kitchen, packed away the leftovers in the containers, and had loaded Fred's car. Hugh and Polly and Freya had headed off to London. Robin and Alberto were on their final walk around the grounds. Sonia was waiting by the gravel drive for her taxi. The boys had brought out her bags and promised to stay in touch.

'How are you going to get home?' Fred asked Charlotte.

'Oh, I'll take a train with Sonia, although I may have to listen to baby-talk all the way back to London. It was an absolute treat to stay in a place like this. And your friends are good people. I can see why you like them.'

'Are we OK, Lottie? Still friends?' he looked at her anxiously.

'Of course!' said Charlotte. 'Please don't worry. What happens in Threepwood, stays in Threepwood. I'll be in touch.'

'Are you going to be OK?'

'For sure!' she said, bravely. 'Look, it was on the cards. And this way, I get to be the injured party.'

'Although, it looked very much as if my brother was the injured party this morning!'

'Serves him right!' said Charlotte. 'Good luck to him. The boys will cope. He's not a bad dad, really. I'm going to enjoy life again. I'm going to find out who I am. Which probably means the single life for a bit.'

'It has its advantages!' said Fred. 'But whatever happens, do make sure you stay in touch!'

Charlotte gave him a warm hug. Sonia also gave him a squeeze.

'Thanks, and well done,' Sonia whispered, in his ear. 'Get in touch when you've written something else. Now, go for it!'

A few minutes later, Sonia and Charlotte were waving out of windows, as the taxi moved off down the drive and Fred sat waving gratefully after them. It hadn't gone so badly. Even the failures had been good for someone. Maybe the next forty years would be OK. Although, sadly, his literature career had fizzled out before it started. And he was still waiting for love. Robin and Alberto returned from their walk and gave him warm embraces as they too set off.

Fred had one more thing to do before locking up. He stowed the dog and his own bags in his car, leaving the window open the statutory crack, and wheeled away towards the kitchen garden.

'Hello?' he called cautiously, as he reached the sty without spotting Nel. 'It's Fred!'

Vin Pong looked at him with interest. Where was his friend Humphrey?

'Round the back,' came the answering call.

Fred wheeled past the container, and into the kitchen garden. There was a rug on the only tiny patch of grass. There lay Nel, tanning herself. In a bikini, which was equally tiny. Fred looked at her. Nothing. No nausea. No fainting.

Attractive woman in tiny polka dot bikini has no deleterious effect on Twistleton psyche, he noted gratefully.

'I've come to apologise,' he said. 'Please believe I had nothing to do with it.'

'Hello,' she said. 'I'm just glad it's you. Not pervy boss man. Please don't worry.'

'I see you're enjoying a free Sunday?' said Fred, greatly relieved.

'Very much so,' said Nel. 'At least while the globally warmed sun is shining, I thought the academic paper could wait. You off?'

'In a minute. Everyone else has gone already.'

'Just us left, then?'

'Yup. And Humphrey is locked up in my car. Sleeping, obviously. With the window down, I hasten to add. I am so sorry for all that nonsense. I can't wait to give him back to my neighbour to look after, frankly.'

'Let me make you some tea. I have a little something for you. A late birthday present.'

'There's no need!'

'Just wait before you say that.'

Nel got up from the blanket, slipped on her Crocs, and put on some sort of a kaftan. She sloped off towards her container-cum-office-cum-dwelling. Fred took her place in the sun.

Ten minutes later she was back, carrying the tray with the familiar chipped cups, and a padded envelope under her arm. She carefully put the tray on the grass, and handed Fred the envelope. She sat back down next to him.

Fred drew out the contents. The top page looked familiar. With increasing disbelief, he flipped from page to page. He looked at Nel, stunned.

'It's my book!'

'I rather thought it might be.'

'I'd given up on it! Where did you find it?'

'I rescued it from the sty. Vin Pong had decided not to eat it…'

'Oh, what a blessed relief!' Fred realised how glad he was to be reunited with his magnum opus.

'…although he did decide it made a good toilet.'

Fred noticed that the pages were stained and wrinkled, as if they had got damp and dried out.

'You rescued it!' he said.

'Yup.'

'Did you have to clean some pig poo off?'

'Yup,' she said. 'Quite a bit, to be honest.'

His heart sank. 'Every page?'

'Almost.'

He looked at her in disbelief. 'You carefully cleaned every page of the manuscript belonging to the man you thought had stolen your pig?'

'If you want to put it like that.'

'You're an angel,' he exclaimed, passionately, and flung his arms around her. What a woman, he thought. He kissed her warmly on the cheek. He enjoyed it so much he did it on the other cheek too.

'Hardly!' she said, politely disentangling herself. But not pushing him away, he noted.

'I don't know how to thank you!' He was, for once, almost lost for words.

'Just drink your tea,' she said, smiling at him.

'But really. This has made my weekend. It's the best possible present. Sonia will be really pleased too.'

'My pleasure. Happy birthday. Glad I could be of help. And the book's not bad either. I had time to read a few pages.'

They sat in silence, drinking their tea. Fred looked from the print-out to her and back again. She smiled. He smiled. The birds sang. Vin Pong grunted in his sleep. It felt calm.

'I don't live far away,' he began. 'Maybe an hour?'

'I don't get out much,' she said, at exactly the same time. 'But I can borrow the estate's car from time to time...'

They stopped in embarrassment. She indicated him to go first.

'Because I was thinking...' said Fred. 'You know. We could go out for dinner?'

'Sorry, not really my thing,' said Nel. 'Dressing up,' she clarified.

'Well, a pub lunch then. At long as it has something for vegans on the menu. And a walk.'

'A walk?'

'I have this all-terrain thing. Like a tractor, if you will. Bolts onto the front of my chair. Means I can go for twenty miles, if I want. Across country.'

'Steady on, tractor boy!'

'But it would be nice, wouldn't it? You and me...'

'Yes,' she said simply, and smiled at him.

'Maybe you could come and see my place?'

'I'd make a comment about running before walking, only it would be hideously un-PC,' said Nel.

'Sorry. But it's quite near. Next to the winsome Wensum.'

'The glamorous life of a rural solicitor?'

'The Bure nearby is also rather special. Otters and that. You might like to come for a professional visit. As a scientist, I mean. We could kayak. If you'd like,' he added, hurriedly.

'I think I might like. But give me some time to be sure.'

The conversation petered out. Nothing more to say, really. He reached out and squeezed her hand. She smiled back at him.

'What are you going to do with the book?'

'Well, I will probably give it back to Sonia to finish reading. Her being a literary agent and everything.'

'And now you can! You might have to type it out afresh, And for God's sake, save it somewhere safe!'

'Yes, I can – and I will. But I've also got an idea, for my second book. A bit soon really, but I thought the story of this weekend might work well as a novel.'

'This weekend?'

'Maybe. Not sure if I can do it justice. I'm not very good at the comic stuff yet. But it's probably safer than raising the lid on all my friends' disreputable early lives.'

'And what would you call it?'

'Ah, yes, that's the very first thing I decided,' he said, proudly. 'I think it's rather neat.'

'What, then?'

The Ha-Ha.

Acknowledgements

For obvious reasons, I apologise to P. G. Wodehouse, who has filled my days with joy for more than forty years. Apologies may also be due to Sara Bragg, Joanna Cox, Mark Erickson, Helen Frankenberg, Jonathan Norris, Oliver Phillips, Dan Cochran, Jon Simmons, Annie Kane and my family (all of whom would nevertheless be entirely wrong to think that this novel has anything to do with them or with my fiftieth birthday weekend). Thanks to Alice Whieldon and Alana Officer for making that weekend so successful, and for happy days kayaking. Thanks also to Mary Wickenden, who may remember a certain punctured boat.

Jonathan Lee and Anne Meadows gave hugely useful guidance at an Arvon Foundation course, and came up with the title. My agent Emma Shercliff has helped me and *The Ha-Ha* in a multitude of ways, particularly by laughing. Clare Alexander, Mark Haddon and Lissa Evans supported me to stay the course. Sally Phillips dressed Roderick and Charlotte Twistleton, and her inspired suggestions included spoiled pigs, hallucinogenic frogs and much more. Thanks to Lucy Bastin and Jon Norris for pointing out what Nel and Hugh might really have done, and to Hannah Kuper and Susan Shakespeare for nomenclature. I blame Humphrey on Pam Henderson, Richard Fredman and Lisa Askem. Thank you, all.

Over the years, Tom Phillips, Julia Darling, Bill Albert and Romi Jones have been the best of writing buddies. More recently, Katherine Quarmby, Kate Beales and Lissa Evans have been the close readers I needed towards the end of the journey. Being able to talk literature with my neighbour Paul Bilic has sustained me daily, as has the piano playing of his partner May Kersey, and the companionship and support of Julia Redhead. Thanks are due to Pete Duncan and everyone at Farrago, particularly my editors Sarah Lambert and Daniela Ferrante.